"Is that what you want? An affair?" Kelsey asked.

Rorke's eyes narrowed. "Forget it. If you want a straight, fast answer, you got it—*no.* I don't want a short, sweet affair."

"I have a problem, Rorke," Kelsey said desperately. "And it's not going to go away if you pretend it isn't there. You don't seem to realize what you'd be getting into."

"No? Well, it's pretty obvious you're dying to tell me, so you just go right ahead."

The humor was back in his tone, as if he were coaxing her to lighten up and take it easy. It only upset her more. He wasn't going to understand...unless she made absolutely sure he had no other choice.

So she told him all of it. Telling her story was no source of pain. She'd done it before. But it was different, baring her soul for Rorke's judgment. It was different, because Rorke was proving an increasingly impossible man not to love.

Dear Reader,

For years, Silhouette Intimate Moments has worked to bring you the most exciting books available in category romance. We were the first to introduce mainstream elements, to make our books themselves something out of the ordinary for romance publishing. Next month we'll take another step in that direction when we introduce an extraordinary new cover design. At last our books will "look as big as they read." Our commitment to quality novels hasn't changed, but now we've come up with a package that we think does our stories justice. I'm hoping you'll think so, too, and that you'll share your thoughts on our new cover with me just as, all along, you've been sharing your thoughts on our books themselves.

But let's not forget the excitement this month in the middle of anticipating next month's big change. Veterans Jennifer Greene, Alexandra Sellers and Kate Bradley are in this month's lineup, along with talented newcomer Joyce McGill. Actually, Joyce has written young-adult novels before, but this is her first foray into adult fiction, and I know you'll be glad to hear that it won't be her last.

That's it for now, but keep your eyes open next month for the newest look in romance—only in Silhouette Intimate Moments.

Yours,

Leslie J. Wainger
Senior Editor and Editorial Coordinator

Broken Blossom

JENNIFER GREENE

Silhouette Intimate Moments

Published by Silhouette Books New York

America's Publisher of Contemporary Romance

88002

SILHOUETTE BOOKS
300 East 42nd St., New York, N.Y. 10017

ISBN: 0-373-07345-3

First Silhouette Books printing August 1990

Printed in the U.S.A.

JENNIFER GREENE

lives on a centennial farm near Lake Michigan with her husband and two children. Before writing full-time, she worked as a personnel manager, counselor and teacher. Mid-1988 marked the publication of her twenty-fifth romance. She claims the critical ingredient to success is a compassionate, kind, patient, understanding husband—who can cook.

Her writing has won national awards from Romance Writers of America, *Romantic Times* and *Affaire De Coeur*. She has also written under the pen name of Jeanne Grant.

For Jean
There was no problem too big
for her to understand.

bare as her long, brown legs. Maybe she'd brushed her hair last night, and the scrubbed face had freckles.

A real calculating hussy, all right. Rorke awkwardly cleared his throat . . . and lost the last chance he had to get a coherent word in for some time.

"Good heavens, come in, come in! No question you're Rorke. Walt told me you'd look like you'd tangled with the bulldozer. He didn't mention that the bulldozer won. Are you sure you're up for this? And I don't know how you could do this to me—"

"How I could—"

"You're on time." She delivered a stunning grin, full of sass and sparkle. "I wasn't on time for my own birth, and nothing's changed since. I *do* try—actually, I only got home from school fifteen minutes ago, so I was just changing clothes . . . I teach history. Did Walt tell you that?"

She extended a hand warmly and her gaze perceptively swept his rangy six-foot frame and military-rigid posture. She didn't look impressed. Actually, she seemed to miss noticing the man altogether because her soft blue eyes focused only on his injuries. She made a sympathetic clucking sound that offended Rorke. Okay, he looked a little battered, but he was nobody's lost lamb.

He slapped his hand in her palm, intending the handshake to be stiff and authoritative. Only her cool, slim palm didn't shake. They squeezed, her hand communicating a distinctly feminine warmth and welcome as she bossily herded him inside.

"The very first thing we have to do is get you comfortable. I know I have lemonade and iced tea. The only hard liquor I have around is a little bourbon—that's my father's drink—and I know someone left beer in my refrigerator at some time or another, but it's an odd variety. Hannibal, Heineken, some name like that? In this heat, I'll bet you could use a beer, but maybe you're not fond of the imported kinds?"

"They're fine, but—"

"Heavens, don't waste any time worrying about being formal or polite around me. All you have to do is say so if you don't like imported beers."

Again, he cleared his throat. "I like imported beers just fine, but—"

Her eyes met his. He felt the connection as though someone had just shoved the key to his ignition, and then her lazy, easy magnolia drawl swept on. "So that's one problem solved. Now comes the challenge of finding you a place to sit. I swear every year I'm going to get organized, but I never do. Maybe you could sort of develop tunnel vision while you walk through?"

"Everything looks fine."

"You're either the last of a dying breed of Southern gentleman or you need your eyes checked. And how swollen is that wrist? It'd be nothing to put together an ice bag while I'm getting the beer...and understand that the only reason I'm waiting on you is because of the shape you're in. Nobody maintains guest status in this house for long."

Before he knew it, he was inside her light-filled living room, installed in a creaking recliner with his feet up and feeling the impact of three or four slammed bullets.

Soft bullets. She was good, he gave her that. For the brief time she was out of sight in the kitchen, Rorke swiped a hand over his face. He dropped his hand when the smile was gone. Smiles! Rorke was far too tough and experienced to be taken in by a good acting job.

He'd walked in knowing exactly what to expect: a brazen hussy who'd put on the dog to sell him her sob story, undoubtedly with a little display of calculated vulnerability to woo his sympathy.

Kelsey meandered back from the kitchen, carrying a tray and still talking—God knows what about now, but undoubtedly *something* to badger a stranger into feeling comfortable and at home. She was one tough cookie, all right.

Her appearance was a sure tip-off to her calculating nature. She barely reached his chin in height, and her hair was a disordered tumble of silky-fine curls that skimmed her shoulders. The color was indefinable, kind of a streaked taffy with a little blond, a little brown, a little goldish red. If she ever wore makeup, there was no sign of it now. Her face was a delicate oval with feathery brows, a tipped nose, high cheekbones and possibly the most fragile mouth on a woman he'd ever seen. She'd left the top two buttons of her shirt open. She shouldn't have. He could see three freckles where he had no business looking in the first place.

She was so smart that she'd probably planned showing off those freckles, and Rorke wasn't likely to underestimate her intelligence. In spite of all her gregarious chitchat, he saw quickness and perception and sensitivity in her eyes . . . blue eyes, the smoke blue that made a man think of hidden fires and hot embers and sex. She'd probably planned the color of her eyes, too.

Kelsey set down his beer—the one he'd been trying to tell her he didn't want—and then a plate of chocolate chip cookies. There were clearly no limits to the effort she was willing to make to enlist his help, he thought dryly. The cookie bottoms were so black that a dog would reject them.

Her gaze flew to his. "They're a little crisp."

"They look real good," he said gruffly.

"I love to bake. It's the only relaxing hobby I have, and my favorite thing is scrounging around for old-fashioned recipes, but somehow... Look, you don't have to eat them."

He took a bite and tasted char. "Terrific," he said firmly.

"Honestly, you don't have to be polite. I knew you were tense when you walked in. Good heavens, so am I. I always talk too much when I'm nervous. We're both stuck with this being a slightly awkward situation, but that doesn't mean you have to feel obligated to eat my cookies."

"Kelsey."

"What?"

"I like your cookies." Okay, it was a lie, but Rorke had to get her to settle down somehow, didn't he? If she offered him any more hospitality, he'd be moved in.

"If there's anything else I could get you—"

"Nothing," he promised her.

She pushed a hand through her hair, which left a flopping cowlick on her brow. She didn't seem to care. Slower now, softer now, she straightened her slim shoulders and took a breath. "Then I won't waste any more of your time. I'm grateful you were willing to come here, Rorke, and—" Somewhere in the distance a phone rang. She closed her eyes and silently mouthed the word *damn*.

"It's all right. Go ahead and answer it."

She shook her head. "It'll stop in a minute if I just let it ring." She added humorously, "I swear that phone is hostile. It knows the exact minute I walk in the door and the exact moment I climb into a bathtub. I meant to take it off the hook before you came, but I was just so rushed. I'm sorry."

The phone company had created an unignorable jangle. "Go ahead," Rorke insisted.

"This is more important."

"And we'll deal with it, but your call could be important, too. I'm not going anywhere. Go ahead, it's okay," he repeated.

Still she hesitated, but the fifth nerve-racking ring finally got to her. The jack was in the kitchen, but her telephone had one of those long cords that traveled room to room. Rorke guessed from the opening track of the conversation that it was one of her students, because she strode for the dining room in the far corner and started leafing through texts and grade books. She hadn't talked for thirty seconds before the phone cord was completely tangled around her waist.

He caught himself smiling again . . . and this time he was irritable because of it.

Okay, the image of the calculating brazen hussy wasn't going to make it, but he still, very honestly, had to be tough. Where Rorke's professional ethics were concerned, he never lowered his guard.

His eyes narrowed in deliberate critical judgment of his surroundings. A woman's life-style always reflected her character. Rorke didn't have to search hard to find faults and flaws to nitpick.

Her living room was all color, all chaos. A dozen projects were half-started, a dozen books were half-read. Two shelves of her bookcase were jammed with

Civil War lore. Plants occupied every lighted spot. She'd started with a color scheme of peaches and cream but somewhere along the line lost control.

Neither control nor organization was obviously important to her. She was halfway through refinishing a garage-sale end table that was never going to be worth the price of the stain. And she was midway through sewing fringe on some curtains that were evidently going to end up on her French doors, because right now one door had a set of curtains and the other didn't.

It was a room to make a man like Rorke crawl the walls. He hated clutter and confusion. He liked order; he needed it in his own life. What nagged at him, though—what really struck him—was that she was thirty-four years old and didn't seem to *have* a damned thing.

Her cheerfully slipcovered couch had a sagging spring; even her books looked secondhand or were library editions. If he had a choice, he'd be sitting with a rigidly formal posture. Instead, he'd been swallowed up by the sinking-soft cushion of her recliner. The torture device had no support. A teacher's salary didn't extend to Rolls-Royces, but unless she was a total spendthrift she should have been able to accumulate something of value by this time in her life. And then his eye caught the gleam of silver.

Sun streamed on the cache of Victorian carved silver frames on the top bookshelf. There had to be a dozen of them. The light was wrong, and a double reflection made it impossible for him to make out the subjects of the photographs. He would have gotten up—he *wanted* to see them—only the moment he leaned forward, his cracked ribs stabbed at his lungs.

"They're pictures of my daughter. Janey."

Rorke hadn't heard her hang up the phone or walk in. Without a word, Kelsey cradled one of the miniature frames and handed it to him.

He forgot the bite of chest pain as he studied the photograph. The little girl was around four or five and definitely her mother's clone. The imp had Kelsey's same vibrance, the same lustrous eyes, the same fey and feminine energy; it was all just packaged pint-size.

The tyke was wearing shorts and waving wildly at the camera, a straggly brown braid bouncing on her neck, her small mouth covered with something orange. A dripping Popsicle? Kelsey was also in the picture, looking at her daughter, laughing, the shine of love in her eyes, her back swayed from the weight of holding the far too heavy little one.

Kelsey wasn't laughing now. She tucked herself into a corner of the couch, her bare legs curled under her. For the first time Rorke noticed the sketch of lines around her brow and eyes. Her skin was a faultless cream except for those lines, so they weren't caused by age. She'd known pain. From the moment she mentioned her daughter, a quiet had taken her from the inside. Her natural warmth and light diminished. She sat still—too still—and her voice had a strained, hoarse quality.

"Your detective friend, Walt, was wonderful to talk to, but he was also honest with me. He said that unless a crime was involved, my problem simply wasn't police business, so I'm especially grateful that you were willing to come. Frankly, I'd given up hope that anyone could help me."

"I don't know that I can," Rorke said cautiously.

She nodded. "I understand. Walt explained—it's not as if you're looking for work in the sense of being unemployed. You're still a state policeman even if you're on medical leave. And it's likely my problem is something you can't, or won't, want to be involved with.''

Rorke felt an irksome, off-balance sensation. She was stealing his lines. He'd intended to get out of this mess by using the excuse of his job. Kelsey was letting him off the hook before she'd even tried to reel him in. Where was the sob story, the sad tale?

"I also have to confess that I can't pay you much—"

"It's not a question of money," Rorke said flatly.

"No." She studied his face and then repeated softly, "No. With you it probably won't be . . . but I'd still like to get that subject out of the way. Like I told your partner, I have some money set aside for this—"

"Kelsey, forget money for right now." He knew he sounded impatient, but he saw the sudden tilt to her chin. They were going to run smack into her pride if he let the subject continue.

She was the one who dropped it. There was obviously a subject that mattered to her far more than pride.

"I need to locate my daughter, Rorke." Her voice was calm, quiet, grave.

Rorke didn't hear any emotion, but he saw it. There was pain in her eyes, so naked, so raw, that it made his stomach twist.

"As I told your partner," she continued, "I haven't seen Janey in eight years. It's that span of time that has complicated finding her. I've tried on my own, but it just isn't working. If you're not willing to help me, I'm hoping you might be willing to offer some ideas, some advice on what I could do from here."

"I didn't say I wasn't willing to help you. I said I wasn't sure I could. There's a difference."

"Is there?" she asked gently. "I could have sworn you walked in here with every intention of turning me down."

Rorke never moved...but he wanted to. He was aware of an itch crawling up his spine that made him feel like squirming. There was no challenge in her eyes, just acceptance. Kelsey was too perceptive for her own good. She also had him. He hadn't really come here to help her. He'd come to hear her out, which was all he'd promised Walt. Then he'd fully planned to walk right back out her door.

So far she hadn't given him a single reason to change that game plan.

Walt had seen the situation as a natural pairing. Rorke not only had time on his hands but had been brooding his way into a depression without something to take his mind off the robbery. And Kelsey "desperately" wanted to find her twelve-year-old daughter, which was no big sweat of a job for Rorke. Finding missing persons could be a hellacious project, but that was only because the average missing person didn't want to be found. Kelsey's ex-husband and daughter weren't missing or hiding. She'd simply lost track of them. Leave or no leave, Rorke had the obvious resources of a state cop at his disposal, such as access to unlisted phone numbers and the cooperation of the IRS. The entire affair could be a piece of cake.

That was how Walt had seen it. It wasn't how Rorke saw it. The use of his resources, however easy, was at his professional discretion. Ethics was where it all got touchy for him.

Kelsey had admitted that she hadn't seen her daughter in eight years. That was one heck of a long time, and Walt had already told him that the ex-husband had custody of the kid. Straight up, if the guy had legal custody, he also had every legal right to disappear off the face of the earth if he pleased. Ethically and professionally, Rorke had no right to mess with that.

More relevant, nice ladies didn't generally lose custody of their kids. Walt had taken one look and decided the sun rose and set with Kelsey Whitfield. Rorke was older, tougher, wiser. Over the years, he'd just seen too many sweet-faced, Bible-quoting women who beat their kids on the side. They never failed to turn his stomach.

Rorke had walked in believing Kelsey was one of them...that if she wasn't a child abuser, she was something just as bad. No way could her loss of custody and that long time span add up to good news.

"Rorke?"

Yeah, he knew. The silence was growing and it was time he said something, but his head was starting to pound. Ever since he'd left the hospital, he would sometimes feel attacked by this stupid, engulfing sensation of physical weakness—especially if he pushed too hard. He'd been pushing too hard all day, he felt like hell and all he wanted out of life was to be in his own apartment, sipping a tall whiskey with the curtains drawn. Alone. He had his own mistakes to live with. He sure as hell didn't need hers.

Impatiently he groped for conversation. "If I understand it right, you lived in Vicksburg eight years ago?"

"Yes." Kelsey sent him a measuring look, but there was no hesitation in her answer. "Andrew and I were married for seven years, and we lived in Vicksburg that whole time. Janey was four when we were divorced, which was the last time I had contact with her. Andrew got full custody—"

"Yeah. So Walt told me." Rorke couldn't keep the edge from his voice. He didn't need to hear about her loss of custody again. *Come on, blue eyes. Give me a reason to be involved. You're not working very hard to stack the deck in your favor.*

But she didn't seem to hear him. "I don't know where or when Andrew moved with Janey after that. I just know they're not at the old address. About a year ago I started spending nights at the library, poring over out-of-town phone books, but I couldn't find him listed anywhere."

"About a year ago? That's when you started this search?"

To Rorke, it seemed a long time for her to wait to find her daughter. If she heard the censure in his voice, her only response was to meet his eyes squarely. "Yes. And when the phone books failed, I called Andrew's attorney, the one who handled the divorce, but he wouldn't help me. And then a few months ago, I got the brilliant idea of hiring a private detective."

Rorke had no problem filling in that blank. "Five hundred dollars a day plus expenses?"

She nodded. "That ballpark. I could have done it for a while, but there was no way I could handle that kind of money for long and he wasn't offering any guarantees."

"Okay. So you tried contacting this lawyer, then this P.I., and you ended up at the cops' because you had a friend who knew Walt," Rorke said impatiently. "Unless I'm missing something, you took all the indirect roads when the direct ones were your better choice. What about all the obvious people who could have helped you? Your ex-husband must have had parents, relatives you could have reached—"

She plucked a frayed couch pillow and hugged it to her chest. "Andrew didn't have a big family. There were just his parents—Andrew senior and Mary—and since the divorce, they've both reached retirement age and moved, too. At least I assumed they moved. Neither are in the Vicksburg phone book anymore." She hesitated. "I have to be honest with you, Rorke. I never spent a lot of time trying to locate them because it wouldn't have helped. They wouldn't have talked to me. As far as they're concerned, they never wanted me to see Janey again."

Swell, Rorke thought wearily. It sure made her picture look rosier to know that she'd totally alienated her ex-in-laws. "Didn't anyone ever teach you to play poker?" he murmured.

"Pardon?"

"Nothing." He was briefly inclined to tear out his hair. He may have walked suspicious of hearing an embellished tale of woe, but Kelsey—for reasons he couldn't begin to fathom—wasn't even trying to present her side of the story.

"I also want to be honest with you about something else. Something I didn't discuss with your partner." She couldn't twist the pillow any tighter. "I want, desperately, to find my daughter. But I don't want to make any direct contact with her myself."

"I don't understand."

She took a breath. "What I want is for Janey to have something from me. Money. It's just over forty thousand dollars, which may not sound like a fortune to you, but it's taken me eight years to save it, whenever I could, however I could. Andrew's wealthy, so I've never been worried that Janey would want for anything, but I'd like her to have this nest egg from me. She's only twelve now, but she's heading into the years when she can plan her life. I want her to know she'll have some independence, some choices." She took another breath. "And there wouldn't have to be anything difficult about that, except that it has to be given to her directly. My ex-husband would never acknowledge or take anything that had my name on it. But I think it could matter to Janey—she had such rough beginnings. I think it might help her to know this was from me."

"Hold on there. You're moving pretty fast. I'm still back at the fence post. You want me to find your daughter, give her this nest egg—"

"Yes."

"But you don't want to see her yourself?"

"There is no way I want to see her," Kelsey confirmed.

Rorke had never seen another woman try it—look him straight in the face and lie. She was so bad at it that he might have been amused, except that the look in her eyes was enough to make a man lose his sense of humor...and maybe a nick off his heart, as well.

The look of strain in her eyes had nothing to do with some "nest egg." Kelsey Whitfield would die and go to hell for a chance of ever seeing her daughter again. How could she not know it? The truth had to be in her face every time she looked in a mirror.

"I'm aware this may change whether or not you're willing to help me. It is more complicated than just locating an address for Janey."

"Yes." Rorke tried to shift and felt his ribs cut into his chest. The loathsome sensation of physical weakness was getting worse, not better. If he was going to be able to cope with the twenty-minute drive home, he had to get out of here.

"You're not going to help me, are you?"

"Yeah, I am."

Her eyes filled up with hope. If she started crying, he was going to get *real* nervous. But then that hope died, and her lips started moving again. "You don't know the whole story—"

"Yeah, I do."

When it became clear that Kelsey wasn't going to fill in the blanks, Rorke had had to. He never made an impulsive decision, never made a judgment call based on emotion—he was too wary of making a mistake. In this case, that wasn't a worry.

One last time he briefly scanned the room: the garage-sale table, the heaping stacks of books, the scuffed sandals tucked under the couch, the plants she'd nurtured into a jungle of life. She had nothing, because she'd been saving every damn nickle and dime for her daughter.

Rorke didn't know the details, but he had no doubts about the two facts that mattered.

Kelsey loved her daughter more than life.

And Andrew Whitfield was a bastard.

Once he'd reached those conclusions, other hows and whys had fallen into place. Rorke believed in the system—he lived by it—but he also knew its flaws. Her ex-husband had money, and in far too many divorce cases, custody went to the parent with clout.

As to why she'd waited so long to search for her daughter, Rorke had no answer, but he had a good guess. The bastard had hit her around. Kelsey wasn't likely to admit that to a stranger. She didn't have to. As a cop, Rorke had seen plenty of women spinning in the abuse cycle. Fear kept them from fighting back and a low self-esteem kept them quiet. A woman with enough courage eventually found the strength to climb out of the abyss, but those kinds of emotional wounds took years to heal. Rorke was positive Kelsey had been there. It was the only reason that explained the long time span, the holes she hadn't filled in, those blue eyes that could turn too soft and too old at the turn of a dime.

Rorke's gaze riveted back on her. Sunlight caught in the froth of curls on her shoulders. She wasn't tiny, but she didn't have any spare ballast. Her loose-necked shirt displayed delicate collarbones. His hand could easily circle her wrists. Rorke thought of a man raising a hand to her and tasted grit in his throat. He was going to have a picture in his mind of that fragile mouth and those eyes for a long time.

"We'll find your kid," he said gruffly. For now, though, he just wanted and needed to get out of here. Quickly. He leaned forward and stopped.

"What's wrong?" she asked immediately.

"Nothing. Maybe you could get a few things together for me before I leave. Your ex-husband's business, his last address, his social security number, if for any reason you have it. And maybe I could take one of those photographs of your daughter."

"Rorke, what's wrong?"

Nothing that burying his head in the nearest hole wouldn't solve. He was trapped in the damned recliner. He'd settled into it easily enough, but the supportless cushion was making it impossible for him to get out. Again he tried to push forward. Shark's teeth clamped around his ribs so sharply that moisture sprang out on his forehead. "You just go ahead and get that stuff together for me," he said irritably.

"In a minute. First I'm going to help you, which is a little tricky to do when I don't have the least idea what we're dealing with."

"We're dealing with an idiot who's stuck in your chair."

"I can see that."

Rorke tried to lurch forward again. It didn't work. He could have worked around the sprained wrist if it wasn't for his ribs. He could have worked around the ribs if he just had some pushing strength in his wrist. And an iron-red flush climbed up his throat the longer she looked at him.

"You're also dealing with a man who doesn't like to do anything halfway. When I'm making a fool of myself, for example, I like to do it whole hog." He could see she didn't want to smile, but he caught the tip of one, which was a lot better than her looking frantically worried. "It was entirely my own fault that I got knocked around two weeks ago in the first place, but then I had to add insult to injury. The doc offered me a painkiller, but I said no way. Hey, only a sissy can't take a little pain. I'm a real tough guy, right?" She was definitely smiling now. He faked a baleful look when she started to chuckle. "You think that's funny, do you? You won't think it's so funny when I start having my mail delivered to this chair."

"I think we can get you out of there before it comes to that. Come on, tough guy." She swooped down on him and wrapped his injured wrist around her shoulder. "Hold your other arm around your ribs. I'll take your weight."

"Dammit, no! I'll knock you down."

"I'm sturdier than I look."

But she wasn't. She smelled like all the fragile blossoms in her yard, like spring and silky softness. And she was warm. He could feel that warmth and the weight of her breast when he heaved out of the chair.

For a moment he was swimming-dizzy, but the pain quickly eased once he was upright. A few brief seconds passed when they were in a close embrace, and when her face was tilted up to his. She was looking at him, assessing how badly he was hurting. Then she was looking at him in a different way.

The smile faded from her lips. Her eyes locked with his. Rorke had already known the sexual charge was there, but it seemed to take *her* by surprise. The hum between them blocked out sunlight, a cluttered, crowded room, an off-the-hook phone buzzing somewhere. The hum was soft, sweet, secret.

God, she was trouble. He'd known that before he walked in, but he hadn't known how much and how dangerous that trouble was going to be. He looked at her mouth and knew at that moment he could take it. She hadn't moved, was barely breathing. But then, neither was he.

A man didn't feel like this when he was thirty-seven. A man felt like this when he was fifteen, had just found his first girl and felt his pulse skyrocketing on wonder and life from just being with her. You never got that magic back again. You got smarter and tougher and older; life slugged you around and experience taught you the lessons you had to know to survive.

Rorke had gotten more of those life slugs than any ten men, but for the cadence of a few seconds he was back ... back at a time when the magic was as fragile as innocence, as blinding as sunlight, as compelling as the texture of his girl's soft cheek under the stroke of his fingertip. Kelsey didn't move away from the touch of his hand. She looked at him with those deep, dark blue eyes, and he felt her shiver.

The absent thought dawdled through his mind that he'd kill anyone who ever hurt her again. That irrational thought was followed by another: she was so special that she could seep into a man's soul without half trying.

Kelsey moved first. She took a gasp of breath, briefly closed her eyes and then gently removed his arm from around her shoulder. "You're okay now?"

"Yes." But when she moved away, he wasn't. Contrary to what he'd told her, he wasn't in the habit of acting like a fool. The opposite was true. He had no patience for fairy-tale emotions, no patience for weakness in a man...yet how many times did a man ever feel a pull so powerful it was like a stroke on his soul? And the emotion tenaciously lingered. What he'd felt for her had been real, something he'd never expected to feel again, not at his age, not in this life.

"I'll get together those things you asked for." Kelsey moved swiftly to her bookshelves and chose one of the photographs to take out of its frame.

She handed it to him, but he didn't look at the picture of the four-year-old girl. He looked at Kelsey. Hectic color streaked her cheekbones and she was all nerves and motion. The sparkle and sass were gone from her eyes; in their place he saw the brittle shine of anxiety...and maybe fear.

"I need to tell you one more thing, Rorke—"

"No, you don't." He wanted to run his hands through her hair and hold her—anything to take that look out of her eyes. "I need to get some details straight, yes. But not right now, and nothing of a nature that's going to pry into your private life—just information on your daughter."

"Yes, well…" Her arms fell limply to her sides. "One of the things you need to know is that I believe—I'm almost positive—that my ex-husband moved to make it deliberately harder for me to find Janey."

"Honey, I guessed that." He didn't mean to let the endearment slip out; it just did. "You don't have to talk about it. It didn't take much to figure out that he was a bastard."

"Then you figured wrong," she said slowly. "Andrew is and always was a decent man and a good father…and I can't ask you to be involved without being honest about what you'd be getting into. I'm the bad guy in the piece, Rorke, not my ex-husband."

"Sure you are," he murmured.

"What I am," she said gently, "is an alcoholic."

Chapter 2

When Sherman sent in a whopping thirty thousand men to take Vicksburg, the rebels sent him back with his tail between his legs. The South not only *wanted* to win the Civil War—they *were* winning it, and Grant knew he was running out of chances. Unless he turned things around *real* quick, the pole outside this school today would be waving the confederate flag instead of the Stars and Stripes—Daryl, would you please take the gum out of your mouth?—so taking Vicksburg *mattered*. Niles, bring your group up here. You're General Pemberton and the Southern troops. And, Sharon—if you wouldn't mind waiting to French-braid your hair until after school—you and your group are Grant and the Union men. Come on, people. I want to see some minds working here. I want to see strategy. I want to know what the South had to do to win."

Kelsey heard a few grumblings and "Aw, Mrs. Whitfields," but those were obligatory ninth-grader complaints. The class was huddled over the relief model at the front of the room within minutes. The kids were of an age where their entire lives were run by hormones. Their interest in history was zip...but heresy was something else. Refixing history so the South could win—that was something they could sink their teeth into.

Rebel and Union caps were donned. Lights flashed on the relief model, simulating gunfire. The siege of Vicksburg had begun—give or take some private bickering between Marie and Annie, who'd been battling for the same boy all term. Kelsey relaxed, leaning back against her desk.

Teaching salaries in a private school couldn't compete with those in a public school, but she had a ton more freedom. She valued it. It took a lot of creativity and imagination to challenge kids these days. In this case it had taken her hours with papier-mâché, a friend with a borrowable pickup truck to transport the heavy model and an electrician willing to wire all those little lights so the kids could really pretend there was gunfire.

It had been a lot of work, but it was worth it. This way the kids thought they were playing a game, and she could sneak in the real history lessons painlessly.

Kelsey was quite aware that all the lessons she'd had to learn in life had been—historically—extremely painful.

"It's just no good, Mrs. Whitfield. There's just no way the South could win once the city was under siege—"

"And that's a very logical conclusion to reach, sugar, but you can do better than that. Couldn't Pemberton have anticipated the siege? Couldn't he have outguessed Grant's plan? And if he'd known what Grant had in mind, what exactly would he have done to stop it?''

"Oh."

Kelsey ruffled Niles's mop of fuzzy brown hair. "Yeah, *oh*. Go to it, General."

He went back to it. Her gaze drifted to the clock. Thirty more minutes before the bell and freedom for the day. Outside the clouds were hanging low and hemmed with dark edges. The sun peeked out, then in. An old catalpa stood just outside the window, its leaves flapping in a sudden fretful, restless wind. It had been an equally fretful, restless day.

She couldn't get him off her mind.

Heaven knew she'd tried, but every time she closed her eyes, she could see Rorke's face when he'd first walked through her door. Meeting him, she had expected to feel uncomfortable, but he was the awkward one, standing there looking so tense, so rigid, so battered. Her heart had gone out to him.

It hadn't taken her long to realize that Rorke didn't want to be there, didn't want anything to do with her. It had taken her even less time to realize that he was hurting. Kelsey had made the only choices she could. She'd taken him in the way she'd take in any wounded critter who landed on her doorstep, and she'd given him every out he could possibly want as far as involvement with her problems.

There was no way it was going to be an easy encounter, but it never had to get complicated. And it wouldn't have . . . if Rorke had listened to her.

He hadn't listened. He'd just kept looking at her with those clear dark eyes, until she felt something fragile and potent and totally unexpected affect her pulse rate.

She had *never* anticipated the emotional and sexual pull. For a few brief moments she'd experienced the heady spell of feeling young again. So young she believed she could do anything: conquer worlds, love with wild and sensual abandon with no consequences, trust that the world would stop if the right man would just believe in her.

The silly illusion hadn't lasted long. Life had taught her better lessons. Life had also taught her that total honesty was the only way to avoid hurting people. Everyone close to Kelsey knew she was an alcoholic—she'd never hidden it, never tried to—but it was hard to tell Rorke, hard to watch that light die in his eyes, hard to watch him fumble with the images that obviously immediately filled his mind.

No one had to tell Kelsey that there was nothing pretty in the picture of a woman drunk.

Before he'd left—and injured or not, he hadn't taken long to clip toward her front door after that—he'd said, "Look, Kelsey. . . it makes no difference."

But of course it made all the difference in the world. She hadn't seen him for nearly a week, so he'd apparently changed his mind about helping her find Janey. It hurt that she'd blown that. And when he'd left so abruptly, he'd walked away from more than Janey—good grief, she didn't blame him! Yet irrationally and indefensibly, that had hurt, too.

For eight long years she'd faced the realities of her life. She wasn't tough. She had never aspired to being tough. But she thought she'd developed a shell harder than enamel where a certain kind of emotional vulnerability was concerned.

"You just have to see this, Mrs. Whitfield. We. . . hey, what'd you do that for?"

She glanced at the broken pencil in her hands then up to the tall gangly teeanger. "Must be my day to be klutzy, Daryl, but what is this that I just 'have to see'?"

"We got Grant pinned at the Big Black River and we're whaling the tar out of him."

"Good grief. Show me." She hopped off the desk, stuck her hands in the pockets of her wild print skirt and entered the war. The next time she looked up, she had a Confederate cap on her head and a Rebel sword in her hand—props shared by the rest of the Rebel troops—but Kelsey knew it was getting close to three. When she looked at the clock, she also caught a glimpse of a man's blue shirt in the open doorway.

When a pair of cold dark eyes connected with hers, she felt a kick in the stomach...not a little flutter but a good wallop.

At first glance, Kelsey guessed Mr. Stoner wanted to be here now no more than he had the first time. Rorke's stance was all aggressive male: shoulders thrown back, one knee cocked forward. When he realized she'd spotted him, he motioned toward her class and mouthed, "I'll wait."

Temporarily trapped as military adviser to both generals Grant and Pemberton, Kelsey didn't have a lot of choice, but her gaze kept straying to the doorway. Five days had made a difference. Physically he looked healthier. His face had some color, and the red stitch line near his right temple didn't look half as angry. The bruises around his nose had faded to a sachet-pretty violet. His wrist was still bandaged and the ribs still had to be bothering him, but the white lines of pain were gone from around his eyes.

His physical healing was coming along, so Kelsey had no idea why she sensed that there were deeper wounds infecting Rorke. She didn't know him. Whatever she "sensed" was none of her business or ever likely to be. He scowled every time he caught her sneaking another look at him...and still she sneaked those looks and felt her nerves go squish every time.

Battered or not, he was a rogue. The stamp of loner was in the cut of his jaw. The stamp of lover was in the emotive depth of his eyes. He was as tall as the devil, with a lean, hungry build and the muscular legs of a runner. His skin had the weathering of fine leather, with sun and laughter lines crinkled around his eyes, but there were deeper groves wedged on his brow...the grooves of a hardheaded man who took on the world. Alone. The way he wanted it. His eyes could be a steel-cold, stubborn gray, but not always.

She'd already seen his eyes darken to the devil's own smoke when Rorke wanted something. For the briefest moment in her living room, he'd wanted her so strongly that she'd felt his sensual power like a slam...an electric, explosive, vital slam. Rorke was a man. No woman could conceivably forget that.

If it was as simple as exposure to sexual dynamite, though, Kelsey would never have been drawn. She liked men fine, but her personal life was hardly whistle-clean. She'd had years of experience in tuning out sexual feelings, not by choice but by necessity. To ask someone else to take on her bad baggage was out of the question.

The blood-and-guts battle was still raging. The rebels in 1863 should have had such enthusiasm. Kelsey automatically removed Sharon's sword—the girl was taking her role a little too seriously—and nudged Tony back into the group. He always hung back unless pushed.

When she glanced up again she caught Rorke studying her, and again felt her pulse surge...less in sexual
awareness this time than in instinctive compassion. As
at their first meeting, Rorke's shirt was immaculate, his
pants creased, his dark sandy hair meticulously
brushed. His shave hadn't missed a whisker. Mr. Perfectionist, she thought wryly, but the label troubled her.
All those laugh lines...yet there was no smile. And
those beautiful dark eyes were driven. Something had
whipped the life out of Rorke. She saw it in his eyes—
the total restraint, the unshakable control and the discipline he demanded of himself.

Do you even know you're hurting, Mr. Stoner?
And, damn you, stop looking at me like that.

A bell rang, strident and insistent. Any other time her
students would have stampeded for the door. But not
when she wanted them to. "Hey." No response. "Come
on, people. There are buses waiting for you out there.
You can finish the battle tomorrow. Leave the props on
my desk." It was like herding sloths. They were capable of moving. They just didn't want to.

"I'm not leaving if you let Niles stay. We just got our
guys all set up on the other side of the river—"

"Niles isn't staying. No one's staying—Daryl, don't
you dare stick that gum under the chair. Come on,
buses and moms are waiting for you. There won't be a
thing moved until you come in tomorrow—"

"What about your other classes?"

"I promise to protect the battlefield from my other
classes. April, you forgot your sweater, and who left
their books on the windowsill?"

Why did the end of the day have to be so chaotic? It
was another five minutes before Kelsey could turn back
to Rorke. He'd been watching but he hadn't moved,

hadn't smiled, and, as far as she could tell, hadn't breathed.

Starting a conversation with a brick wall was going to be tricky; she'd probably look foolish flying all over the room. But walking toward him, Kelsey had suddenly had enough of feeling nail-biting tense. She propped a grave expression on her face to match his. "Believe me, it's not usually like this. Normally, I'm a model teacher, a paragon of authority and organization, heavily into respect and control—I mean, these kids jump when I say jump." She confided, "They're terrified of me."

It was the right tack to take. Somewhere, deep in those formidably austere features, was a crack. "Yeah, I could see how tough you were with them."

"Give kids this age an inch and they'll take a mile. Any other day and you'd see how it really is. I stand on my desk with a whip and I crack that thing over their heads—"

"Yeah?" A grin sneaked out, lopsided and slow, but for that brief moment Rorke forgot to be stiff. "I hate to doubt your veracity—"

"Then please don't," she said primly.

Now she had a chuckle from him. "But when I went to school, Vicksburg and Gettysburg had something in common. The Union won both battles."

"Not the way I teach history."

"That's what confused me."

Belatedly she realized she was still wearing a Confederate cap. When she whipped it off, her hair flopped every which way, propelled by static electricity. All her life, Kelsey had hated her hair, but never more than at that moment. "The kids have a hard time relating to dates and history. Go back a few centuries and it's all so remote, nothing like the electronic age we're living in now, so they don't see the relevance. If I can get them to act something out, they can forget the dates and relate the events to real people, human beings no different than they are. No matter what period they lived in, people have a habit of making the same mistakes, and that's what the study of history should be—a way to recognize and learn from mistakes that were already made.'' She was just warming up to the subject when he interrupted her.

"They love you."

"Pardon?"

"The kids. They think you move earth and water."

"You can fool some of the people some of the time," she murmured, but that was as far as she could take the irrelevant conversation. "It couldn't have shocked me more to see you in the doorway," she said quietly. "I never expected to see you again."

"Why? I told you I'd be back."

"I know, but..." But she remembered the look on his face when he'd left her. He just wanted out—clean, clear and fast—from anything to do with her.

"I told you I'd need more information on your daughter. You knew that. And I told you I'd help you find her—you knew that, too."

She wondered if he heard the belligerent tone in his voice. He was here for Janey. Nothing else. He could have stamped the message in cement. Kelsey was briefly tempted to smooth his hair, comfortingly, the way she would for a child. It had been hard for him to come back; did he think she was blind? And she understood—probably better than he did—why he wanted it clear that he had no personal interest in her.

"I apologize if coming to the school was a bad idea. It seemed like a logical time to catch you when the kids were just letting out—'' He glanced around. There were two doors to her classroom. So far, no more than thirty seconds had passed without someone's head popping in. No one had interrupted when they saw Kelsey was talking to him, but it was like her house. No conceivable chance of peace and quiet. One pimply-faced boy had walked in and just glared at him. He brought back two sidekicks—girls—who took one look at Rorke and giggled.

Kelsey twisted her head around, but by then no one was there.

Exasperated, Rorke said, ''I just need a few minutes with you. Is there someplace we could go? Someplace quiet?''

''There's a teachers' lounge—''

''I mean someplace where a hundred people aren't going to walk in on us.'' The color changed in his face. ''I mean—''

''I know what you mean,'' she said calmly. No one would have interpreted his comment as a sexual innuendo except someone with sex on his mind. Rorke was the one changing color. To smooth over the awkward moment, she said swiftly, ''There's a place named Maloney's a few blocks from here. Some of us run over there for a steak sandwich on Fridays. It's really quiet.''

''Fine. I'll drive.'' He frowned at her. ''Or we can both drive. Or—''

''We'll both drive. That's easy enough, isn't it?''

''It won't take long,'' he promised. ''Only, Kelsey?''

''Hmm?''

He scratched his chin. ''You might want to take off the Confederate Army jacket before you go anywhere.''

* * *

Rorke had never had a problem with nerves. All the tedious work involved in setting up a drug bust, all the gut-churning emotion when you walked in knowing your adversaries were armed, even the time six years ago when he'd been held hostage by a psycho...all of it was nothing compared to following that rat-trap of a car of Kelsey's for three blocks.

The thing died at the first stop sign, then sputtered and jerked when she restarted it. One tire was low. Wire held up the muffler. The exhaust spumed black—she'd probably changed the oil six, seven years ago, and that red rust heap would have been on the endangered species list even then. He thought of her driving down a highway at highway speeds and aged ten years.

And it wasn't just her car, it was *her*. Watching her with those kids, full of pepper and life, fixing it so the South won the Civil War, for God's sake. She hadn't treated him any differently than she treated anyone else. He could see that now. She was generously warm with men, women, kids and probably dogs.

She hadn't felt anything different with him.

He was the one who felt taken out by meeting her, and that had annoyed him for the past five days. Since the robbery, he'd been living in a self-imposed emotional exile. She'd stirred him out of it, with her burned cookies and sun-swept smiles and those damned floppy pansies. No, he hadn't forgotten the guilt stalking him since the boy had been shot. If anything, the incident was more vibrant and clear in his mind, not less. The dreadful woman had exposed him to the sensation of feeling again.

His zombielike depression had been far less painless.

He was thirty-seven years old. Several women had really mattered to him over the years. His job was hard on relationships, but Rorke had always known that he was the real flaw. He was careful. Too careful. Once past the courtship rituals it didn't matter how good it was in bed—a woman always discovered that he wasn't going to open up. "Talk to me," June used to complain. He thought he had been talking. Andrea's parting shot had been "You're never going to let a woman in, Rorke." That one had hurt the most, because he'd tried.

Within an hour of meeting Kelsey, she had seeped into an emotional niche he never exposed. Except for one occasion when he was a teenager, he'd been at the worst physical and mental low in his life. That was the only rational explanation he could come up with for feeling so... different... with her.

But a drinker?

Cops were particular prey to the problem; more than once Rorke had seen guys lose their jobs and their families over a love affair with the bottle. One of his first partners had been a man named Russ. Russ had a beautiful wife and an eight-month-old cherubic urchin. A *baby*. All Russ had to do was stay off the sauce. How could a man have so little self-control as to throw away everything that mattered to him?

Rorke had told himself that Kelsey's problem was none of his business. Who was he to judge her? But he woke up from dreams where he pictured her slack-eyed and weaving. He pictured her waking up in the morning to a baby in a high chair, and her pouring vodka into a shot glass. He couldn't make the pictures work—not with Kelsey's face, not with those blue eyes. Not without getting violently sick to his stomach.

Kelsey sped into a parking space ahead of him. Her brakes had a sound that made him wince.

Originally ethics had made him suspicious of being involved with her. Those same ethics had driven him to seek her out again—he had no reason *not* to help her. Finding her daughter was an entirely separate problem from Kelsey's being an alcoholic. He'd find her kid. Rorke didn't give a hoot what she'd done eight years ago—she had a right to know where her daughter was. It shouldn't take him more than a few afternoons of phone calls to locate an address, and after that it was her ball game and he was out of it. Caring about her never entered the picture. Involvement with an alcoholic?

He'd been smarter than that since the day he was born.

He climbed out of his car, mentally swearing when his ribs pinched, and strode toward her. "When did you plan on getting a new car?" he asked her peaceably.

"Pardon?"

Totally uninvolved and uncaring, he said firmly, "No way you're driving that thing another year."

She wended her way toward him with a purse bigger than a suitcase and a longish, silky-looking skirt swirling around her legs in the wind. She pushed the hair out of her eyes with an impish grin. "You'd better watch it. I don't take kindly to insults to my family. Bertha's been my baby for seven years, and I know she has a few flaws, but loyalty has to count for something. I would never trade her in for a total stranger—"

"Kelsey, it's a car. A car with bald tires and rust—" He swung open the restaurant door for her automatically. "I didn't like the sound of those brakes . . ." Maloney's, she'd said. He hadn't noticed the wind pick up or the first spatterings of rain, and he hadn't paid any attention to the look of the place.

Now he did, and felt his throat close. The main room was long and narrow and almost empty of customers at this hour. Dark red carpeting cushioned all sound, and hanging Tiffany lamps provided subdued lighting. Red leather booths lined two walls. It was exactly what he wanted: a private place to talk, where no phones were going to ring and no students were going to interrupt a conversation that Kelsey might not want overheard.

Only he never dreamed she'd recommend a bar. Good Lord, could she think he'd have deliberately forced this on her? "A cop could cite you for the exhaust alone—"

"What's wrong with my exhaust?"

He took one look at the gleaming array of liquor bottles and jerked in front of her. "You need an oil change."

"I change my oil all the time."

"Then it's using oil like a freight train."

"That's true. And I know she likes a lot of oil, but she's old. I can't just put her out to pasture because she's old. Would you do that to your grandmother?"

"We're talking about *cars*. Not grandmothers." His palm closed over her shoulder. The contact made her eyes zoom to his. He'd never intended to touch her, but it was the only way he could steer her into the near side of the booth where she had no view of all that alcohol.

"You seem to be feeling a lot better than the last time I saw you," she said gently.

She was wrong. He'd never felt more sick, and that feeling intensified when the frizzy white-haired bartender meandered toward them and leaned over the table.

"Hi, George," Kelsey said warmly.

"Hi, darlin'. My grandson not giving you any trouble, is he?"

"Dylan's doing just great. He's one of my favorites."

"Yeah? But you say that about all the kids. My daughter's got two that age now. She says she's going to end up in a rest home before they're both out of puberty. Well? What can I get you two?"

"A Coke," Rorke said swiftly. He could feel beads of sweat forming at the back of his neck. Kelsey obviously knew the bartender. Well.

"A Coke it is. And how about you, darlin'?"

Kelsey's eyes met Rorke's. "A beer, I think."

Rorke froze.

"You want a list of labels or the house draft?"

"That depends on whether you recommend the house draft," Kelsey teased.

"It'll wet your tongue on a hot day," George promised.

"That's it, then."

George drifted off. Rorke didn't know where to look, how to behave. Kelsey carried on a smooth, calm, ridiculous monologue about Bertha—her damned car. He was vaguely aware of the creak of leather behind him, the distant buzz of conversation from a couple on the far side of the room, George moving around behind the brass-and-mirrored bar.

Rorke had been to a few bars in his time—but never with an alcoholic. Never with a freckle-nosed woman with wispy hair and unforgettably sexy blue eyes. Her violet blouse had a V neck. God, those three freckles. He was dying.

He died even more when George returned. Napkins and a bowl of peanuts were served with a flourish and a grin. "One Coke and one beer..."

"My tab," Kelsey told him.

"Mine," Rorke corrected her.

George winked and placed the bill midway between them. Once he walked away, Kelsey calmly switched his Coke for her beer. "Rorke?"

"What?" The beer was in front of him, not her. She wasn't going to drink it. He had to mentally repeat that three times to himself before it registered.

"Would you please look at my mouth?"

Could anything else go wrong with this afternoon? What kind of request was that? He'd just started to relax about the beer, and now she handed him another curveball—but his gaze strayed to the two lips. In his most critical, decisive and impartial judgment, they were delectable. *Why did you have to be a drinker, Kelsey Whitfield?* The upper lip was more sharply defined, but both looked softer than petals and cream; both looked as if they'd fit perfectly under a man's mouth....

And at the moment they were moving. "Note there's no froth, no foam. I don't turn rabid at the sight of liquor, Rorke. It's perfectly okay to lighten up. I served you a beer at the house, remember?"

"I remember." He didn't understand, but he remembered. For the moment he couldn't seem to understand much of anything, except that alcohol overshadowed every thought in his head. "I never meant to offend you," he said quietly.

"You didn't." His overprotective attitude had touched Kelsey, so much that her hand reached over to cover his half-closed fist on the table. They were never going to be able to talk while he was this tight, this tense. "Rorke...it's not a cause with me. If I know a friend likes beer, I usually keep it around. I also walk into bars and go to parties with friends where I know liquor will be served. You're perfectly welcome to drink around me."

All he wanted to do was drop the subject—totally—but the gruff words sneaked out. "It has to be harder on you to be exposed to it."

"Harder or easier has nothing to do with it. I've been dry from the time my daughter was taken away from me—that's eight years. Ample time for me to realize that temptation is in the head, not in the availability of a glass of Chardonnay. Either way, no one's responsible for my problem but me."

He heard her, but his attention was distracted. Her fingers squeezed and then slid away, yet not before he noticed that her hand was soft, supple and white, with four short, well-manicured nails...and a thumbnail she'd bitten to the quick.

A nail biter who raised pansies and wore a moth-eaten Confederate coat to teach classes. He told himself he felt relief. She had absolutely nothing in common with any woman he'd ever been attracted to. Ergo, it should be easy to move on to what he'd come for. Only when he cleared his throat, he found himself still hanging on the same limb. "Eight years is a long time. I'd think anyone would consider that a total cure."

"Then that 'anyone' would be wrong," she said cheerfully. She scooped up a handful of peanuts and nudged the bowl closer to him. "There is no cure. I'm going to be an alcoholic when I'm a hundred and three. That's the way it is. Actually, I think you already know that's the way it is, and I have to believe you're going to be amazingly happier once you drop this subject."

She had that right, but one more time he had to try. "You still want it? That glass of Chardonnay?"

She didn't respond for a moment because her mouth was full of peanuts. Flecks of salt coated her bottom lip, just like a little kid's, but when her eyes met his, he saw all the shrewd perceptiveness of a woman who knew him too well in far too short a time. She murmured softly, "Don't ask questions you don't want the answers for, sugar."

She let that sift in before saying, "Dammit, Rorke, can we please talk about my daughter? That's the only reason you came here, wasn't it?"

Chapter 3

The minute Kelsey mentioned her daughter, her whole focus diverted away from him.

That was just as well, because Rorke had no ability to make casual conversation for the next few moments. She was right. He'd sought her out for the honest reason of needing to discuss her daughter. But he'd also wanted to know if Kelsey's laughter still had that sassy catch, if her eyes were really that incredible blue. She couldn't be as natural to be around as he remembered. He couldn't feel a burst of life and emotion for a woman he barely knew.

And Rorke had his answers. She was just as captivating and complex as he'd found her the first time. *But she still wanted that glass of Chardonnay.* He felt as if a door had just been slammed in his face.

She did it deliberately, Stoner. She's been nothing but honest with you. Damn you, let it go.

Kelsey obviously had. Her head was dipped over her purse. "If you'd happened to call, I had all the stuff you asked for ready by the phone at home. Unfortunately, I didn't plan on seeing you out of the blue." Out of Pandora's box came a pair of spindly framed reading glasses, which she propped on her nose, then a two-year-old cleaner's receipt, four pens, a hairbrush, keys, a box of chalk, the week's paycheck...she lifted her head and grinned. "I knew I had a pad of paper in here somewhere!"

Rorke had the brief suspicion that her exuberance was a way of steering him, gently, protectively, away from deep waters. The oversize frames only magnified the sensitivity and perception in her eyes. Kelsey, he guessed, had a long-standing habit of taking care of people in her wake. Men who momentarily fell off the wagon of common sense, for instance.

Taking her cue of humor, he dryly motioned to her purse. "Do you pack in the morning expecting to be kidnapped for three weeks at a stretch?"

"There's nothing in here that isn't absolutely essential."

"I'll bet this old Christmas card comes in real handy during an emergency."

"If you tease me, tough guy, I'm going to remind you of how silly you looked stuck in the recliner in my living room...darn." The first two pens didn't work; she tried the third and then scrawled an address on the dog-eared pad of paper. "That's a Vicksburg address—the last one I knew where Andrew and Janey lived. Also, here's the phone number." She dug in her wallet and slipped out a photograph. "There's another picture of Janey, but you'll be careful with it, won't you?"

"I'll guard it with my life."

She lifted her face, her gaze suddenly stricken, and his smile died. She seemed to face life with an indomitably light heart—she even made jokes about her drinking—but her whole world shifted as volatilely as quicksand anywhere near the subject of her daughter. He shouldn't have joked, not about Janey. It was a mistake he wouldn't make again.

"I meant it," he said quietly. "I won't let anything happen to the photograph."

"It's just that I don't have that many of them."

"I understand. It's okay."

It seemed to be, because she immediately concentrated on the business of repacking her purse. "Andrew's Social Security number is sitting on the counter in my kitchen. You nearly had me in a pickle when you asked for that. I wasn't sure I could find it, but I started digging in a box in the attic and came up with an old tax return. Anyway, if you call me, I'll give it to you over the phone."

"Fine."

"What else did you ask me about? I remember...his business." She tucked her knuckles under her chin and frowned. "I think that's probably a dead end, Rorke. At least I don't see how you could locate him through his work. Andrew was born with a silver spoon just like his dad, old Southern money, and he doesn't work in the same way most people do. He has a business degree and a real estate license, and what he handles is land—big estates—but he doesn't work for anyone. I mean, there's no company name, no office telephone number. It's just him. Unless he's gotten into something different over the past few years."

"All right. We'll work from that," he said abruptly. He scribbled "real estate license" on her pad, but the lead didn't catch his attention. Every time she mentioned her ex-husband, he found himself waiting. Kelsey wasn't likely to admit the bastard had hit her around, started her drinking, but Rorke had come to his own conclusions. He kept expecting her to hear a nuance or inflection in her voice—bitterness, anger, stress—something that nailed down her history with the creep.

"He's likely to have Jenny in a private school. A day school, though. He wouldn't send her away," Kelsey said thoughtfully. "And wherever he's living, he's likely to belong to things. Country clubs, men's clubs... He likes boats. Maybe membership lists would make it easier for you to find him?"

She might talk as if the guy were any man on the street, but Rorke wasn't fooled. "Sounds like he likes living pretty upper crust."

Kelsey glanced at him, then dipped her fingers in the peanut bowl again. "My dad used to say that if you had it, flaunt it. Believe me, Andrew has it. Why shouldn't he live high?"

"Why are you finishing a garage-sale table so you have a place to put a lamp on?"

He could have bitten his tongue. Kelsey lowered the glasses to the tip of her nose and studied him. "By any chance," she said gently, "do you have my ex-husband pegged as a too-rich, spoiled, wastrel-type son of a gun?"

"You haven't given me any reason to think that shoe doesn't fit," he shot back.

"Of course I have. Janey's with him. You think I wouldn't have fought for my daughter—drinking problem or not—if I didn't believe he was the best of fathers? I'd have stolen her if I had to, Rorke."

He wiped his face with his hand. "Maybe you could try and keep in mind that I'm a cop, toots. You don't tell a cop that you'd be happy to kidnap a kid."

"I wouldn't have hesitated two seconds."

Rorke couldn't remember a time when he'd been more desperate for a taste of beer. His throat was as parched as a withered cactus, but somehow he couldn't make his hand move to the foaming pilsner. It wasn't that he'd have died and gone to hell before drinking alcohol in front of her. He just knew that anything less than a triple whiskey wasn't likely worth the effort.

Kelsey lifted her hand and motioned to George. Rorke thought fleetingly that if she ordered another beer, even if she intended to switch it, he would strangle her. "New subject, Rorke," she said darkly.

Please, God, no.

"We have to get this money thing settled. I never expected you to help me for free. I told you I had money put away."

"Good. Put it into brakes, fresh oil and a new muffler and we'll call it quits. Better yet, put it toward a down payment on something without rust."

"No."

He waited, but that was her entire comment on the subject. How was he supposed to handle that? Wary of her pride, he downplayed the subject by shifting—regrettably—to the even tougher subject of the reason he'd sought her out. "We need to get something straight before going on," he said carefully. "I spoke too quickly the other day. The truth is that I can't do exactly what you asked me to do, Kelsey. It's not—"

Her eyes froze on his face, but he couldn't finish what he was trying to say because George interrupted them. She never glanced at the bartender even while she was delivering her absent request. "He's dying of thirst, George, but the beer just isn't doing it."

"You don't like my draft?"

Rorke never glanced at George, either. Did she have to look as if he'd hit her? "I don't want anything, George."

George looked at the two of them, threw up his hands in a comical gesture and ambled back to polishing his glasses.

Rorke jumped back in. "Kelsey, I'll find your daughter. That's not the problem."

"I thought you were trying to tell me that you couldn't help me."

He shook his head. "There are a dozen ways to track down your ex-husband—tax records, unlisted phone numbers, his real estate license, whatever. We'll hit on one of them."

"You sound so sure."

"I am that sure that I can locate your daughter, meaning that one way or another I'll get you an address. It may take a little time, but very little effort—and that's what I meant about the money, okay? If I thought I was going to add up expenses, I'd ask you for something, but this just isn't like that."

"Of course it is."

For whole stretches of time he could forget she was a drinker. For whole periods of time he was shamelessly distracted by how special she was. Little details kept capturing his attention, like her long white neck and those freckles, like the wisp of a sun-kissed curl on her brow, like the fragile angle of her eyebrows, like her mouth. She was quick, dangerously perceptive, a woman who flaunted her softness and had a man wanting to peel past the complex layers to really know her.

But she did have a head harder than a baseball bat. There wasn't any way he could take money from a woman who couldn't afford more than cast-off furniture, and he didn't give a duck's behind how proud she was.

"The point," Rorke said quietly, "is that I can locate your daughter, but not contact her. You wanted me to give your daughter this nest egg, and that's what I can't do."

"Why?"

"Honey, your ex-husband has total custody."

"Yes."

"She's a minor."

"Yes."

"He has legal rights, which are intended to protect your daughter's legal rights. Maybe the bastar— Maybe your ex-husband doesn't deserve to have the law on his side, but right now he does. Right now, no stranger can walk up to your twelve-year-old daughter without the threat of a penalty, and that's the way it should be. Sure, you know this circumstance is different because it's you involved, but I have to see this as a cop. I can't cross that legal line."

Kelsey started to respond, then tugged off her reading glasses and pinched the bridge of her nose. She swallowed, hard. When she found her voice again, it had softened and deepened like the nap side of velvet. "I'm sorry. Really sorry. It never occurred to me that I was asking you to cross a legal line, and it should have, because you're right. Normally I would *never* want a stranger to be able to approach Janey. Good grief, I *want* her protected. It's just . . ."

"Honey—"

Kelsey shook her head, needing to explain. "It's just that if it wasn't a stranger, there was no other way. Andrew would never let me near her. I could always put the money in Janey's name—it might even reach her—but he'd never let her know it was from me."

Her voice caught. "She was four when I left. She has to believe I abandoned her. I've stayed out of her life— I *belong* out of her life, Rorke. But she's not such a little girl now. She's old enough to start thinking about things. She never needed my stupid nest egg in the sense that she needed money, but I thought . . . I thought it might help her to have something from me. There was just no other way I had to tell her. I thought she might need to know that I think about her all the time, that I love her, that I've always loved her."

He was dying. The bar was starting to fill up with people. Her voice was too low to be overheard by anyone else, but it wasn't a place for her to be talking like this. The love pouring out of Kelsey was so private and painful that he wanted to snatch her up and take her off, shield her.

"Rorke . . ." Kelsey hesitated, then said swiftly, "I *need* to know she's all right. I wouldn't be asking you to do anything unethical by just getting a look at her, would I? I don't mean *talk* to her. I just mean—look. Tell me what she looks like, what she's wearing and if she has friends, what her friends look like, if she looks healthy, if she looks *happy*."

Rorke rubbed his tense muscles at the back of his neck. About five hours ago, he'd been positive how this meeting was going to go. His fascination with those blue eyes was supposed to disappear as soon as he saw her again. He'd planned to agree to find the kid, qualify the details and walk away clean. That she desperately wanted to find her daughter wasn't his problem. It wasn't his problem, the hunger in her voice every time she mentioned Janey. He had it all settled in his mind before he came here. He wanted to feel anything personal for her as much as he wanted a case of the bubonic plague.

"Okay, okay," he said finally. "I'll find her and I'll get a look at her if that's what you want. But then I think you should do the obvious."

"The obvious?"

"Come on, it's killing you. You have to know that. God knows how long you've bottled this up, but you're never going to be satisfied with some report you get from a stranger. You want to see her yourself—you're *dying* to see her yourself."

"That's absolutely not true."

"No?"

Kelsey pushed two fingers at her temples and closed her eyes. "I know it sounds cold, Rorke, a mother who wants no contact with her daughter. You have to be thinking I'm some kind of inhuman monster, but there's nothing I can do about that. You're going to have to think what you want. This is the way it has to be."

If she'd been an inhuman monster, he wouldn't be half as tempted to shake her. She was nuts. She framed every photograph of the kid she had, couldn't even talk about her without getting a catch in her throat, had deprived herself for years to save the nest egg, treated the wallet snapshot as if it were sacred. This for a woman who wanted no contact with her daughter?

Horses should fly so high. Rorke was real glad he'd brought the subject up. It was like trying to get through to a steel wall.

"I hurt Janey once. I'll never risk hurting her again," she said simply.

"It doesn't have to be that way."

"There's no chance—*none*—I would ever take that risk."

Rorke had the annoying feeling that the shadowed pain in her eyes was going to haunt his dreams, but eventually he had to give up trying to reason with her. She was tearing herself up talking about it. Nothing he said was getting through.

Preparing to leave, he reached back for his wallet and winced. The pain in his ribs was getting real old. He'd catered to this injury business about as long as he was going to. Feeling frustrated, he slapped a greenback on the table. His eyes dared Kelsey to argue with him, but she scooped up the handles of her purse and led the way to the door.

The meeting was done; the pressure was over. Rorke didn't realize how much stress he'd felt in the bar until he got outside. A steady mist was falling from the sky, soft and quiet, making the grass smell fresh and the trees glisten emerald.

He hauled a gulp of fresh air in his lungs and immediately felt better, calmer, totally in control again. The stress didn't matter. He was about to accomplish what he'd planned, which was to walk away, clean and uninvolved. Self-discipline was the key. He didn't look at Kelsey and he didn't look at her car.

"I'll call you for that Social Security number," he told Kelsey, his tone all business.

"I'll have it."

"Otherwise, I won't call unless I have something. Count on it taking a few days. If I think it's going to take a whole lot longer than that, I'll let you know."

She nodded. "I don't know your address, so I'll send some money through your department."

"No, you won't." He said it cheerfully. He didn't want her to think he was going to strangle her if she didn't quit bringing up the subject of paying him. *Keep it calm, Stoner, keep it cool.*

"Rorke?"

"What?" Ten measly more feet and he'd have been safe and sound in his car, and trust the darn woman to stop in the middle of the parking lot. She didn't even know enough to get out of the rain, and no raincoat. Hell, why would the woman carry a raincoat when the Natchez forecast had been a ninety percent chance of rain? Crystal drops were beading in her hair and on her eyelashes; her blouse was starting to cling. Did she run for cover? No. She just stood there, getting meltably wet and looking so damned fragile she took his breath away.

"It's okay to back out," she said gently. "That's what you're feeling, isn't it? Uncomfortable, uneasy, angry at the situation, angry at me. You've been hurt and you have your own troubles. You don't need a stranger's to add to those. If you feel some obligation to help me—that's nuts. You don't owe me anything. It's perfectly okay to say forget it and walk away. Why shouldn't you?"

There you go, Stoner. Not for the first time she'd plugged into his feelings with brilliant perceptiveness. He was feeling uncomfortable, uneasy and madder than a spitting cat. He wanted out. He wanted to have never heard her name, never met her and she had it just right. He had no obligation to her in any way.

"It's okay," she repeated.

He didn't answer. The mist was making her hair curl in crazy little corkscrews. One lock escaped the rest and flopped down over her right eye. She blinked, looking almost comically startled. She lifted her hand to push it away at the same time he did. As soon as he brushed back the errant strand, he told himself he'd walk away.

He brushed it back and saw the look in her eyes change. He heard her breath catch, and her lips parted just slightly. A clear pearl of water started to slide down her cheek. He told himself he'd walk away as soon as the pad of his thumb dried that droplet of rain.

He chased the drop off her cheek. He still didn't move. She seemed to know what he was going to do before he did, because there was a sudden awareness in her eyes, a luminous sheen that had nothing to do with the rain.

As if he had no choice, his palms slid into her hair and became trapped in all those tangled damp curls. As if he had to, as if he'd die if he didn't, he lowered his head and closed his eyes.

Her sweet, soft lips yielded under his, and she tasted like rain. She tasted like magic. There was nothing else—just that sweetness, innocent and free, and the texture and smell of her seeping into his senses. It mattered where she'd been. It mattered who he was. Just not then.

Years chased away. He hadn't always been hard; he hadn't always controlled his life with rigid self-discipline. A million years ago he'd been a brash and arrogant kid with no morals and no sense and his entire life had been ruled by whims. That shameful history had been buried a long time ago.

She brought it back, but not the bad parts. He'd almost forgotten that time in his life when he couldn't wait to wake up each day. There was a whole life out there to be tested and challenged, and the flavor of danger just added to that excitement because, dammit, she tasted sweet. She tasted good. Kelsey made a small sound—a whimper, not a word—and he felt her hands tentatively touch his waist and then clutch it when his tongue found hers.

Desire ripped through him, wilder than a summer storm, more blinding than sunlight. She was precious. She'd gone all still, shivery still, at the first contact of his mouth. She didn't seem to know she'd made that little sound of hunger, of desire. Maybe she'd been to hell and back, but she didn't know how to kiss. Not the way she should be kissed. Not the way she *needed* to be kissed.

He could feel the moment she lifted up on her toes and yielded, this time completely, to the possessive crush of his mouth. He felt the softness of her breasts against his shirt and imagined her naked, all innocence and fire. Her lips moved beneath his, luringly responsive, and he imagined her bare legs wrapped around him, luringly responsive when he took her. He would take her. He had to. His loins ached for the stark desire that shot through him, and his head . . . the only thing in his whole damn head was the utterly alien emotion of tenderness.

Eventually he lifted his head because he had to breathe. Reality was waiting for him. Reality always was. He heard the hiss of wet tires in the distance, felt the bite in his ribs from bending over her, became aware of the weight of her purse against his hip. The silky mist was still coming down as he framed her face in his palms and frowned.

She couldn't be this much trouble. She just couldn't be. Between the ages of seventeen and thirty-seven, he had to have kissed dozens of women. More than a few had sent sexual need rippling through his bloodstream. None had threatened his sanity.

Kelsey's hands dropped from his waist. Her wet lashes swept up. The look in her eyes was intimately revealing. She hadn't expected to be caught up in a lightning storm. It had stunned her, scared her... but her mouth was a soft bruised red. Not because he'd been rough, but because of her own generous response. "Rorke..."

He was incapable of hearing that voice without thinking of magnolias.

"You don't want this," she said desperately. "Believe me, you don't want this."

Kelsey was right. Magic was not reality. The reality was that she was already having a love affair with something he couldn't possibly compete with. She still wanted that glass of Chardonnay. She'd told him, she'd been honest with him, and she'd done everything a good woman could do to warn him off.

But Kelsey was also wrong. He *did* want this. Maybe she was a witch, maybe she had a sorceress's powers hidden in those itsy-bitsy freckles, but he knew damn well he felt something for her he'd never felt for another woman. Maybe it was need. Maybe he hadn't realized he could still feel need, so rich, so potent, that it made him feel alive again. Rorke wanted that feeling back. He wanted it badly. He brushed a raindrop from her temple, smoothed her hair and then dropped his hands.

"I'll contact you when I have something on your daughter," he said gruffly.

And then he walked away.

Two nights later, Kelsey was wakened in the middle of the night by the jangle of the phone. She groped in the dark for the receiver by the bed.

"Kels?"

Immediately recognizing the other woman's voice, Kelsey pushed back the covers and switched on the bedside lamp. The clock read 2:00 a.m. "Take it easy," she murmured into the phone. "I can be there in fifteen minutes."

"I'm not going to make it." The other woman's voice shook with defeat.

"Maybe you are and maybe you aren't, but you can hold off fifteen minutes, can't you? Come on, Maggie. Promise me."

"I—"

"Promise me."

Even before Kelsey hung up the phone, she'd tugged on jeans and sandals. In full view of God and her nonexistent neighbors, she was still pulling on a Garfield T-shirt when she pelted down her front porch steps. Stars peppered the warm, quiet night. Natchez was asleep. There was no reason not to run the red light on Jardin Avenue, and outside of eighteen minutes she turned into the circular drive that led to the Redeaux mansion.

She parked Bertha behind a silver BMW and a gleaming Lincoln town car. Without needing to think, she left her keys and purse on the seat. Thieves that passed in the night had lots better choices around here than an aging gas guzzler and anything that belonged to a woman in a Garfield T-shirt.

The three-story, white-pillared home was reminiscent of plantations days. Manicured English gardens surrounded the place. A white marble fountain decorated the front yard. Every March Natchez had a "spring pilgrimage," where owners of some of the more special historical homes were willing to open their doors to the public. Kelsey knew the Redeaux mansion was on the tour and could guess how Maggie had spent her day. How she spent her night was Kelsey's concern now.

Every light was on and the front door was hanging open when Kelsey zipped up the porch's dozen marble steps. She didn't waste time knocking. Maggie Redeaux was just inside, and Kelsey's heart turned over at the look of her.

She was still dressed as she had been for the tourists that day, in an 1850s-style hooped skirt with lace at the bodice and wrists. Her graying brown hair was neatly caught back in a chignon. A cameo had been threaded in a ribbon of black velvet at her throat. No tourist would have seen anything but a woman who typified Southern gentility and charm. But then, Maggie's dragons only came out after dark. There was a rage and a despair in her dark brown eyes when she spotted Kelsey, and her hands were violently shaking.

"I shouldn't have called you. There was no point."

"No? I take it you poured the bourbon?"

"I don't care," Maggie said.

Kelsey understood. At the moment, Maggie really wouldn't care if a hurricane destroyed all her antiques, if a ghost wandered down the elegant stairway, if she was miraculously pregnant with quintuplets, if the world was ending. There was only one thing in Maggie's head.

That glass of bourbon.

Kelsey reached out a hand. Maggie shrank back. She didn't want to be touched, probably couldn't tolerate being touched right now. Sometimes talk helped, but having to make the judgment in seconds, Kelsey guessed she was past that, too.

"Just go home. Leave me alone. I'm sorry I called. It was wrong. I don't want you here. I don't want anyone here—"

"Shut up, Maggie, and come on."

"Come on where?"

Kelsey had no idea where, but she herded Maggie through the black-and-white paneled hall, past the pantry and butler's station and endless kitchen. Outside was fresh air and an acre of English gardens, every rose perfect, every weed plucked . . . but it was the pool that caught Kelsey's eye.

"When's the last time you took a moonlit swim?" Kelsey asked lightly.

"You've lost your mind." For a brief moment Maggie's voice regained a sense of dignity—the same dignity that undoubtedly cowed servants, a problem Kelsey had certainly never had. Maggie wasn't quite so proud when Kelsey spun her around, unsnapped the velvet band with the cameo and started working on the thousand hooks and eyes on the back of Maggie's dress. The yard lights were bright, but the night was still shadowed. It wasn't easy to see the hooks. "You have lost your mind."

"Because we're going swimming?"

"I'm not going swimming."

"Sure you are."

"I don't even have a suit. There are servants in the house. James . . ."

"Good. We'll give them quite a show." Kelsey already knew that except for the servants, Maggie the same as lived alone in that three-story historical monstrosity. Her children were grown and gone. Her husband traveled months of the year with his business. Loneliness was Maggie's newest excuse to drink. Heaven knew, that loneliness was real.

Heaven knew, it was an asinine excuse, just like all the others.

"I *can't* swim. It's too cold and I'm too tired and it's not going to make any difference. I thought you if anyone would understand—"

"I do," Kelsey said flatly. And then she pushed Maggie in the pool. The older woman came up sputtering, shaking, her chignon coming apart in dripping ringlets, her eyes more haunted than ghosts. Kelsey was already in the water by then herself, wearing the Garfield T-shirt only because she hadn't taken the time to remove it, and annoyingly aware that she now had nothing to go home in. Maggie was reaching for the handles of the ladder. Kelsey said softly, "You want a drink, Maggie? I'm not going to stop you. I'm just asking you to do one lap first."

"I can't."

"One lap? Of course you can. You're already wet, you're already in here. Why not?"

"One lap, and then I'm going in."

"Fine," Kelsey said. But after one lap, she coaxed Maggie into swimming another. After the second lap, she bullied her into doing a third, and a fourth, and a fifth.

"I'll have a heart attack. Catch pneumonia. You're being hateful and cruel and I wish to God you'd go home and leave me alone!"

"Just a few more," Kelsey coaxed.

Her own arms ached and she was chilled to the bone before she let Maggie out of the pool. Neither had a towel. It was just two women in a bleak dark night, soaking wet in various states of underwear, one crying. Maggie, by then, was crying hard.

Kelsey put an arm around her, and the two dripped all through the Aubusson-carpeted downstairs to the staircase. Kelsey found towels in the mosaic-tiled bathroom on the second floor and rubbed the shaking woman down before tumbling her into bed.

Maggie didn't want to sleep. She wanted her bourbon, but the dragon—this one night—proved less powerful than simple, basic exhaustion. Within ten minutes she closed her eyes.

Kelsey covered her, turned off the light and tiptoed downstairs. Somewhere she guessed that servants were awake, but no one stopped her from wandering around the house. She found the poured glass of bourbon in the velvet-draped parlor, dumped it in the kitchen sink and let herself out.

Within a half hour she was home, stripped of wet clothes and wrapped in a blanket. She needed to sleep and knew she wouldn't. Carrying a mug of mint tea, she curled up in her creaking recliner.

Through the whole encounter with Maggie, part of her mind—and heart—had been on Rorke. She could picture his expression if he'd seen Maggie. She could picture those dark eyes ice with disgust, contempt. Maggie had everything. More money than she knew what to do with, the education and background to do anything with her life, children who loved her and a husband who'd tried—not once, but a dozen times—to help her.

The peripheral details were different, but Kelsey, eight years ago, could have been Maggie. Shaky and wild-eyed, selfish and self-pitying. She could turn the picture in her mind in a dozen different directions. From any direction, the pictures were ugly. There had been nights she would have sold herself to a stranger for a drink—anything to please her dragon lover, anything to take the clawing craving away, anything for that first smooth, soothing sip of wine.

Kelsey took a sip of tea, closed her eyes against the welling of tears and thought, *damn him*.

Maybe there was a level where Rorke simply couldn't understand, but she'd *told* him. She'd been honest with him. She'd done everything she knew how to avoid that kiss, and still she'd known it was coming. The chemistry had been volatile from the first, and Rorke, being Rorke, was always going to test it. Some men had the sense to run from trouble. Rorke was always going to turn around and face it.

She guessed that he was trying to dispel trouble when he kissed her. He'd tried to obliterate the attraction by reducing it to reality, tried to prove to himself that there was nothing there that he couldn't handle.

Only he hadn't handled that embrace well, and neither had she. Eyes still closed, she gulped more tea.

Forty-eight hours later and she could still remember the feel of his arms around her, the texture of his mouth, the look of his face in the rain, and his eyes, lonely and dark. She'd never intended to respond.

She'd never expected to find a man so desperate for warmth, a man with such buried tenderness, a man who came apart with such little exposure to caring.

From the first, she'd sensed he was troubled, that he was hurting—not physical hurts but the kind of emotional hurts that put dragons in nightmares. He was so tightly controlled. The longer you leashed a panther, the more dangerous the animal became when he was finally set free.

A little of that restraint had slipped when he'd kissed her, and she'd felt the lure, for the first time in eight years, of a man who tempted her into feeling abandon. She had never felt so wanted, so needed, as if nothing else mattered but that she be there for him. She had never felt pulled under by a man's dark, powerful, sexual draw.

And she had never let herself forget who and what she was. An alcoholic.

Kelsey let the last of the hot tea scald her tongue. A long time ago she'd learned to live with shame. The shame was real. So was guilt. Both had determined her choice of celibacy. There was no way she would ask a man to share her private hell. And there was no way she could live with a man who was shamed by who she was, ashamed of loving her.

Leave me alone, Rorke.

I've already judged myself a thousand times more harshly than you ever could. I can't fall in love with you. I know what I'd be letting myself in for. Even worse, I know what I'd be doing to you. I'll be strong for both of us if I have to be, but you have to help.

You have to leave me alone.

Chapter 4

At four o'clock on Saturday, Rorke pulled in his driveway to find a familiar white Camaro parked ahead of him. Just inside the front door he found his mail neatly stacked and his newspaper already brought in. Further in, he found the drapes opened, making his gray-and-white living room so light and bright he almost winced. Walt's red head popped around the kitchen doorway. "Where you been?"

"Don't hesitate to make yourself at home, Walt," Rorke said dryly.

"I never do." The fuzzy red hair disappeared. "Brought you some beer," he called out.

Rorke wandered through as far as the doorway. "And food, I see."

His partner was bending inside the refrigerator, shelving vegetable and fruits that came out of a grocery sack. Walt was four years younger, too inches taller and ten tons better looking than Rorke. He was muscled like a freight train, but at heart, no question, he was a little old woman. He meticulously washed the lettuce before popping it in the refrigerator, and the apples were already lined up just so.

"I could swear I asked you not to do this," Rorke mentioned.

"Yeah? Well, I got a mom and three sisters to do it for me. You don't have any close family, and you're not supposed to lift anything until the ribs are healed. What's the big deal? I get food for myself at the same time." Walt closed the refrigerator door and looked Rorke over as thoroughly as any mother. "The captain loaned me Baker on our drug project. *Baker.* You put a beard and a clown suit on Baker and anyone walking down the street would still know he was a cop. You *have to* get stronger a lot faster than this, and where you been for the past two hours?"

Rorke could have ignored the question, but there was no point. Walt could nag answers out of a deaf and dumb suspect when he was in the mood. "I was at the hospital."

"You have the doc check you over again?"

"No. I went to see the kid." If he stood there and didn't make any hospitable overtures, there was always the possibility Walt would go home, but no. Walt twisted the top on a Dixie Longneck and took a leisurely swallow, settling back against the counter where he could easily glare at his friend.

"When the hell are you going to let it go, Stoner? You didn't put the gun in that kid's hand. If the captain believed you were in any way to blame for what happened, he'd have had you on report so fast it'd make your head spin. How come you're the only one who thinks you're responsible?"

Rorke didn't respond. He and Walt had been through this too many times before. No amount of talk could get the look of that sixteen-year-old boy out of his mind.

Rorke had been sixteen once, hell on wheels, the devil incarnate. Good home, good family, all the advantages—and he'd still been so wild he'd nearly worried his father to death. Literally.

Every time he walked in a hospital, the smell of alcohol and antiseptic corridors twisted his stomach. He'd spent hours in a hospital room when he was seventeen, promising God he'd change if his dad would just recover. His dad had recovered, and Rorke had kept all those promises. He'd gone as straight and narrow as a slide rule, made self-discipline his creed, lapped up responsibility that had earned him medals first in the Navy and then the police force. He'd guaranteed God that he'd be as good as a saint, and dammit, he'd done his best... until that night less than a month ago, when yet again he'd made the kind of mistake a man couldn't forgive himself for. The twist of his hand had ignited the explosion of gunpowder, and a straw-haired kid lay bleeding.

Everyone agreed the kid was trouble. Everyone missed the point. The kid was a *kid*. Stupid enough to smoke grass, young and arrogant enough to believe that carrying a gun made him a man. Somebody needed to turn the kid around—fast—but he sure didn't deserve to die because he was a damn fool.

"You actually talk to him?" Walt asked.

"No." Rorke saw Walt's look of relief, but the relief was unnecessary. Obviously he would give testimony at the boy's trial, and that testimony would be jeopardized if he saw the boy ahead of time. Rorke knew the law. He also knew that the best chance to help the teen-ager was in the courtroom.

"So why do you go?" Walt demanded irritably.

Again, Rorke didn't answer. There was no answer. He went. That was all.

Walt took another draft of beer and abruptly switched gears. "Anyway, ten bucks on the table says you talked to the doc. So, is he gonna be all right?"

"In time. Bullet hit a bone. He's going to walk real slow for some real long months, but they're going to let him out in another week."

"They set a court date?"

"Not yet."

"It's kind of nice to have one that's open-and-shut. Two eye witnesses, a clear-cut armed robbery, posses-sion of stolen weapons... 'Course, get you up in front of the judge, you'll probably tell him it was all your fault—okay, okay." Walt lifted his hands in a "forget it" gesture. "I'm dropping it, I'm dropping it. I really knew better than to bring the subject up to begin with."

"Could have fooled me."

Walt grinned, uninsultable. He finished up his beer with the standard chitchat—what was going on in the department, who'd been arrested, a case that had gone down in court and, last, department gossip. No one loved the juicy details like Walt. "I'm telling you, he's sleeping with Bartholomew's wife. I saw his car right in the motel parking lot at high noon. Word has it she's into handcuffs."

Rorke clawed a hand through his hair. "Maybe Bar-tholomew's wife is Bartholomew's problem?"

"The way I hear it, she's no problem at all. Hey, it's nothing to me. I steer right clear of ladies wearing rings." Walt drained the last drop of beer and wiped his mouth on his sleeve. "Whoa!" He neatly deposited the empty bottle under the sink and straightened again. "You went to see Kelsey Whitfield the other day, didn't you? What happened?"

Rorke took offense at Kelsey and Bartholomew's wife being mentioned in the same conversation, but that reaction was irrational, he knew. Walt could put elephants and butterflies in the same conversation. There didn't have to be a relationship. "Just what you thought would happen. I'm going to help find her daughter."

"Any luck?"

"Some. It's a little more complicated than I thought it'd be. I pulled some addresses together, but—"

"I didn't mean luck with the *daughter*. I meant luck with the *lady*. And don't tell me you didn't notice those legs." Walt's smile shriveled. "I'm batting a thousand this afternoon. I could have sworn you would hit it off. She's got a smile on her that could thaw an iceberg, and not like your sense of humor's been a little murky lately, Stoner, but—"

"How about if you lay off this whole subject?"

Again Walt threw up his hands. "Okay, so you two didn't click. You think I'm complaining, you're out of your tree. You got a problem being deaf, dumb and blind. I sure as hell don't. When it comes down to it, I saw her first." Again he read Rorke's expression. "So..." he drawled like a kid pulling taffy. "You're not at *all* interested, but may death strike any man who dials her phone number. Have I got it about right?"

"When these ribs are healed, you and I are going to meet on a handball court," Rorke said pleasantly.

"I notice you're still not answering any questions about the lady."

"Were you going home soon?"

"I also notice for the first time in three weeks you've got something on your mind besides the robbery."

"If you'll drop this subject, I'll stake you to a week of lunches when I'm off this blasted medical leave."

Walt mouthed the word "mum" and sauntered in total silence toward the door.

"Matthews—thanks. For the beer, for the baby-sitting, even for driving me nuts. I owe you."

Walt sent him a finger gesture in acknowledgment. Smiling, Rorke stood with one foot cocked in the doorway until his partner's car had disappeared from sight. At times Walt's humor was adolescent, but the man wasn't. In a crisis situation, both knew precisely how the other would react. Both had tested each other's trust, competence and judgment. Rorke would have stood in front of a firing line for his friend, and if Walt had been the one injured, Rorke knew damn well he'd be the one carting in food.

Not, perhaps, quite so old-woman fussily.

Once Walt's car was out of sight, Rorke frowned distractedly. At a certain level he didn't share easily with people, yet he'd never deliberately hidden anything from Walt. Life's events were automatic grist for a chitchat. Even a taciturn clam eventually opened up over the long, lonely, tedious hours of a stakeout. Cops who worked as partners had few secrets.

The moment Rorke saw Walt again, he intended to lay reams of grief on his head for setting him up with Kelsey. For that matter, he wasn't sure why he hadn't told his partner exactly how it was, except that he could guess Walt's reaction. Walt's blue-green eyes would blink. "Her? A boozer, a tippler, a drinker? You gotta be kidding." And then he would back off fast and say something tactful.

Even the thought of that scene made Rorke cringe. *Are you ashamed of her, Stoner? Ashamed of the idea that you'd fall for a boozer?*

Rorke let the screen door slam closed. He was confused as hell. He wandered the house, looking for things to do. There wasn't a thing. By nature he cleaned up after himself. The gray-and-white living room accumulated only so much dust with a man living alone. The navy sheets on his bed rumpled only so much when a man was sleeping alone. The kitchen refused to accumulate dishes when a man wasn't hungry, and silence—loneliness—lapped at him from every room in the house.

He'd made blind, stupid mistakes as a kid. When he'd realized that, he'd changed his ways. That's what Rorke assumed good people did. You faced your mistakes on the chin, owned up, prayed to God you had the strength to change and then did, because with or without God, that's what you had to do.

Rorke had lived his entire adult life on those principles, and dammit, he *didn't* understand Kelsey. She'd kept on drinking to the point where she'd destroyed her marriage and lost the one person who meant more than life to her—her daughter.

So are you ashamed of her, Stoner?

Rorke scowled at the glare of the living room's light. What he knew—*all* he knew—was that Walt was his friend, his partner, the man who'd covered his behind countless times. And if Walt had called her a boozer, Rorke was regrettably positive he'd have socked him in the jaw.

Kelsey had been hurt enough.

Impatiently he paced back toward the kitchen. When he noticed the stash of beer Walt had left on the counter, he lifted one long-necked bottle and unscrewed the top. He tilted his head, took a long draft and closed his eyes.

He'd always loved beer. Walt had purchased his favorite brand.

The stuff tasted as appealing as battery acid.

Rorke shook his head, set down the bottle and reached for his car keys. Two days of pacing and insomnia were enough. The answers obviously weren't going to come out of his head.

He had a perfectly good excuse to see her. Wheels weren't turning as quickly as he wanted, but he'd managed to pin down the unlisted phone numbers for every Andrew Whitfield in the country. He'd have preferred more efficient leads—unlisted numbers took time to track down—but at least a dozen were in the South. If it wasn't Saturday, he'd have already started pursuing them. Monday he planned to do that. He could also inform her about what he'd come up with so far.

Climbing in his car, Rorke tried to remember a time when he'd contrived a flimsier excuse to see a woman. There wasn't one. He wasn't even positive he *wanted* to see her, but he wanted to be able to sleep again. To be able to drink a beer without thinking of her. To quit reliving that damn kiss in the rain every time he closed his eyes.

Maybe he just wanted to be with her. The most complex of motivations had a way of reducing down to basics when it came to Kelsey. The moment he pulled in her driveway he discovered that was both disastrously and humorously true today.

Her ankle-high grass had a power mower standing in the middle of it. The lawn was two-thirds finished. The rusted mower had clearly stalled—no surprise. The company who made the vintage mowing machine had probably gone out of business when Studebakers were still on the road.

He could hear the phone ringing as, dodging the pansies, he took her front steps. He also caught a vague whiff of smoke. Any other time he would have knocked. The smoke changed that option. He barreled in, and nearly collided with an open can of stain, a paintbrush and a stripped-down table set on newspapers. When he was angling around the debris, he saw her.

Actually, what he saw was her fanny waggling in short shorts—burnt orange, *too* short shorts—where she bent over the cluttered dining room table. She jerked up, catching the phone receiver between her shoulder and ear as she spotted him. If she said something in greeting, he didn't catch it. He was too busy moving toward the smell of smoke.

Two frayed hot pads sat on her stove. He grabbed both, opened the oven and coughed. His damn ribs still didn't like him to bend, but someone had to take the smoking pan out of her oven. Possibly it had been chicken. Possibly beef. Whatever, it was only fit for a eulogy now.

A smoke alarm had the courtesy to acknowledge the smoke. Beyond that screaming noise a buzzer sounded. He knew that buzzer sound; his dryer had one. She was doing the wash.

"Rorke? I'll be off the phone in a minute."

Who had time to worry if the woman was a drinker? Rorke neatly deposited the charred dish on her back porch and came back to drag a kitchen chair under the smoke alarm. Even after he removed the battery, his ears continued to ring. She had the cheap model of dryer. The buzzer wasn't going to stop until someone opened the door.

He didn't even know where her dryer was. He got down from the kitchen chair—did his ribs need this?—and found the blasted dryer in the room just off her kitchen. As fast as he opened the door, the buzzer ceased—and a violet wisp of bra, too hot to handle, flew out at him.

"*What* are you doing?"

At that moment he was trying to undrape his arm from the clinging bit of lingerie. It seemed a little late to go for dignity. "I don't confess this to everyone," he said gravely, "but I have a bra fetish. Had it for years. First thing I do when I go into anyone's house is check their dryer, just on the off chance they were washing bras that day."

"Ah." With a solemn expression and eyes full of dance, she ambled over to the dryer in bare feet and peered in. "I think I washed three. If you're not real partial to purple, I'm pretty sure I can find you a blue one."

"That's okay…um…I'm afraid there's a black dish decorating your back porch."

She murmured, "Thank you."

"I'm also afraid it might have been your dinner."

"Chicken in a herbed butter sauce," she agreed sadly. "It wasn't supposed to be done for another half hour, but my oven has an impulsive streak where heat's concerned. I was just coming to check the chicken when the phone rang, but the caller was a woman named Maggie, and—"

"You don't have to explain."

"Of course I do. I don't want you to think I live like this all the time. Normally my house is like my classroom—neat as a pin, immaculate, total order and control. This is the first day in absolutely years that I . . . um—"

"Totally lost it?" he supplied helpfully.

"I have a slight tendency to do ten things at once."

She had a slight tendency to disarm a man without even trying. Rorke was quite sure he'd concocted a fairly good reason for coming here. It was a good thing she didn't ask, because he had no idea what it was.

Her right hand was entirely coated with pecan stain. So was half of the loose khaki shirt she obviously reserved to wear for painting. She'd scraped her hair back and tied it with string into a ponytail. A bit of stain on her cheek was her only makeup. Any other woman would have been embarrassed to be interrupted in the middle of such an unholy mess. Not Kelsey. She seemed to have adopted a what-you-see-is-what-you-get philosophy.

What he saw beyond the sassy humor in her bright blue eyes was wariness and worry. Her eyes were as reflective as a mirror, filled with the memory of a kiss that had disturbed and shaken her—no differently than it had him. If she was unsure what to do with him, though, she was not unhappy to see him. In a cluttered laundry room, in an atmosphere of detergent, she looked at him the way a man dreamed a woman might look at him, sometime, somewhere, just once . . . as if nothing else mattered. As if the world had just got brighter. As if black and white converted to Technicolor when he was around.

"Did you—" they'd been teasing easy a moment ago; now Kelsey had a hard time making her lips function "—have any special reason for coming here? I know you'd have called if you had any news on my daughter, so you couldn't be here for that.''

"No." Rorke scratched a sudden itch at the back of his spine. "Actually, I was sitting in my house and had this sudden flash of ESP. Someone, somewhere, was having carburetion problems with their lawn mower. My car turned in your driveway of its own volition, so I guess it must be your mower having the problem?''

"ESP, hmm?"

"Don't you read detective novels? Cops have hunches. That's how we solve crimes.''

"Rorke?"

"Hmm?"

"The carburetion is fine. I just ran out of gas.''

"Sometimes these hunches can be a little vague.''

Anytime now he was going to stop looking at her as if she were the most precious woman he'd ever seen. As soon as he did, Kelsey promised herself she'd get real tough and hard and distant. It was hard to think when a man's gaze swept possessively over you head to toe, finished, then prowled the same territory all over again.

His eyes had been the same smoky gray the afternoon he'd kissed her. He was back for another. She knew it, and that wasn't going to happen because she was too smart to let it happen again, yet her heart couldn't seem to whip up a good seal of hardness. Not just then. He was having such a fine time teasing her— it was the first time she'd seen him even try to let down his hair and relax. Yet there were dark smudges under his eyes. He looked so tired. He looked tired and hungry and as though he were afraid she was going to send him away.

She should.

"So, you gonna point me to your gas can or make me find it all on my own?"

Her heart sighed uneasily, knowing the decision was already made. Probably the wrong decision. All her life she'd been good at those. "I'm going to point you to a glass of spearmint iced tea. You go anywhere near my lawn mower with that sprained wrist and those broken ribs and I'll beat you."

"You know what the charge is for threatening a cop?"

"You think that's a threat? I'm not even warmed up. I'm warning you, Rorke, if you even go near that lawn mower—" She didn't finish because the phone rang. As quickly as she sprang to answer it, she heard the screen door close in her kitchen. The next time she looked out the window, her mower was on its side and Rorke was sharpening its blades. He'd taken his shirt off; she could see the glint of grease on his hands and he was whistling.

What are you going to do with him, Kelsey?

But at the moment she couldn't do anything with him. She had a table that *had* to be finished before the stain dried. Mississippi Bell left her in peace for an entire half hour—a record—before the phone was jangling again. Before she could get off her knees to answer it, Rorke jogged around the kitchen corner with a rag in his hands. He picked up the receiver.

"This is Miss Whitfield's temporary answering service. She'd love to come to the phone herself, but her hands are covered with paint. Any chance I could relay a message for her?" He covered the receiver with his hand. "Janet would like to know if you want to go shopping next Thursday after work," he said gravely, and then rolled his eyes. "It seems there's a sale on jean skirts at Rictor's that is not to be believed."

Kelsey chuckled at his perfect mimic of her friend's voice. "Thank you, Mr. Stoner. Please tell Janet I'll call her back when I can."

"Yes, ma'am." When Rorke hung up, he ambled over to the table and circled with a critical eye. "Is this the same termite-ridden rickety thing that was leaning against a corner last time I was here?"

"The same."

"I thought you were nuts."

Kelsey grinned. "She's turning into a beauty, isn't she? When the stain dries, I'm going to give her a nice satin sheen of varnish."

"This isn't the first time you've worked with wood. You're good, lady." He was still rubbing his hands with the rag, but suddenly stopped. "What's that sound I hear?"

"Nothing."

"I think it was your stomach grumbling."

"My stomach would never be so impolite as to grumble in public," she assured him.

"Then it must be mine. You realize it's past seven o'clock?"

She realized that he hadn't put on his shirt again and that he'd worked up a seal-slick sheen of sweat mowing her lawn. Tufts of sandy hair glistened on his tanned chest. His upper arms were all corded muscle, his torso hard as iron...except where his ribs were taped. The injured skin surrounding the tape was still purple and blue. The look sobered her. She held the paintbrush in one hand, suspended, as she raised her eyes to his. "I don't know how you could have been walking around at all last week."

"This? No big deal. Didn't I tell you I was a tough guy?"

"Sometime, tough guy, I'd like you to tell me what happened to you."

Something flickered in his eyes, then was gone. "I thought we were talking about dinner."

"As soon as I get done with this, I was going to put something together."

Rorke didn't want to hurt her feelings, but he'd already seen her cookies and her chicken. "How about if I take you out for something quick instead?"

"You have to be kidding. I have stain under every fingernail, my feet are black, and I don't even want to know what my hair looks like. Even a fast-food place would lock their doors if they saw me coming. I think I'll just hole up in here with a sandwich, Rorke."

He saw the fingernails and feet, but she was wrong about her hair. Soft evening sunlight spilled through the open door on her kneeling figure. Her ponytail had gotten loose. Fine, silky strands were wisping around her face and neck, a little caramel, a little taffy, a little butterscotch.

For all that softness, there was just an itsy-bitsy trace of steel in those blue eyes. She'd spoken without thinking when she mentioned putting something together. Now she was thinking just fine, and the idea of their having dinner together had aroused her wariness.

There were a lot of things Rorke wanted to arouse in Kelsey. None of them was wariness. "You still have to eat," he persisted. "You've also been working all day. You have to want something more substantial than a sandwich."

"Rorke—"

"I'm not talking fancy, just food. The best I can do to clean up is use the soap and water at your sink and put on my shirt. And while you're taking a shower, I'll get that battery back in your smoke alarm."

"Rorke, I just don't think—"

She was going to turn him down. He could feel it, taste it. "I'll leave right after that, but a quick dinner'll give me the chance to tell you what I've found out. The weekend nipped the chance to pursue it, Kelsey, but come Monday I have a few leads to follow."

Her head whipped up from her paintbrush. "Already? You've already found—"

"I'll tell you over dinner."

He could tell from her face that he'd won. All he'd had to do was hint at news of her daughter. It didn't do a whole lot for his ego that it took bribery to coax her to dinner, but he'd taken worse blows to his pride.

She finished the last stroke on the table and went off with her brush to find turpentine. He replaced the battery in her smoke alarm and, while she was in the shower, answered her phone. God, the woman could hire a full-time secretary just to answer that phone. If he had a BB gun he'd shoot the thing.

The whole time he was soaping down at her kitchen sink he stared at her stove. Once he was cleaned up, he wanted to look at the connections. Maybe she wasn't that terrible a cook. Maybe there was something honestly wrong with her stove—the thing was old, its white enamel dented in spots. He was rubbing a towel on his chest, studying the stove, when he heard a caterwauling meow at the back door.

The cat was the most bedraggled thing he'd ever seen, with one torn ear and mangy fur. Rorke scowled at the thing. "Even Kelsey would be smarter than to let you in," he began, and then noticed the small empty bowl on the floor. With a sigh, he opened the screen door and changed his litany. "Kelsey *should* be smarter than to let you in. God, it's like the phone. The interruptions around here never stop, and I suppose you want milk?"

Wrong. The cat wanted to get into the bottom cupboard next to the sink. Rorke shook his head when he found the cans of cat food. "She should have brought you the cheap dry stuff—assuming she was nuts enough to feed you at all. She is nuts, you know." He was interrupted by a breathless feminine order delivered from the other room.

"Rorke, if you have a shred of decency in you, do me a favor and close your eyes for a fast two seconds!"

"Sure," he said. He immediately looked, and saw a towel-wrapped figure streak barefoot from the bathroom to the laundry room, snatch a wisp of violet from the dryer and fly back to the bedroom.

"You can look now!"

So, he thought, she was going to wear the purple bra. "She's nuts," he repeated to the cat, but he was fairly positive that the condition of insanity was his problem, not hers. Her place was a war zone of noise, confusion, interruptions and clutter. He couldn't stand noise, confusion, interruptions and clutter—never could. Yet when he let the cat out and started pulling on his shirt, he discovered himself whistling.

He was happy.

That extremely rare emotion had started to seep into him when he was tinkering with her lawn mower, taken hold when he'd finished her grass and had been steadily accelerating just like the cat's purr. The place needed a man. Given enough time, he could check out the stove, get a coat of paint on her porch, maybe hire a bull-dozer for her entire yard.

How long had it been since anyone needed him?

He buttoned, tucked and ran his hands through his hair in lieu of a brush. Any minute now the door to that bedroom was going to open. He'd been virtuously careful not to think about her sliding her arms through those bra straps, fitting the violet lace to those high-tilted breasts, snapping the front. By now she was cov-ered in something. Hopefully something that covered those three freckles, because he didn't want to jump her the moment she came out.

The sudden disquieting thought occurred to him that Kelsey hadn't been "jumped" in a long time. Not made love to, not wooed and wined, not even kissed. Her life-style, busy as it was, shouted "alone." In the parking lot she'd been smart enough to know he was going to kiss her… but not smart enough to defuse a response that sprang free from a generous and lonely heart.

Are you playing with her, Stoner? his conscience de-manded of him.

But Rorke wasn't playing. He never played. He'd never been with a woman where he didn't feel "on," tested and testing, careful, bogged down by unknown expectations that he was always worried about meet-ing. There was no test to pass with Kelsey. She had a gift of making a man feel accepted, valued no matter who and what he was. When he was with her, for the first time in weeks—maybe years—he felt easy within him-self.

Hurt her?

Never.

And that issue at the moment was moot. All he intended to do was take her to dinner. How could he possibly hurt her in the process of simply sharing a meal?

Chapter 5

Kelsey felt peculiarly disorientated. During the drive into town, Rorke had apologized for not finding Janey as quickly as he'd expected. He couldn't press the contacts he usually worked with because, ethically, her problem wasn't official police business. "What I did come up with are unlisted phone numbers. One of them will pan out. I just have to warn you that it could take a few more days."

Rorke talked about a few more days as if the case wasn't even challenging. Until that moment Kelsey had never believed the search would be successful. She'd believed for too long that she'd never find her daughter again.

She told herself she felt elation...and she did. Yet on this warm spring night, her skin was suddenly shivery, as if a ghost had stepped on her shadow. This wasn't the first time she'd felt this way. A year ago, just after she'd started her private search for her daughter, she'd begun waking in the dead of night. She'd been drenched with sweat, and her heart was pounding with anxiety that told her Janey needed help.

"Uh . . . Whitfield? It's perfectly okay with me if you want to sit in the car all night, but the last I knew you were starving. Raving about eating horses, elephants, that kind of thing," Rorke said mildly.

Her gaze zipped up to his smile. How long had he been standing with the car door open? Cheeks flushed, she climbed out of the car in a rush. Hokey premonitions were shelved in the back of her mind, where they belonged. Even if her daughter was actually in trouble, Kelsey was the last one who could help her. To believe otherwise was a fairy-tale illusion *and* a sure route to heartache.

She'd been down that road too many times, and tonight she simply wasn't going to allow herself to travel it again. All thoughts of Janey were promptly wrapped and ribboned and secreted back to the cache in her heart reserved solely for her daughter.

She had plans for Mr. Stoner this evening, and none of them included any heavy subjects. Rorke was so sure that he'd conned her into this dinner. The truth was that she saw it as an ideal occasion to refuse and defuse the cavorting hormones between them. She'd picked the place, Cock of the Walk, on Silver Street. By no stretch of the imagination was it a place for tête-à-têtes. The specialty of the house was blackened catfish. Drinks were served in tin cups, the place mats were paper and the atmosphere was dependably casual, rowdy and fun.

Rorke needed the fun, and, if he needed an honest friend, she intended to provide that for him, too. So far his involvement with her had only added to his troubles. That was about to change. Kelsey was good at

taking care of people, and Rorke, poor baby, was about
to be taken under her wing. "Only it's like I told you.
The treat's on me or we're not going in," she said
firmly.

"Yes, ma'am." Rorke's tone reeked humble obedience.

Kelsey wasn't fooled. "Don't try that respectful act
on me, sugar. I catch you even *trying* to reach for your
wallet and you're going to see some real violence."

"Yes, ma'am."

Ignoring the mischief in his eyes, she hooked her arm
through his and steered his six-foot frame toward the
restaurant. When his hip bumped hers, she felt like Eve
buried in apples. The inexcusable rush of pure feminine sexual awareness made her almost heady. Willing
those winsomely seductive hormones to drop off the
nearest cliff, she persevered—as a friend. "Someone
should have taken you in hand long before this," she
scolded. "Honestly! To live in Natchez your whole life
and have never eaten here before."

"Hey, I've driven down here, I just never stopped. I
thought the place was a tourist trap."

"Tourists are at least smart enough to clue in to an
area's history," she said darkly. He gave her a long-
suffering look—Rorke's appreciation of history left off
when Columbus landed—but she was hungry for him to
see that this was different.

Silver Street bordered the banks of the Mississippi,
and the riverfront was steeped in keelboat lore, most of
it wicked, rowdy and wild. Natchez proper had a rich
and elegant past, but Natchez "Under-the-Hill" was
something else. As they mounted the steps to the restaurant, she motioned expressively with her hand.
"Smell that river...and can't you just see it? Keel-

boats crowded at the dock, pirate shirts and fistfights everywhere you look. The gambling and the vice and the ruined women.''

"If I'm going to get a history lesson, I'd appreciate it if you'd concentrate on the ruined women."

His tone was skeptical and teasing, until she gave him a thorough, unabridged history on ruined women that had him in stitches. His laughter set the tone for dinner. They both ordered the catfish with riverfries, and they were lucky enough to catch a table outside, overlooking the riverfront. The Mississippi stretched as far as the eye could see, and as the waiter served their dinner, the sun was dipping over the horizon and spearing the river with the color of jewels. Kelsey watched Rorke gradually relax with a feeling of smug feminine satisfaction.

That changed. She wasn't sure when. There simply came a moment when she wasn't "taking care" of Rorke anymore, and the opposite was true. He was taking care of her in the most dangerous of ways.

As darkness fell, the breeze picked up, ruffling his dark hair. His collar was open, and the waiter had placed a candle in a red glass on their table. The light flickered and glowed on Rorke's tanned throat and bare arms. He hadn't shaved—how could he? Neither of them had planned on going to dinner, and his cheeks and chin were beginning to form a shadowed, disreputable stubble.

Rorke, relaxed, was half pirate and all sexy rogue. The darker the night, the more that rogue's gaze drifted over her. Kelsey's white jeans and silky red shirt were nothing special and certainly not provocative. Possibly he kept looking because he was that astounded that a ponytail and pecan-stained hands could transform into something he wasn't ashamed to be seen with in public.

Only he didn't just look at her as if he were remembering ponytails. He looked at her as if he'd like to kiss her, long and thoroughly.

Years had passed since she'd felt the stomach-melting kind of desire that made her feel bewitched and beguiled and dangerously happy to be a woman. She wanted to enjoy it. For just once, just one night, she wanted to be just like any other woman alone with a special man. She wanted to be wooed. She wanted to see desire—not in any man's eyes, but in Rorke's.

Maybe he didn't realize what a gift he was giving her, but Kelsey did. The evening had become a date, because he'd converted it into one . . . and she couldn't let that go on. She was too conscious of what he was doing. Unlike the afternoon in the bar, when he couldn't get his mind off alcohol to save his life, he hadn't once mentioned the subject tonight.

If you never opened the envelope, you never had to face the bill. If you blocked the view of the cobra, maybe you could pretend it wasn't really there.

Kelsey had avoided involvement for eight long years. She'd done that, always, by being immediately honest with the men who asked her out. Lots of those men had become friends, but every one of them had had the sense to drop the pursuit once they understood the background.

She'd been just as honest with Rorke. Only he hadn't run from, but toward, her. Suddenly she felt very sad, and very scared.

"Hey."

She looked up.

"Where did I lose you?" Rorke murmured. "All of a sudden you looked like a dark cloud walked on your shadow."

Immediately she smiled. "A dark cloud on a night like this?" Her mood abruptly shifted. She'd agreed to dinner for Rorke's sake, not hers. The undeniably feminine instinct to take care of him stemmed from an obvious source. He took rotten care of himself. He pushed himself too hard. He had to be coaxed to relax, to laugh. He took on the world—the stern, austere lines in his face attested to that—and he most readily took on other people's troubles, as well. Tonight, she'd hoped to take on his instead.

A waiter paused to ask if they needed anything else, then wandered past, a young man in black pants with a jaunty red feather in his hat. "You know why he's wearing that red feather, don't you?" she asked Rorke.

"Is this another history lesson like the ruined women?"

"Now, be patient. This one relates directly to you." At his amused and speculative glance, she continued. "A zillion years ago, the men who ran the keelboats were a tough bunch. They had to be. It was a tough job, poling their boats back upriver after they'd delivered their loads in Natchez. So on the extremely obnoxious excuse of needing to stay in shape, they used to get into a lot of fights when they were in port. Not nice fights. We're talking ear biting, eye gouging, real down-and-dirty stuff."

"Is this the part that relates directly to me?" Rorke asked dryly.

Kelsey grinned and forked the last of her riverfries onto his plate. "The relevance is not the fights, Stoner, but the pecking order. See, each boat had one man who'd established himself as top gun. He was called the cock of the walk.''

"Like the name of the restaurant?"

She nodded. "Anyway, so everyone knew he was top gun, he wore a red turkey feather in his hat. That feather, unfortunately, earned him a lot of trouble. It used to be an unwritten law that one red feather had to challenge another the moment they met. So when there were a lot of boats in port, you can imagine how often each red feather had to prove himself.''

"Every hour." Rorke pushed aside his empty plate and leaned back. His eyes danced at hers across the table. "I think I'm feeling maligned and wounded and insulted. I mean, which was the part that was supposed to relate to me—the eye-gouging fights or the guy running around wearing feathers?''

"Am I sorry I brought this up or what?" she asked the ice cube in her water glass.

"Come on. Fess up what was in your mind."

"I just thought you might see yourself in that historical scene," she admitted. "I mean, if I close my eyes and picture you living a hundred and fifty years ago, I think you'd be in the thick of it. You'd have been bored living up on the hill, with nothing to do all day but supervise the family's fortunes. And below the hill, I doubt you'd have settled for being just a boatman, a bystander, part of the herd. I think you'd have had one of those swashbuckling mustaches, and you'd have worn a red feather in your hat sure as you breathed. In fact—''

"You're out of your mind, but go on."

Something goaded her in those dark magnetic eyes. "I think," she said softly, "that you'd have thrived on those physical challenges. That you'd have fought to win, to stay on top. That you would naturally choose a life-style where you had to constantly test and prove yourself.''

Rorke shifted restlessly. ''You wake up with that imagination, or does it just come on you like that?'' he teased lightly. ''You're describing a pretty wild life-style—wild, amoral, lawless. Take a look across the table. I'm as straight as they come. Past or present, there's no way that whole scene could fit me.''

''No?''

''No.'' He swilled the ice cubes in his glass and finished the last sip of his drink.

Kelsey could see he was more amused than annoyed, but that trace of annoyance was there. She'd hit something close; Rorke didn't like it.

Let it go, she told herself, yet she wished she didn't have to. More and more she saw a man driven to prove himself—physically, mentally, emotionally. He was injured as hell, but his shirts were still starched, his posture still erect—and he still took on other people's problems. But should anyone come close to him, Rorke closed up tighter than a clam. He sent an impatient scowl across the table.

''Might as well spill it,'' he said gruffly. ''There's obviously something else rolling around in that creative mind of yours.''

''Nothing that's any of my business.'' She reached for her purse. The waiter had slipped the receipt on the table, and they were both done. Her hand closed on the bill. Rorke's hand closed over hers.

Contact with a light socket couldn't have startled her more.

''You can pay for your dinner if you'll tell me what you were thinking.''

"Just . . ." She had to be losing her mind if the simple contact of a man's hand was causing the blood to shimmer in her veins. It was just the dark night, the smell of the river, the wild flickering candlelight on his hard, strong face. He *was* a pirate in another life. "It was just an impression. Just a feeling . . . that you were wild as a teenager. A swashbuckler, 1970s version. And that I thought something might have happened to make you so hard on yourself." She took a breath. "Nothing like a woman putting a foot in her mouth, is there? It's not like I know you from Adam—"

Something in his dark eyes stopped her from chattering—a flicker of something dangerously, sinfully warm. And then he shook his head. "You're scary, Kels. Worse than scary, and . . . dammit all." He filched the bills from under her hand and flipped it over. "When did you do this?"

"I slipped him a credit card early on. Good heavens, sugar. You didn't think I'd take your word about keeping your wallet in your pocket, did you? I told you this treat was on me."

She shot him a gloating, feminine smile so full of satisfaction that she was damn lucky he didn't kiss it off.

Outside, she handed him more trouble. She got it in her head that they both needed a stroll down the riverbank to walk off their dinners. He figured she was going to deliver another Natchez history lesson—a reasonable assumption, since that's what she told him. A half mile later they passed a freshly painted white gazebo that was some historical landmark. He didn't know what, and Kelsey didn't inform him. By then he was on to her. She hadn't lured him on the walk to give him a history lesson.

She'd lured him out here so he could make a damn fool of himself talking himself dry. He'd never met a more calculating and maneuvering woman. In full view of Natchez, she kicked off her sandals and started walking barefoot. Worse, she goaded him into doing the same. She steered him up a grass bank and over a knoll. There, the city lights and sounds disappeared as if they'd never existed, and the Mississippi swelled in front of them, satin black and still. Kelsey seemed to have arranged that. She arranged the crescent moon and she arranged the huge leafy oak to be in the exact spot where she demanded he stretch out.

The ebony night, the dark private shadows and the lap of the river were all conducive to seduction, and when a woman coaxed a man to lie next to her in the grass . . . Hey, Rorke wasn't born yesterday. He knew what was on her mind.

It wasn't the same thing that was on his mind.

She stuck a blade of grass between her teeth, Thomasina Sawyer fashion, buttoned her shirt to the neck— it was cool—and then sat up and rearranged her legs in a lotus position that made his spine cringe to look at her. And then she did the unforgivable. She listened.

And it just kept coming out, stuff she couldn't possibly want to hear. He was the youngest, with two perfect older brothers. He'd been the renegade in the family, the devil, the one to wrap a cycle around a tree, the one to date the wildest girls. He'd worried his father right into a heart attack, then set about changing his whole life, permanently burying the rebellious streak, becoming someone else. A man. And, thank God, a helluva lot better man than he'd been a kid.

He'd have quit talking—he *hated* talking about things like this, *never* talked about things like this—if she'd just had the good sense to quit listening. She didn't argue, didn't analyze, didn't play amateur psychologist. She didn't do anything at all but sit there with the breeze tangling her hair every which way and the starlight playing on her face. It was as if she were absorbing his feelings, not judging him. She was just being there—as a friend, if he wanted one. Somehow or another he found himself spilling the whole story of the robbery.

"I'd just walked in. I'd been at it twelve hours, and the only thing in my head was getting a can of something I could open for dinner. It was pitch-black outside and not much brighter in. This little old guy was behind the counter. He'd already turned off some of the lights, ready to close. It was like a nightmare coming at me all at once. I saw the two kids, saw the blade of a knife, saw their eyes. They were high—not out of it— just high enough on something to think they owned the world."

He shut his eyes, feeling the same sickness tighten his gut the way it did every time the memory closed in on him. "I should have walked right back out. Called for backup. I had a unit in the car. That's the rule, to call for backup, and it's a good rule. I was an off-duty cop and alone. There's no way to make a mistake in a situation like that."

He felt the damp, cool grass beneath his back, felt the river breeze, felt *her* next to him, and out it came. "But that's what I did—made a mistake. I didn't call for backup. I stayed. This thing was going down *now*. All I could see was that if I didn't do something, it was going to be too late. Those kids weren't going to wait around for another patrol car to show up. The captain saw it the same way when he read the report and heard me out. Nobody gave me any grief. But—"

"But there was more to it?" Kelsey asked softly.

He opened his eyes. Kelsey's face was in shadow, her hair whispering around her shoulders in the wind. "One of the boys who was in there—I couldn't take my eyes off his face. I don't know why. He was blond, not like me. He was a scrapper and I was always a brawler in height. And I was never into drugs or real trouble when I was his age. I was just so high on life, so arrogant that I never saw I was causing other people heartache. I was too damned stupid, and that kid—that stupid, stupid kid—he wasn't even old enough to have whiskers."

"You feel you reacted because of him? Let your judgment be affected because of him?"

It was an unnerving sensation to have Kelsey put words to the feelings he hadn't known how to express—not to anyone else, not even to himself. He said slowly, "I know I did. Given the same situation again, I'd still stay. It wasn't a scene I could walk away from, not as a cop, not as a man. That's not the problem. It's knowing I let that kid get to me emotionally."

"Of course you did," she said gently. "He reminded you of you, didn't he?"

"I…" He frowned at her. He hadn't considered that and wasn't sure he wanted to. "Maybe. But that's hardly an excuse."

"Just tell me the rest."

She heard his voice cool and harden. According to Rorke, it was a measure of his biased judgment that he didn't guess that two boys that young wouldn't have a bigger source of courage. The rest of the gang swarmed in from the back door. The blond boy pulled a gun, and Rorke lunged for him. The gun went off. The boy was shot. After that, it was five on one, all trying to elude capture with the sound of sirens wailing in the distance. Kelsey could too easily picture it. She'd already seen Rorke's bruises.

But they weren't the real source of his pain.

A seventeen-year-old boy a long time ago had learned to be so hard on himself. And for a brief moment in a small country store, a gruff, tough, by-the-rules cop had dared to react emotionally. He'd dared to let blind emotions color his judgment. And he was so damn sure that it was wrong to do that.

"No comment, Whitfield?"

"Nope."

"I got a whole department on my tail, telling me to put it behind me and forget it. Every cop's walked into a scene where he couldn't make it right. You put kids, drugs and weapons together and no matter what you do or who does it, that's going to explode sometimes. I've had advice coming out of my ears like that. You want to add to it?"

"No."

He said low, hard, "It's my fault the kid was shot."

"That's obviously what you believe," she agreed. "If you're looking for an argument from me, you're not going to get one. You're a grown man. You know what you feel, what you believe." She'd been sitting absolutely still for a long time. She uncurled her legs, stretched and scooted over to his supine figure in the shadows. "Guilt and I are old friends, Rorke. Sometimes I think that if guilt were gold, we'd all be kings. The best I can tell you is that there's a certain kind of wrong you can't make right until you forgive yourself."

"Ah . . . Kelsey?"

She'd hoped he was listening, but his voice had deepened to a husky, distracted murmur. His mind had definitely moved away from the robbery.

"Honey, what in God's green earth are you doing?"

Although her technique was certainly rusty, she was quite sure Rorke knew exactly what she was doing. He was lying with both arms behind his neck when she crouched over him. He never had the chance to move before her head dipped down. His lips were cool and smooth and his eyes unnervingly wide open when she kissed him.

His entire body stiffened. She could have sworn this was what he'd wanted all evening. She could also have sworn this was what she had been successfully avoiding all evening, because physical contact with Rorke was not wise. Talk was wise. Only she'd been talking with him for several hours now and discovered—not for the first time in her life—that some things were more important than common sense.

Someone needed to kiss Rorke. Someone needed to tell him that he was a good man, a special man, that if he'd opened his eyes he'd realize that he'd risked his life to save a boy, not hurt him. No mistakes he'd ever made could make him less of a man but more of one. You couldn't love a perfect statue. A statue didn't hurt, didn't need, didn't bleed. She cared for him just as he was, a man who saw himself as unforgivingly fallible. And if all those things were just too complicated to communicate at that precise moment, a kiss would do.

Every thought in her head was loving, not sexual, when she lowered her lips to his a second time. All she intended was tenderness and a woman's natural expression of empathy and caring. The corpse warmed under her second kiss. It also moved. Just as she lifted her head and was about to move away, his arm snaked out from behind his head and wrapped around her. Rorke groaned, hoarse and low, when he shifted her beneath him.

"You hurt yourself—your ribs?"

"Yeah."

"Badly?"

"Shh."

Her kisses had been innocent. His were like time bombs, and they kept coming until her lungs forgot to inhale and exhale. Had she really believed Rorke lacked confidence? The rogue wasn't rough for a moment, but he knew exactly what he was doing. His mouth covered hers, savoring, exploring and, in that shadowed night, claiming.

When he laid his palm against her throat, tipping her mouth to a more alluring angle, she gulped in air. When his lips tried to secure hers again, she bumped his nose, then winced. Her nose didn't hurt, but his had to.

He lifted his head, a black silhouette against the spiky branches and rustling of leaves above him, but she could see his smile. "When," he murmured, "is the last time you kissed a man? Apart from that kiss I stole in the parking lot a few days ago."

"Not that long ago." She was still breathless. Air, oxygen, ozone. Her lungs couldn't seem to get enough of any of them.

"I think it was an unbelievably long time ago."

"Come on, Rorke. I was married!"

He smiled again, a virile, wicked smile, and then lowered his head. "Doesn't count. You were only a baby when you were married. Necking is a lot more dangerous...and a lot more fun...when you're old enough to know how much real trouble you can get into.''

"Rorke?"

"Hmm."

"I don't *want* to get into trouble. In fact, I'm not sure how all this started, but—"

When he raised his head, he was no longer smiling. "You think I'd in any way physically hurt you?"

The question seemed to come from nowhere. She shook her head, immediately and instinctively.

"Are you afraid I'll let things go too far?"

Again she shook her head, immediately and instinctively.

"Then open your mouth for me, Kels," he whispered.

His mouth pressed her into the cool spring grass. When her lips parted, he went after her tongue. A tongue, in a small dark mouth, had only so many places to hide. She found her fingers latched onto his arm, at first repressively, then clutching, climbing, as if she'd lost her sense of gravity and was dependent on his.

She'd necked, about a thousand years ago, with stubble-faced boys taking her home from a date. It was nothing like this. Andrew, a hundred years ago, had taken a virgin to bed. At least in the beginning that relationship had been good.

But it was absolutely nothing like this. Now Rorke's big, warm palm skimmed over her hip, drifted over the swell of her ribs and between her breasts. He never broke the kiss as his finger flipped open the button at her throat, then a second button.

He angled her head and kissed her mouth, then her bared throat, then her mouth again. His whiskered cheek burned the soft skin under her chin. The scraping rubbed against feminine nerves that were already electrified. She could smell Spanish moss, rich earth and river. She could feel Rorke's heart start to pound, slow, pagan slow, its beat as strong as the thigh he nudged between hers as he scooped her closer.

Her response was blind emotion, as instinctive as life and a little frightening. Too much, for too many years, had happened in her life for her to dwell on sexual feelings. She'd been a girl when she'd married Andrew. She'd long since grown into a woman, but it had never occurred to her that her sexual feelings and needs had grown up, as well. She wasn't a girl. It wasn't the same. She didn't know, couldn't have known, that being kissed by a man and a seasoned lover was a thousand times more exciting, more dangerous, than anything she'd ever dreamed of.

The crazy thing was that Kelsey knew she'd started this, under the naive impression that for a few brief moments in time, Rorke needed someone to hold, someone to be there for him.

Crazier yet, she still couldn't shake that notion. The thread of his pulse and the hunger in his eyes moved her far more than his dominant skills as a lover. And those skills were more than enough to take her down where the night was deep and dark, where his needs aroused her own.

Within that first round of kisses, he seemed to know her body better than she did. She was trembling. He encouraged that. His caresses were sure, skilled, easy, slow. Her heart was beating, her knees seemed to have melted and she was all hot and cold. Hot in all the embarrassing places. Chilled where he wasn't touching her.

When his mouth blazed a new trail of fire down her neck, his hand slid under her blouse. His fingers were callused, rough on the tender skin of her ribs. She made a sound, furrowing her hands into his hair, waiting for his hand to claim her breast. Yet he didn't. Leisurely his finger traced the lace edge of her bra, starting at the shoulder strap, dipping to the swell beneath her arm, curving around the white flesh, lingering at the clasp between her breasts.

"Purple?" he murmured.

Her eyes shot open for the teasing question, only he wasn't teasing. Maybe he'd wanted to; maybe he'd planned on saying something light and humorous to lessen the volatility between them, but that wasn't what happened. He looked at her moonlit face and his eyes glowed dark, hot, possessive. Rorke was aroused— heaven knew she'd already realized that—but desire made his whole face harder, the shadows and planes sharpened in intensity. If she felt vulnerable, she understood instinctively that he was more so…and that he'd risked more than he knew by letting her see it. The desire was as raw in his face as need.

The Mississippi somehow stopped flowing just then. The stars stopped winking in the sky. And it was then— watching her, letting her watch him—that he flipped the front catch on her bra. Her heart picked up speed. His fingers pushed aside the skimp of lace and covered her small white breast.

He rubbed a rough thumb over the nipple, back and forth, softly, tenderly, until the tip hardened and tightened and ached. She closed her eyes, feeling more exposed than if she were stark naked, feeling fire lick through her as if she were the match and he were the flame. *"Don't,"* she said fiercely, but she'd have killed him if he'd stopped.

He responded by kissing her, this time with no finesse and no skill, just emotion. That wasn't supposed to happen. It never happened. Rorke took pride in his skill as a lover. He never forgot that he was of a size and weight that could hurt a woman, never lost control because a woman's response was fragile and a selfish man could lose that.

He laid his lips on Kelsey's throat and was tempted to lose his entire mind. She *couldn't* always be this responsive, and he knew it had been a long time for her. She told him that with her hushed breath, the tangle of limbs when her mouth reached for his again, the feel of her fingers clutched in his hair, holding him . . . holding him. He would be the one, that's all he knew. When she made love again, it was going to be with him.

He wrapped his arms around her. His left wrist screamed weakness; he didn't care. He skimmed his hands down her slim sides, drawing her closer when they were as close as they could be fully clothed. But he had her pictured in his mind: naked, wearing nothing but moonlight—or better yet in sunlight, because he could imagine his tongue on the three freckles that crested her breasts, could already see her hair tumbling on his pillow and her long supple limbs wrapped around him. . . .

Rorke abruptly realized that he was out of control.

He wrenched his lips free from her and rolled on his back, breathing in gasps. Damnation, they were on a public riverbank. He wasn't just hard; the whole blood flow of his body had coiled beneath his belt. He was hot and, more unforgivably, he didn't want to cool down.

Then he twisted his head—and saw Kelsey.

Chapter 6

The moment Rorke rolled away from her, Kelsey closed her eyes and wound her arms around her chest. The transition from drowning sweet desire to burning hurt had been lethally swift. If she hugged herself hard enough, maybe the ache would go away. If she breathed just right, maybe she could forget how fast, how suddenly, Rorke had jerked away from her.

"Kels..." Rorke reached over to touch her cheek. Her skin had been so warm. Now it was ice. "I'm sorry, really sorry. I didn't mean for it to go that far."

"I know you didn't." There was no question in her mind of that. "It's okay."

"I didn't plan this when I asked you for dinner." He hesitated, then added with gruff honesty, "I'd thought about it. I wanted it. But I swear the only thing I intended to push for was more time with you."

"Rorke, it's all right. I understand. I lost my head, too." Her lips twisted in a smile. "You're pretty heady stuff, tough guy," she whispered.

But her voice was oddly hoarse and her smile barely a shadow, making him frown. She lurched to a sitting position and buried her hands under her blouse, trying to rehook her bra. Her hair tumbled in front of her face, blocking her expression, but he could see her hands were shaking.

"Let me," he murmured, and shifted closer.

Her eyes shot up. "No!"

He froze, not so much by the rebuff as by the wounded hurt in her eyes. He would have understood anger, even distress. His own body was still screaming stress; every pump of his blood was still heated with desire. But that wasn't what he saw on her pale, drawn face. When and how had he hurt her?

Her voice immediately lowered. "I just meant—I can do it myself."

She couldn't. He watched her fumble, fail and give up. She tucked in her shirt as if it didn't matter, looking everywhere but at him. Rorke had defused more than one bomb in his years on the force. The real danger was if you didn't know the nature of explosive you were working with. Carefully he chose a tone that was soothing and light. "You're going to have to help me find my shoes, lady. I remember dropping them, but I have no idea where and my night vision's worth about a zip and a kanoodle."

"I'll find them." She stood up immediately. "I'll bet you have trouble putting shoes on with your ribs."

"I'd have trouble putting shoes on with my knees, too," he quipped, but there was no smile. She scouted around in the shadows and came back with both her sandals and his shoes. "Good grief, you realize that it's two o'clock in the morning?"

No question about it—she wanted to go home. He kept up the conversation on the half-mile hike back to the car. Her responses to his token humor were unenthusiastic, not like the Kelsey he knew, but she had some color back in her face by the time he was navigating the dark silent streets toward her house. As he had the first time, he nearly missed her driveway because the brush was so tangled and thick around the mailbox and narrow drive. "Once I get a little stronger," he offered as they climbed out of the car, "I could bring a chain saw over here."

"Stop it, Rorke. It's not necessary. Honestly."

He closed his car door quietly, carefully, as if he were doing the best he could not to detonate a grenade. "What's that supposed to mean?"

"Come on." She lifted her hand in a helpless gesture as if to say, Please, let it go. Then she buried her head in her purse, fishing for her house key. Since she hadn't left on the porch light, it was hard to see. Her purse was loaded with half of what she owned; one small house key was extra hard to find. Next week she was going to buy a key ring. A *huge* one. Of course, she'd told herself that before and never done it, but thinking about key rings now was a lot easier than crying.

Rorke came up behind her, quieter than a panther. She didn't realize he was there until his knuckles grazed her throat. He lifted her chin. With both her hands trapped in the juggling act with her purse, she felt as vulnerable as glass.

"You think I'm not coming back, is that what's going on?" he said sharply.

"I don't *think*. I *know*, just like I know why you jerked away from me at the river."

"Kels, there is no way you could misunderstand why I stopped things at the river." But he could see there was. She didn't seem to have the least comprehension of what she did to a man. "Okay," he said on a thread of patience, "how about if you tell me why you think I 'jerked away' from you?"

"Because you realized who I was." She twisted her head away from his grasp and ducked again. This time when she dug in her purse she came up with a house key. "Believe me, I don't blame you. I don't even know how I let it all happen to begin with. My whole life is Janey. She's my world, everything that matters to me, and the last thing I can afford is for you to be angry with me."

"Dammit, I'm not angry with you." He was furious with her, partly for doubting his integrity, mostly because he still didn't have the least idea what she was upset about. "I don't welch on my word, and I told you before, I'll find your daughter. Your daughter has nothing to do with you and me."

"There is no you and me." She tossed back her hair and headed for the door. "There was just two people. Maybe two lonely people, and they shared something, and it was special and it felt good and, dammit, you're a good man, Rorke. But you're not going to get involved with an alcoholic!"

She bolted up the porch steps to stunned silence behind her. Fumbling and jerking, she finally got the key in the lock, only to discover she hadn't locked the stupid door to begin with. She heard a slammed footstep on the porch behind her—it sounded as emphatic as an elephant's—and then a booted toe connect with a pansy pot.

He said a single succinct word. Any other time on earth she would have smiled. Poor Rorke, he was injured already. And he didn't have a clumsy bone in his body; it was just around her pansies that he developed this bullish streak.

She pushed open the door and dropped her purse inside.

"Turn around."

She didn't want to turn around. She wanted to be inside, in her dark living room, where she could think about Rorke bumping into her pansies while she cried in peace.

"Then don't turn around. I'm just telling you—I wasn't kissing an alcoholic, Whitfield. I was kissing a woman, and she sure as hell was kissing me back. And I don't know about you, but that was the best thing that's happened to me in just about forever, and I'm not walking away from it."

He made her eyes brim. She had to swallow hard to even talk. "Rorke, that's exactly what you have to do. Walk away. Let it go. And that's exactly what you're going to do once you go home and think about it."

"Kelsey—"

But she quietly, firmly closed the door and, as she should have done earlier that evening, latched it.

Click, click, click.

The distant, odd metallic sound was as annoying as the buzz of a bee. Kelsey raised one bleary eyelid, noted the disgusting bright sunshine and read the clock—7:00 a.m.

Seven o'clock Sunday morning.

Most Sunday mornings she roused to make a church service, but she wasn't always so perfect. This morning she didn't feel perfect at all. After Rorke had left she hadn't gotten to sleep until 3:00 a.m. She felt physically and emotionally battered and sluggish, mean and so exhausted that she decided she was imagining that strange little metallic sound. Fluffing the pillow over her head, she settled her cheek in the cool sheet and nestled back in bed.

Clip, clip, clip.

Her lids opened under the pillow. Nothing was out there but birds. Originally she'd bought the house because the mortgage was cheap. It should have been cheap; the place had been in terrible shape—and still was, she thought glumly. She was fixing it as fast as she could, though, and she specifically loved the place because of its surrounding half acre of land. The original owner had fenced the property. The fence was in as disreputable repair as the house and lawn, but the whole thing was hers, secluded and private and loaded with the flowering bushes and trees she loved. The relevant factor, however, was the privacy. No one could be clip, clip, clipping. Not within her hearing range.

Clip, clip...

With murder in her heart, she threw off the pillow, ripped off the sheet and stomped stark naked to the window. Nothing from the west view. Her bare feet tromped on white jeans, the comforter lying on the floor and a shoe before she reached the east window and threw up the sash.

Nothing. Zip, zero, zilch. Just early morning sunshine soft as butter, an oriole fluttering on the telephone wire and her favorite magnolia in spectacular flowering glory. She was just about to turn away when she saw something fall. A branch. A branch from the rose-hued azalea just beyond her myrtle tree.

Her eyes narrowed as if she were sighting a gun. Another branch fell. And if she wasn't mistaken she caught a gleam of color—flesh color—like the flesh color on a man's upper arm.

Another body part flashed in front of her. A man's jean-clad behind as he was bending over. Beyond the sound of clips she heard a groan, which was a very helpful means of identifying this particular man but not necessary. She'd have recognized that particular man's tight muscular fanny anywhere, anytime.

She grabbed a vibrantly printed robe that an old friend had brought her from Hong Kong, belted the sash to stomach-constricting tightness and marched barefoot outside.

Rorke had turned the corner on her azalea by then. He was wearing work boots and jeans, nothing else. He'd reapplied his wrist bandage, evidently to give the joint some strength. The hand clippers glittered in the sun as he mercilessly pruned another twelve inches off her azalea. His forehead was beaded and his shoulders oiled gold with sweat. It was humid and sticky this early, but not hot. He'd had to toil like a demon to work up that sweat; he'd also worked up pain, because the lines around his eyes showed stark white against his tan.

Something constricted in her throat at the look of him. Hurt? Love? Because she couldn't deal with either of those emotions, she did the best she knew how to make her voice sound angry and irritated. "You're certifiable, Stoner. You know what time it is? *Seven o'clock.* And neither of us could have gotten to sleep before three!"

"It's not seven o'clock. It's 7:10." He turned his head, gave her the once-over in the orange, green and yellow satin robe and winced. "Somebody gave that to you for a present, right? I have drawerfuls of ties that must have come from the same place."

"There's absolutely nothing wrong with this robe—"

"There's definitely nothing wrong with what's in it, but just to prove my mother raised me like a gentleman, I'm going to stay turned around until you get something decent on."

"I'm as covered as a nun, and I'm not going anywhere." She shoved back her hair, which immediately flopped forward again. "At least not until you tell me what you think you're doing here."

"Now, Kels." He flashed her a grin, but he also kept working. "All I'm doing is obeying your orders."

"My orders?" she asked blankly.

"Yeah, your orders. You ordered me last night to go home and think things over. I did. I decided there wasn't a damn thing I could do about your daughter until business hours tomorrow, so that left today free." He motioned expansively around him. "I don't want to hurt your feelings, sugar, but this place is a mess. Your mailman can't see your mailbox for the brush. People miss your driveway for the branches. Can't mow your lawn without being attacked by either a bush or a tree that's been let go so long it's gone wild."

"If you like yard work so much, did it occur to you to concentrate on your own?"

"It did, it did . . . but mine's already in golf course shape. My house is just as bad. Everything in its place, no clutter, no dust. Nothing to do. And telling you that shouldn't surprise you. You probably already have me pegged as a neatnik perfectionist." Again he motioned expansively. "This is so hopeless, it's a neatnik's dream. At four in the morning I was pacing my floors thinking about these bushes. By five in the morning I was getting all hot and excited just fantasizing about bringing my chain saw over here.''

He checked to see if she was smiling. Kelsey tried to maintain a stone face but his nonsense was getting to her. Not a lot. Just a little. ''You seem to have had the good sense to sublimate your . . . ah . . . fantasy.''

''Had to. No way my wrist could handle a chain saw. Maybe in two or three more weeks, but in three more weeks this yard could have covered the house. No one would have ever found you again. You'd have been starved for oxygen, no way to get out and get food. Cobras—long extinct in Mississippi—would have found their way here when they discovered their natural habitat of jungle.''

He clipped an absolutely gorgeous branch of flowering azalea. Mournfully she watched it fall. ''I was going to get to the yard. I was just waiting until the spring flowering season was over.''

''I'm sure you were 'going to get' to the yard. Only the way you seem to have five thousand constant irons in the fire, I figured your timetable was more realistically around the year 2000. Like I said—''

''The cobras. I heard you.'' But, she thought, he hadn't heard her last night. Silence fell between them. It didn't seem to bother Rorke. He just kept pruning. He was as stubborn as a hound and just as hardheaded. One out of three movements he made caused him an unconscious grimace.

He was going to kill himself from trimming her vines, and she stood there watching him with a feeling of helplessness. His golden shoulders and spine sheened with moisture were a daunting sight for a woman barely awake, but she also saw the winces, the circles under his eyes.

He'd been up all night because of her, and because he was the kind of frustrating man who had more determination than sense. Last night he'd told her he'd been kissing a woman, not an alcoholic. Those words had haunted her dreams, troubled her sleep and absolutely riddled her with guilt.

What he'd said was true. Last night she'd made the unforgivable mistake of letting herself feel no differently than any other woman alone with a man she cared for. Last night it had felt perfectly natural to coax Rorke to open up, to feel trust and sensitivity for each other burgeon and grow. Last night she'd felt exhilarated and reckless and wonderful in his arms, caught up in a cyclone of emotion that made her feel richer as a woman than she'd ever felt before.

Last night Kelsey knew damn well she'd been falling in love.

Until he'd jerked away from her. Then, reality had slammed at her with all the delicacy of a bulldozer. She *was* a woman, which Rorke had forced her to remember in the most powerful way. But she was also an alcoholic. The two were not separable, no matter how much Rorke wanted them to be.

No matter how much she wanted them to be, either.

"You have a wheelbarrow around here, princess?"

"Rorke," she said quietly, "I can't keep warning you off. I know I was guilty of encouraging you last night—but that was a mistake. I'm outstanding at making mistakes, which I've tried to tell you from the beginning. No one in my shoes would ask someone into their life, ask someone to take on the kind of problem that I have."

"If you don't have a wheelbarrow, how about some lawn or trash bags? Something to pile the debris in." He stopped clipping long enough to wipe the sweat from his brow with the back of his arm. For a brief moment he hooked his fist on his hips, standing still just long enough to catch his breath—and let his gaze rove over her with a lush masculine intensity. "And while you're getting those trash bags, maybe you can let a grown man decide what he can handle and what he can't."

Her bare feet hit the grass. With the satin robe flapping around her knees, she dug up some lawn-and-leaf bags, then went searching for the rusty wheelbarrow in the toolshed. The shed was dark and cool and cluttered. Naturally the wheelbarrow was at the back, behind all her potting tools. She set her jaw and angled the unwieldy thing back to the yard.

Rorke's mouth twisted with humor at the look of her in the satin robe and bare feet, pushing the wheelbarrow, but she wasn't smiling. "If I have to make you listen to me, I will. You don't know me well enough to jump into any kind of relationship."

He calmly, firmly, corrected her. "I haven't known you long, but I know you plenty well." He went back to clipping, his tone conversational. "That first afternoon, I saw what a real tough cookie you were. You put yourself on the line for anyone who needs you, you're a sucker for any kid. Actually, you're a sucker for anything living, starting with pansies. You're totally disorganized and sometimes you're too perceptive for your own good. I know how you feel about your daughter, and anything else I needed to know I found out last night. You went to my head so fast that it's only by the grace of God I didn't take you in the grass." He turned his head. "I wish I had."

The look in his eyes made all the air whoosh out of her lungs. "That's just . . . sexual attraction."

"You bet it was." A wicked grin.

"It'll go away—"

"You sashay over here in that robe about five feet closer and we'll see how fast it's going to go away."

Yesterday, Kelsey had thought him such a good man. Now she changed her mind. He was a dreadful, un-principled devil. Too fast the image slinked into her mind of his long brown arms around her, his clever hands peeling off her robe, sweat and sunlight and the taste of him. . . .

She swatted, hard, at a mosquito on her neck. The sting of reality—and real unhappiness—was in her voice. "Rorke, there's just no way I can deal with this lightly. If I asked you a question, would you answer it straight? No teasing, no smiles, no embarrassment—"

"Ask."

She took a breath. "Do you want an affair?"

Again he straightened to look at her. His jaw muscle tightened and his gaze narrowed on her face. Softly, dangerously softly, he said, "Honey, you have this look in your eyes. Like you're hoping if you offer me a stick of candy I'll forget the whole candy store it came from. Forget it. I'm thirty-seven—way too old to be looking for fast sex, and if that's all I thought you and I had going, I wouldn't be here. If you wanted a straight, fast answer, you got it. *No.* I *don't* want a short, sweet af-fair."

Rorke turned back to work as if the subject were fin-ished—or as if it damn well better be. Kelsey practiced swallowing several times. It had cost her to ask the question. She hadn't realized it would cost her far more to hear the answer. "I have a problem, Rorke," she said desperately. "And it's not going to go away if you pretend it isn't there. You don't seem to realize what you'd be getting into."

"No? Well, it's pretty obvious you're dying to tell me, toots, so you just go right ahead."

The humor was back in his tone, as if he were catering to a woman in a bad mood, coaxing her to lighten up and take it easy. It only upset her more. He wasn't going to understand...unless she made absolutely sure he had no other choice.

So she trailed after him, stuffing branches first in the wheelbarrow and then in leaf bags, and she told him— all of it. Deliberately she weaned all emotion from her voice. Telling her story was no source of pain. She'd done it before, starting with a roomful of strangers at an AA meeting years ago. But it was different, baring her soul for Rorke's judgment. It was different, because Rorke was proving an increasingly impossible man not to love.

She so badly didn't want him to judge her harshly.

She couldn't give him any other choice.

Her mother had died when she was small. Kelsey and her father were alone during her growing-up years. Her dad was a successful engineer who'd never missed a day of work in his life. He'd also started with a double bourbon before dinner and, to her memory, had never once gone to bed sober. "Do you hear me, Rorke? I grew up with it. I sneaked off to Al-Anon meetings when I was a teenager. I knew better than to ever have that first drink."

He didn't answer, but he was taking out the east hedge at the speed of sound. She knew he was listening.

She'd met Andrew when she was a seventeen-year-old freshman in college. He was a senior: older and sophisticated, romantic and fun. She hadn't had so much fun growing up, and Andrew had been like a dark prince, carrying her off in the night of a fairy tale. He took one look at her and wanted her, and it had never occurred to her to say no.

"When I look back, I know exactly how I misled him. He was on that timetable people get into when they finish college, ready to start his life, in a hurry to find a wife he could share that with. Naturally he knew the age difference, but I was never a 'young' seventeen, Rorke. Growing up with my father, I'd had to take on a layer of responsibility and maturity. That layer was artificial, but he had no way to know that, and very honestly, neither did I. I was anxious to please him, malleable, too caught up in my fairy-tale dream to realize I was in no way ready for marriage."

Kelsey straightened, her fingertips rubbing at the small of her back. Rorke had moved from her azaleas to her myrtle tree. If his pruning technique became any more ruthless, her poor tree was going to end up a bonsai. Still, he didn't make any comment, but she hadn't come to the tough stuff yet. She took a breath and waded in, her voice soft, clear, even.

She'd still been going to school part-time, but right off they'd started in a life-style of entertaining. Andrew had never forced her to keep up with his mint juleps. That was her choice. Andrew never realized she was going under. She had, but she drank anyway.

"Every step of the way I knew what I was doing. It took me over. That's how it was. I threw it all away, when for the first time in my life I had it all—financial security, a man who loved me, a home I could count on, and in time, a baby." Kelsey shoved back her hair. "The only time I had it beat was when I was pregnant. I never had a drop when I was carrying Janey, and when she was born I adored her. I loved her more than my life, more than any breath I could take, more than anyone or anything that had ever mattered to me...."

She had to close her eyes to force herself to keep talking. She'd started back in with wine when Janey was a year old. When Kelsey had been living with her father, her excuse had been how hard life was. When she was first married, her excuse had been to please Andrew by keeping up with him at parties. When Janey was a year old, her excuse was that she was exhausted by the time the baby was in bed and just needed "a little something" to relax.

"If a pin dropped, that was enough reason for me to start pouring. Do you understand me, Rorke? I *had* no excuses. I drank. It's as simple and as ugly as that, and there's nothing I can do to make it pretty. It wasn't my father's fault. It wasn't Andrew's. It was entirely mine."

Rorke's only response was to stalk over to her magnolia tree, which didn't in the least need pruning.

"I never exposed Janey to it, which was the only thing I did right." She never drank before her daughter was in bed, but that didn't alter the whole picture. Her life was the bottle by then. She cared about her daughter, but nothing else. Not Andrew or the house or their life, and certainly not about herself. "My husband took a drunk to bed and woke up to a wife with a hangover. I had blackouts. I lost thirty pounds. Andrew was a warm, fun-loving man with a laugh that could spring out of nowhere—or he was when he put the ring on my finger. Marriage to me cured him of that. You have no idea what hell I put him through.''

Her magnolia tree was fast becoming a shambles.

"When Janey was four years old, he came home late one night. I'd cooked dinner hours before but had forgotten it. Smoke was billowing out of the kitchen. Janey was long asleep by ten o'clock, and I was predictably passed out. He filed for divorce—I have yet to understand why he waited so long. The only thing he felt for me by then was contempt and disgust. That was mutual, because that was all I felt about myself. Rorke?''

He didn't answer. By then, Kelsey no longer expected him to. She looked down at her hands as if they belonged to someone else. She was shaking like a fool, and on a warm, humid Sunday morning with the sun beating down on her like a halo. A halo for a woman who'd never been an angel.

"It took me," she said softly, "almost as many years to rebuild my life as it did to destroy it. I lost my daughter, Stoner. You don't get lower than that. And if I can't live with that, I'll be damned if I can believe that you could." She took one last breath. "Eight years ago I had two things to learn. One is that I'd run out of excuses . . . and the other is that I can't make guarantees. There's a dragon in my life and that threat will always be there.''

Rorke was silent a moment, then turned to face her. "Are you done talking?''

"Yes.'' She was more than through. She told herself it was a relief to have it all out in the open—for Rorke to have any illusions about her could only hurt him—yet she also felt breakably fragile. She wasn't proud of the woman she'd been. Learning to live with who she was and what she'd done was her problem, no one else's and certainly not Rorke's. But it wasn't easy to admit the nature of her giant mistakes to a man who crucified himself for his own.

"Are you sure you told me everything you wanted to tell me? That you don't want to add anything else? Are we really all done with this subject?"

She stared at him in confusion. Rorke set aside the clippers and started walking toward her—not walking, stalking. The sun cast a glint of dark fire in his eyes, and his stride was an all-male aggressive gait. Like a looming giant, his bronze shoulders shaded her face entirely from sunlight before she had the chance to answer. "We're done, yes," she said uncertainly.

"Good." He swooped down, a falcon for prey, and stole a kiss from her...a kiss so fleeting, so tender, that it felt like the brush of wings. "You can relax now, Kels. You did your absolute best. It's in no way your fault that I'm not scared off. And if we've got all that settled once and for all, I'd really appreciate a glass of orange juice."

"Orange juice?" she echoed vaguely.

"Juice, pop, water. I'm not fussy—just thirsty as hell." He took another look at her face and said just as gently, "It's okay. I can find the orange juice for myself. Trust me, you're going to get used to me raiding your refrigerator."

He waited. Not long. A split second passed when she understood he was giving her a choice, one time, one last time, to decide whether she would let him into the house—into her life.

Then the moment was gone. When she didn't immediately respond to the negative, he lithely zipped up the porch steps and opened her screen door. "You want a glass, too?" he called over his shoulder.

She wanted to shoot him. *Why do I have the feeling you just railroaded me, Stoner? Like, could we talk about terms? I'm not even absolutely sure what I just agreed to.*

But her heart called her on that small fib. Her heart, at the moment, felt recklessly open and unbearably full. After hearing her story he could have reacted in a hundred ways, some of which would have crushed her. Instead he'd kissed her in a way that made her feel washed in gold.

Kelsey knew herself to be strong. Over the years she'd gained the resilience and fortitude and just plain grit it took to make something of her life. At the moment, though, she simply wasn't strong enough to pretend she didn't care.

She more than cared.

She was falling in love with Rorke.

And she'd never in her life been more afraid.

Chapter 7

Yeah, thanks.'' Rorke hung up the phone and dragged a hand through his hair in frustration.

Rorke liked order. He liked habits. He always started his day with a set of masculine rituals.

It was now past four in the afternoon. He had yet to shower, yet to shave, yet to put on shoes. It was a rare occasion that his kitchen couldn't have passed a military inspection. At the moment, cupcake wrappers had taken over. Cold coffee cups littered the counter, cupboards hung open and a forlorn-looking package of cold French fries topped off the overflowing trash. The phone cord trailed across the room, making a waist-high trip cord from counter to table. Surrounding the telephone on the table were stacks of lists and stubby pencils and more coffee cups.

His stomach was churning from an overdose of caffeine and he wanted a cigarette so badly he could taste it. He'd given up smoking seven years ago.

Nothing was going well. He irritably hooked the phone receiver between his ear and his shoulder and checked the next number on his list. As he poked the digits with the blunt end of a pen, he figured his long-distance phone bill for the day was getting real close to the national debt. The phone rang at the other end, then rang again. "Come on, come on," he growled impatiently.

When a hoarse woman answered, he hooked his bare feet on the chair rungs and leaned forward. "Sadie? Rorke Stoner... Yeah, I know we haven't talked for a long time. You been okay?... Listen, I could use a favor...."

About a thousand years ago Sadie Jenkins, who worked records in the courthouse in Biloxi, had needed an extremely obscure favor from a cop in Natchez. Rorke's whole day had been an exercise in calling in obscure favors. Sadie put him on hold, and he glanced at the clock. Most places would shut down at five, leaving his hands tied until the next day.

He'd never figured it would take this long. By noon, absolute latest, he'd expected to have located Kelsey's ex-husband. It wasn't as if he were short on leads. The average cop would climax for the thrill of this many leads. Unlisted phone numbers. IRS. The real-estate-license background.

Rorke could have had his answers hours ago if he'd even implied that Andrew Whitfield was a police problem. The noose around his neck was ethics. There were laws about privacy. There should have been laws about bastards in general, but Rorke had already checked those. If her ex had just done something obligingly simple like rob a bank, Rorke could have had a make on the guy faster than the flick of a computer. Whitfield didn't have the courtesy to have even a speeding ticket on record. *Mr. Pure-as-the-Driven-Snow,* Rorke thought darkly.

Kelsey had called him a dark prince. That grated every time Rorke thought about it. In fact, it grated so much that he'd like to get his hands on her "dark prince" for just a few short minutes.

"Rorke? You were right. This Greenwoods is a private real estate firm in Biloxi, a partnership registered to two Andrew Whitfields—apparently father and son. That's what you wanted?"

Rorke's hand tightened on the receiver. Adrenaline started pumping through him. *Finally.* "Yeah, that's what I wanted. You wouldn't have a home address listed for either of those Whitfields, would you?"

"Not that it's kosher for me to give out." Sadie hesitated. "This official police business, sweet pea?"

"Nope." He closed his eyes and wondered why the sam hill he just didn't lie. Sadie would never know and neither would anyone else. The moment she'd pinned down the real estate firm to a Whitfield, he knew he had it. Two of the phone numbers on his list were Biloxi exchanges. He washed his face with his hand. What he wouldn't give for an unfiltered Camel at the moment defied all sanity. "I knew I was pushing when I asked. Forget it, Sadie. You've been a great help, and don't sweat it. I'll find another way to get the addresses."

Sadie sighed. "Listen, I'd help you if I could, but I can't just give out the addresses at 1332 Summerton and 37 Charles Street. You don't know my boss. He's a real stickler for going by the rules."

Rorke blinked, then let out a bark of a laugh. "Sadie?"

"I'm still here, sweet pea."

"I owe you. Diamonds, rubies, whatever you want."

As fast as Rorke disconnected, he was redialing. It took one more call to differentiate father from son, and then it was done. He had Janey's father. He had Janey for Kelsey.

He made his last phone call standing up, trying to shove dishes in the dishwasher and debris in the trash at the same time. Unfortunately, Kelsey's number was busy, which didn't surprise him. He tried two more times, then gave up and jogged off for a shower. Waiting for Kelsey to get off the phone could take weeks. He could undoubtedly drive there faster.

Within minutes he was showered, shaved and climbing in the car in a fresh pair of chinos and a short-sleeved white shirt. Rush hour in Natchez might not compare to that in a big city, but it was stop-and-stall enough to make him duck down Melrose and find the more obscure streets.

He wanted to picture her excitement when he told her about Janey, yet the picture dominating his mind was the memory of Kelsey, yesterday, standing in the yard with that crazy robe and her chin in the air, so proud, so fragile, and God, those eyes. A fawn couldn't look that hopeless, even if it was trapped and waiting for a hunter's bullet. Still, she'd told her story without making one effort to soften it. She'd made no excuses, no apologies, no explanations. *This is it, Rorke.*

The hell it was.

He understood she was trying to protect him from becoming involved with her, but all he could think of was who had ever protected her? She'd grown up alone with a drunk. That was one hell of a childhood, and Rorke didn't wonder she had been easy prey for a "dark prince"—or any other man who'd taken her out of that environment. She was too young for marriage, especially marriage to a selfish creep who sounded pure playboy to Rorke, and a baby would only have added to those pressures.

A frown creased his brow as he zipped up her driveway. It bothered him that he'd felt enormous relief when he could finally pin down reasons for her drinking, reasons he could understand, reasons he could live with. It bothered him that he couldn't keep his mind off the bottle of Chardonnay she kept in her cupboard.

It bothered him that when he'd invited himself into her house yesterday morning, he'd the same as promised her he could handle it.

Rorke shook off his sudden uneasy mood. He knew what he had in Kelsey. It wasn't trouble, but riches. When he was with her, the whole world was tipped right. She took on a man's worst secrets, darkest guilts, and started the healing process with her understanding and acceptance. He'd never felt so closely tuned to anyone else, and he was well aware she'd been wary of spending the day with him yesterday. He'd wanted the day to be good for her. She'd turned the tables on him.

The witch had gotten it in her head to tease him mercilessly about loosening up and relaxing. She had a thousand things to do around her house, but instead she'd unplugged her phone and rented some old silent comedies—*Safety Last* and Chaplin's *The Gold Rush*. She'd served burned popcorn and later destroyed pork chops on a rusty grill. Later yet he'd caught her cheating at a game of cards so he would win. She'd vociferously argued her choice of watching the Disney movie and then fell asleep in the middle of it, crooked in his shoulder on the couch, so sleepy she didn't know her own name.

Give her up? There was no way.

She was good. Good clear through to the bone, loving and honest and real—he'd never seen her less. He'd never wanted a woman more, nor ever had a woman respond to him with half her sensuality and passion. If Kelsey hadn't planned on being landed with a habit-prone neatnik, there were benefits to their differences. Life had handed her a hell of a load, but that was done. She was a hopeless softie. He wasn't. He would make sure she was protected from the rough side of life. He would love her so damn much she'd forget anything that had happened in the past.

Gee, Stoner. Has it occurred to you that you're planning out the next fifty years and you haven't even gotten her in bed yet?

Wearing a grin, he took her porch steps two at a time, neatly sashayed around the pansies and banged on her open screen door. The only answer he got was a yelped "Come on in!" from the distance of her kitchen. He let himself in and waded past the usual clutter and chaos until he reached her kitchen doorway.

One look inside and he judiciously decided that taking her to bed at the earliest opportunity was absolutely necessary. Men living in cavemen times had it so much easier. You saw a woman you wanted, dragged her off by the hair and from then on claimed the protective right to chain her by your fire. Everything about that image appealed to Rorke. Kelsey, left alone, could clearly get into no end of trouble.

There was no chance he was going to be able to tell her about Janey just yet. He'd thought *his* kitchen was a mess. Hers qualified for disaster relief funds. Her counters were mounded from one end to the other with dry baby formula, measuring devices, doll bottles, nipples and broken eggshells. Kelsey was sitting cross-legged on the floor on a pile of old newspapers, her hair looped in a top knot, wearing a short-sleeved red sweatshirt and a frayed pair of shorts.

She was also surrounded by puppies, most of whom were mewling at the top of their undersized lungs.

"Hi."

"Hi back," he murmured. He was hard-pressed not to sing the greeting. For the briefest moment her eyes searched his, but then she smiled, a rapt, soft, welcoming smile that ignited a few more caveman urges. She wasn't going to fight his right to be in her kitchen again. That victory smelled sweet, but he was well aware how close he'd come to failing her yesterday morning. She still wasn't sure of him. Later he hoped to take care of that, but right now he simply cleared his throat. "What have you gotten yourself into now, toots?"

"Babies."

"I can see that."

She chuckled at his appalled expression. "There's nine—"

"I can see that, too, although from the decibel level, it sounds like there's three or four dozen. I hate to mention this," he said delicately, "but you don't have a dog."

"I know, but Jim does. Jim runs a shelter, but he was already overrun with stray litters this spring. These little ones lost their mother to the road last night. He found a family who'll take them, but not until tomorrow afternoon. Aren't they beautiful? They're barely a week old, still have to be fed every three hours—"

He had to raise his voice to be heard. "They have to be fed every three hours, including all *night*?"

"It's only until tomorrow. Rorke, you don't have to help. They really make a terrible mess."

He'd already moved to the sink. Maybe he didn't have to help, but there clearly wasn't a prayer of talking to her if he didn't. The only quiet mutt was the one being cradled by Kelsey with a bottle plugged in its mouth.

Fixing another bottle seemed real simple; she had the formula all ready. Only the thick mixture didn't want to pour into the tiny bottle opening, and then he couldn't figure out how the nipple attached. The rubber nipple popped out, then sunk in. He had a brief vision of preparing a bottle for a freckle-nosed baby with Kelsey's eyes. The fantasy tugged at his heart, expanded in his imagination...until reality hit. The baby in his vision would likely die of starvation before he ever got the bottle together.

"Having any trouble?"

"Not at all." He mopped up after his mess, not wanting her to see he was such a klutz, and then angled down beside her with the dripping bottle. His knee grazed hers. Every hormone in his body stiffened to immediate attention. *This is clearly not the time and place, Stoner. And get your damn eyes off her thighs.* He scooped up one yelping runt, marveling at Kelsey's claim of "beautiful." He'd never seen a more pitiful species of life in his entire life. "Are you sure there's a dog in there? All I see are wrinkles and ears."

"They're bassetts. They're supposed to be all ears—and they absolutely hate the bottle. You have to coax them, make them think it's a mother's nipple...like this."

In his wildest dreams, his game plan for the day had never once included faking out a week-old puppy into believing he had a mother dog's nipple. It was Kelsey. Something happened every time he was around her that completely corroded his sense of balance. You'd think he was perfectly happy sitting on a pile of newspapers, milk dripping all over him, trying to jam the nipple into the little sucker's mouth. "So," he said casually, "who's this Jim?"

"An old friend."

"A good friend?"

"A very good friend."

"What kind of very good friend?"

Kelsey glanced at him, her eyes suddenly full of mischief. "Jim," she said gravely, "is seventy-one years old, has been married fifty-some years and weighs in at about two hundred and seventy-five."

The pup fell asleep on him, probably because Rorke abruptly relaxed. He reached for another squaller. Its ears were bigger than the first one's, and after that he was out of milk and had to fill another bottle. "Every three hours? All of them are going to be hungry every three hours? You didn't think you had enough on your plate without taking this on?"

"What else could I do?" she asked simply.

"I don't suppose saying no ever crossed your mind?" He glanced at her face. "I withdraw the question."

Four puppies later, his white shirt was filthy; he smelled like dried formula and his legs were cramped from sitting in one position. Unfortunately, he couldn't move. One pup was crooked under his bent knee, another under a foot and Kelsey had dropped two more in his lap. Except for the last one she was feeding, the rest were finally asleep. It was the first time there had been a moment's quiet since he walked in.

"Kels?"

She looked up, smiling at his careful whisper. A yank of a curl had escaped her top knot and spun around her cheek. Whether she was aware of it, her shoulders had automatically taken up a soft rocking motion for the last pup she had cradled in her arms. Her long white neck had a streak of dirt, and so did her chin. She didn't care. The thought crossed his mind that with something in her arms to nurture, Kelsey would never care.

"I found her, honey."

Her smile stilled, like a dewdrop caught in sunlight. "Janey?" Her voice was a whisper, too, but not like this. The bottle slipped from the last puppy's mouth.

"I wanted to tell you when I first came in, but there was so much noise and confusion. Anyway, this isn't so monumental—it's not like I've had a look at her yet. All we have is an address so far. They're both in Biloxi." Horrified, he saw her eyes swell up with tears. "That goes for both your ex-husband and ex-father-in-law." She swallowed and kept swallowing, but suddenly she was crying. "I can't swear yet she's with her father, but it's the middle of the school year so there's no reason to think she'd be anywhere else. Sweetheart, don't do that. I thought you'd be *happy*."

"I *am*. I—" she gulped in air "—am. It's just…I've missed her so much."

"I know."

"I've worried about her so much."

"I know."

"It was like…losing my heartbeat. And I've been so afraid, so terribly afraid, that something was wrong. That she was in trouble. I wake up from these horrible, horrible dreams where I hear her crying."

"Shh." A pup yelped, crushed under his knee. In one fell swoop, Rorke shifted the wriggling bodies off his lap and yanked Kelsey there. On the drive here, he'd imagined her exuberant reaction when he told her. He'd never imagined her crying, and this was more than a few emotional tears. In part he understood that she'd bottled up despair that she'd never find her daughter again. But this was more an explosion of anxiety. She was shuddering; she was shaken.

He dragged her arms around his neck and pushed her cheek into his shoulder. "Schools were all closed by the time I pinned down the addresses, but first thing tomorrow I'll check out every school in Biloxi, okay? Would you please stop crying? I swear I'll find her. I swear she's all right. I swear..." He'd have sworn anything to make those rough gulping sounds stop coming from her throat. He didn't know what to say, what to do. "Kelsey, they were just dreams. Think about it. If there'd been something really wrong, you'd have heard. You'd always have heard. She's all right. I know she's all right. I promise you she's all right."

With her fanny tucked between his crossed legs, he wound his arms around her and kissed her brow, then rocked her, kissed her hair, then rocked again. Eventually she gained control. The tears slowed and then ceased. She was shaky for a while after that; he just let her settle, cradled against him, her cheek in the hollow of his neck.

He closed his eyes, not wanting to move, not wanting her to move. She'd been a real tough cookie from the moment he met her. She'd stayed cool asking for his help. She'd run circles around him in the bar. She'd cheated him out of paying for dinner and she'd told him that whole damn story yesterday morning without a flicker of emotion or self-pity. Never mind that she was a sucker for puppies, his tough cookie was as strong as a brick.

But not always.

Not where her daughter was concerned.

Not, Rorke suspected, where anyone she loved was concerned.

"I don't believe I did this to you," she said finally.

"You didn't do anything to me," he said gruffly. Her voice still sounded like a warble. It still tore at him.

"No? Your shirt looks like a deposit from the Great Salt Lake. Nothing like walking in and having a woman go to pieces on you out of the blue, is there? I have a habit of crying in movies before they even roll the credits, but whether you believe it or not, I don't make a habit of doing this. I'm sorry, Rorke. I've probably embarrassed you to death."

"Good grief, would you stop? Nobody's embarrassed and there's nothing to be sorry for." He said gently, "I think you had that one coming for a long time."

"Maybe. It still feels pretty foolish." She swiped at her eyes. "I have to get up."

He knew she was recovered from the sound of her voice, but still he argued. "No, you don't."

"I need a tissue."

"There's a handkerchief in my back right pocket if you can reach it."

She reached around and dug her fingers in his pocket, found his handkerchief and blew her nose. Listening to a woman blow her nose was a hell of a time to discover he was hopelessly in love with her. Not for the first time, Rorke reminded himself that he wasn't exactly hell-on-wheels successful when it came to serious personal relationships. He reminded himself that she had a small problem that he'd given her to understand was no sweat for him to handle. He wasn't sure he could handle it.

And none of that made a damn bit of difference. He used his thumbs to brush the last moisture away from her cheeks and was tempted to smile. Some women cried...nicely. Kelsey cried the same way she did everything else. Totally. Her eyes were bloodshot; her cheeks were blotchy; her freckles stood out. "You have two seconds to give me a smile," he murmured.

"Two seconds?"

"I can smell dinner."

She flew out of his lap, which gave his cramped limbs and ribs a chance to recover feeling. There were other senses he wished had remained numb.

When Kelsey didn't immediately throw the food out, he understood that this was a "successful" dinner. The carrots had only slightly black edges. The biscuits were indescribably browned. If you poured a glass of water over the meat loaf, it would still be dry. Her eyes flew to his across the table. "I forgot to make potatoes."

"That's okay."

"I didn't realize I'd be feeding anyone but me."

"And I didn't come to mooch. Really, this is terrific."

"You like the biscuits?"

His dentist would. Every bite was a test of his fillings.

Kelsey's smile was back by then...a little sass, a little sparkle and far too much mischief. Whether she knew it, there was also a new closeness between them, sparked when she'd cried and he'd held her. She wanted him there, either because she was still feeling vulnerable or because she was too honest to hide it. He'd take closeness any way he could get it—although Kelsey's teasing hit a little too close to home.

"Are you aware that you haven't used your normal voice through this entire meal? You can stop whispering anytime, tough guy. The puppies aren't likely to wake up until they're hungry again."

"I wasn't whispering because of them," he denied gruffly.

"You were. I've never seen such a marshmallow in my entire life. The first day I met you, I saw the swagger and the scowl and those linebacker shoulders, and I thought, Mr. Rigid Law and Order. You didn't even crack a smile. Good grief, did you have me fooled—"

"Do these chatty moods come on you often?"

"I saw you with those puppies. You *loved* them. Why on earth don't you have a dog?"

She kept teasing him all the way through the dishes. He washed, she dried. She couldn't dry worth a damn, but she could change subjects faster than the flip of a dime. She discussed Greek mythology, the advantages of varnish over linseed oil and whether he'd prefer a setter or a hound. All in the same conversation.

She made him laugh, but he was conscious that she didn't mention her daughter again. That was Rorke's only clue that she was still feeling fragile, and he let it be. In fact, he'd have moved mountains to let it be. Scooting around the kitchen in that monstrous-sized T-shirt, she was full of pepper and vinegar. If it was up to him, she was going to stay that way.

When the dishes were done, she started mixing a new batch of puppy formula, and he took a determined look at her stove. No human being, male or female, could reach the age of thirty-four without being able to cook an edible meal. It *had* to be her oven. "Kelsey? Do you have an electrical tester?"

She turned, cocked one feathery brow, wiped her hands on a kitchen towel and ambled toward him. Natural as you please, she casually roped her arms around his neck and kissed him. It was just a kiss. Her lips tasted like mint iced tea and destroyed meat loaf. Her breasts, bare beneath that T-shirt—now he knew for sure—crushed against him and then eased away. The entire embrace didn't last seconds. She immediately strode back to her formula-making project.

His head was suddenly thick, his blood pressure soaring. The obvious comment for him to make was that the kind of electrical tester he'd had in mind tested voltage—as in appliances. Kelsey was unworldly.

Not that unworldly. She knew precisely how much voltage was between them. She'd still volunteered that kiss. Low as a dare, he murmured, "Hey, you. Come back here."

She didn't turn around. "Don't make a big thing of it, Stoner. It was just a thank-you for putting up with my crying all over your shirt. You want to turn on the tube? The puppies are going to wake up in another few minutes. I really have to get this ready."

She inhaled when she felt his big warm hands slide around her waist from behind. His mouth nuzzled until he found the extraordinary sensitive spot on the back of her neck. The spring night was buzzing with crickets right outside the window. She was suddenly buzzing, too, from his warm breath on her neck, from the masculine smell of him, from the feel of her fanny molding against his hard thighs.

She could sense danger. Rorke took a small potent bite of her neck. The nip was playful, but every instinct warned that Rorke wasn't playing, didn't ever play with a woman. She'd known that before she kissed him.

She'd known that the day she met him.

His hands stroked the length of her sides so that only his fingertips grazed the edge of her breasts. The air rushed out of her lungs on a nameless sound. It happened every time. An extremely complicated world became far too simple when he touched her, but she never remembered desire like this.

"Put the bottles down," he murmured.

Blankly she stared at the two bottles in her hands. There had to be some reason she was holding them, but for an instant she couldn't remember what it was. When she didn't immediately respond, he stole the items from her hands and deposited them on the counter. He pivoted her to face him at the same time he swung her arms around his neck.

His mouth covered hers, and she could taste it. Need. The need of a man to know tenderness, to express it. He didn't take the kiss, he offered it, with his eyes closed and his hands slowly, slowly kneading down her spine.

She hadn't intended her peck of a kiss to start an avalanche. She hadn't specifically intended anything to happen now, not barefoot in her kitchen, not at nine o'clock on a Monday evening when she had to smell like puppies and dish soap.

But she had known, from the moment she let him in the house yesterday morning, that he would ask her to make love with him. And that he wouldn't wait long. Rorke was too hungry, too lonely. Sometimes he reminded her of a half-frozen wolf who'd prowled too many nights alone; he'd forgotten the warmth and comfort of a fire.

He took her mouth again. Hard, possessive. His tongue swept hers, stroked hers. Before he let her up for air, she felt his pulsating hardness against her stomach, felt his hands swirling circles down her spine. "Rorke—"

When he lifted his hand, she forgot what she was going to say. His eyes had darkened to pitch. His hands skidded down her bare arms, making her pulse gallop and her skin heat. It was in his eyes—all or nothing. That's how it was with Rorke, who he was, what he was.

"You're afraid?" he whispered.

She nodded.

"Of me? Or of you, love?"

She didn't have the chance to answer. One puppy stirred, then another. A third yelped ... and woke the others. In a minute flat, the pitiful symphony could have woken the dead.

There was a growl of humor in his voice. "You'd better get the formula ready. It's a cinch no one's going to be able to think—much less talk—until they're fed again."

When he strode from the room, she finished with the formula and the bottles. He strode back in when she was just bending down to reach for the first pup.

"I'll tackle the devils. Faucets are running in your tub in the bathroom. You're headed for a warm bath."

"Rorke, I'm hardly going to leave you with—"

"You worked all day and you're going to be stuck feeding these monsters half the night, so don't tell me you couldn't use some feet-up time. You think I can't handle a few puppies alone? Go on, scoot. The tub will overflow if you don't get in there.''

"Rorke—"

"Don't argue with the law, lady. It's always a losing proposition. Now out. Scram. Vamoose.''

Chapter 8

Kelsey "vamoosed" as far as the bathroom, but all she intended was to jump in the bathtub, soap down at the speed of light and jump out again. After puppy-sitting all afternoon, the chance to get clean was irresistible, but she was far too tense to take a relaxing soak, especially with Rorke waiting for her.

She stripped down, stepped into the swirling water and abruptly discovered that the rogue had sabotaged her bath.

He'd adjusted the water so that the heat immediately seeped into her muscles. And he'd laced it with baby oil and expensive perfume, her one and only extravagant vice, and he'd had to nose through her medicine cabinet to find it. *Stoner, I can't afford to waste good perfume on something as frivolous as a bath,* she groaned mentally.

But the heat and scent and water felt subversively, shamelessly, good. Her heartbeat slowed; her mind stopped racing. Submerged to the neck, she leaned her head against the cool porcelain and closed her eyes.

Rorke would be knee-deep in puppies now. He'd be sitting there looking impatient and annoyed and military-stern...and the babies would be blithely swarming all over him. Animals had an instinct for humans. Rorke might talk a tough game, but he'd cradle those monsters until they quieted. He'd whisper, he'd cuddle, he'd soothe.

Kelsey wished he had half that patience with her. She knew the way he'd kissed her in the kitchen that he was going to push to spend the night. She also guessed he'd set her up with a little space, a little privacy, a little perfume, to give her the chance to think about it.

She already had. Over lunch, she'd made a stop at the drugstore. A package of birth control was hiding behind the hand creams in the cabinet below the sink. She'd thrown out her pills after the divorce and had never needed anything since—or expected to. The sponge was newer technology than she was familiar with. She hadn't read the directions yet. She hadn't had time. She bought it not because she was sure of saying yes but because she never lied to herself.

Sexual feelings had a way of getting away from her anytime she was physically near Rorke. She had a small weakness for the man. It had started the day she met him, but the malady had recently advanced to plague-like proportions.

Yesterday morning she'd laid her whole sordid story in front of him. She'd been blunt. She'd been frank. And instead of taking off at the speed of sound like any sane man, Rorke had stuck by her like glue. He hadn't said the words, but he'd clearly delivered the message.

He didn't give a hoot about her past. He cared about, wanted, believed in the woman she was now.

There was no way he could have given her a more precious gift. But then he had, this afternoon. She'd come apart when he'd told her about Janey. In theory her reaction should have been pure joy. He'd found her daughter—what she'd wanted, dreamed of, prayed for so many times. Yet mixed with that relief had been an explosion of unbearable anxiety.

Rorke, she knew, didn't understand her refusal to see her daughter. He had no way to understand that the measure of her love for Janey—the cost, the measure and the price—was staying completely out of her daughter's life. Her dreams about Janey in trouble were increasing. The real nightmare was knowing she couldn't help her little girl.

Rorke hadn't and couldn't have understood any of that—but he'd held her and he'd been there.

He just didn't realize that he kept doing things, maybe the only things on earth, that made it impossible for her to resist him—and even more impossible not to love him.

Abruptly Kelsey rinsed off, flicked open the drain and grabbed for a towel. She knew exactly what her feelings for Rorke were. She wanted him. She wanted him in her life, in her bed; she wanted to be the one he turned to when the chips were down; she wanted to see the kind of need darken his eyes that had her name on it. She wanted the right to be a woman again—for him, with him.

But she hadn't suddenly turned into a fool, and a woman was foolish to wish for things she couldn't have. Love didn't conquer all, not in Kelsey's life. Asking someone to share her alcoholic burden was its own mountain. With Rorke, that mountain was even higher. He was a man who judged every mistake in his own life on a ruthlessly tough scale of ethics. How could he possibly live with her? He couldn't. She'd been honest with him. It wasn't getting through. He was going to see her as "good" if it killed him, and the measure of his determination was yesterday, when he'd closed the subject as if it were all done and dealt with.

Kelsey hastily swiped the towel over her body and snatched her clothes. Her skin was still warm and damp when she dragged on shorts, and her fingers fumbled with the buttons of her shirt. It didn't matter. Rorke didn't have to deal with the problem; she already had. In her heart, in her mind, she had completely accepted that she couldn't have Rorke long-term.

But that didn't mean she couldn't sleep with him. At five o'clock that morning she'd reasoned it all out. Good grief, she was thirty-four years old. Too young to be celibate the rest of her life, and plenty old enough to deal maturely with a physical relationship. Thousands of women had affairs. Even a short relationship could be positive and healthy. Right now she knew she was good for Rorke. When she'd first met him he was as tight as a stick and far too tough on himself. Underneath the starch was a warm and emphatic man just starting to come out. She could help him. She knew she could. And the moment the relationship stopped being good for him, she'd call it quits. It was as simple as that.

So. It's all settled, Whitfield? You're going to go out there calm and natural and poised, and if he asks you to spend the night you're going to say yes. You just have to make it clear that it can only be a short-term relationship.

Exactly. She ran a brush through her hair, jammed the towel on the rack and lifted her chin as she reached the door. Her fingers slipped off the knob.

It seemed that her palms were slick, her pulse was bouncing like a Ping-Pong ball and her throat was dry. Her limbs were frozen and her stomach was thudding.

None of those imaginary thousands of women who had affairs so easily seemed to be her.

She squeezed her eyes closed and willed her heart to stop hammering. The kiss in the kitchen clung in her mind. She knew Rorke was out there. She knew he was waiting. She knew what he wanted and she knew what she wanted, and a responsible woman made a decision about making love before she was caught up in desire. She'd done that. Her decision had been responsible.

It had also been emotional. If she didn't take this chance, to know him, be with him, love him, turn to him in the night, that chance could disappear. If that happened, she'd regret it the rest of her life.

Haven't you lived with enough regrets, Whitfield? Come on, open the door. Rorke's going to think you're hiding out like a scared virgin if you don't.

Determinedly she stepped out of the brightly lighted bathroom and abruptly blinked. Night had completely fallen in the few minutes she'd been in the bath. Both the hall and the kitchen were toe-stubbing dark, and she had no idea where Rorke was.

When she finally found him, her lips started to twitch. Before her bath, he'd been as aroused as fire. All her nerves and soul-searching had been a prelude to the seduction scene she was so sure was coming.

It was some seduction scene, all right. Rorke was sprawled out on the carpet in her dark living room, a couch pillow behind him, the only light on in the entire house coming from the TV. A blood-and-guts cops-and-robbers flick was the Monday-night fare, and he was so immersed that his hand groped blindly for the bowl of jelly beans on the coffee table.

If he was set on getting naked, he sure didn't look it, and Kelsey felt the relief of a bandit offered a reprieve. "Did the puppies give you any trouble?"

When he heard her voice he raised his arm to motion her closer, but he never looked up. "They ate you out of house and home, but no, they're all asleep. Not to worry."

She wasn't worried—not anymore—but she was certainly amused as she viewed the TV action that clearly had him riveted. The movie was on its third run. She remembered falling asleep during its first. The drug runners were the villains, the cops the good guys. The plot had been done five, six thousand times. "You really like this?" she asked him humorously.

"Kels—"

"How can you really like this?"

"Are you kidding? In the flicks, the good guys always win. You think it's like that in real life? This is wonderful. Sit."

She perched on a corner of the couch, only to hear his tut-tut. Without once lifting his eyes from the screen, he circled her wrist with his hand and tugged. "Can't watch a movie sitting on furniture, toots. You turn off the lights, pull the pillows on the floor and stretch out. If you're going to watch a movie, you have to do it right."

"Heavens, I didn't realize," she said dryly.

She eased down next to him and fluffed a couch pillow behind her, only to hear his exasperated "No, no, no." She glanced at him. His left forefinger was pointed at the crook of his shoulder. When she didn't immediately move, he blindly reached out an arm and playfully cuffed her closer.

She had to chuckle. "Is that another rule, Stoner?"

"Rule?"

"You can't watch TV without someone next to you?"

"Not as well." For the first time he leveled his attention on her, away from the movie. His brow creased in a baleful frown. "Whitfield, if you're one of those women who talk through the whole show and then go quiet as a tomb during the commercials, tell me now."

She couldn't help but chuckle. His teasing made her feel rich. How long had it taken her to make Rorke feel comfortable enough to tease around her? "You wouldn't be trying to politely tell me to shut up, would you?"

"Where I grew up, you didn't use words like 'shut up' around a lady. If the lady was in a chatterbox mood, however, it was acceptable to get up and make her some popcorn—or whatever else it took to appease her jaw muscles." He paused. "If by any chance you would like some popcorn—"

She shook her head. "I'm fine."

But she wasn't for long. Ignoring the movie, she absorbed the feel of his shoulder under her cheek, the weight of his arm hooked around her, the clean, sharp masculine scent of him.

She didn't have to look far to find the reason for all her troubling indecision in the bathroom. Rorke might not be in the mood. She was. All it took was being close to him for a sweet, secret electricity to steal into her bloodstream.

There was the danger; there was the fear. Near him, needs intensified. Anticipation ruled her pulse. Sight, sound, tastes magnified. And she was terribly afraid that she'd have sold her soul for moments like this. Moments with him. Moments when the rest of the world disappeared. Moments when she felt fragile and wonderful for no other reason than being with him.

Moments when she was far too tempted to believe in forever.

I know, I know. No forevers. But the vision of a short-term fling gnawed at her. Not because of morality—she could have jettisoned every moral she'd ever had for Rorke. What worried her was being sure she could keep it cool, controlled, light, when absolutely none of her feelings for him were cool, controlled, light. She wouldn't—*couldn't*—hurt Rorke. And unless she could steer him away from serious involvement, she had no business in his life at all.

The thoughts tumbling through her mind were private. At least she believed they were, until the cops and robbers were careening on the screen in a siren-screaming chase scene. At the peak of excitement, she felt Rorke's fingers sifting, shivery-slow, through the damp hair at her nape.

When she lifted her face, his eyes were on her, not the movie. She didn't know how long he'd been studying her, but he must have read something in her expression. Desire was bold in his eyes, so was a certain dark intensity. Her heart started ticking in double time.

"Your hair is still damp," he murmured. "You never took the time to dry off, did you? Your skin's still warm, and I can smell that perfume."

His voice was so husky and low it raised shivers down her spine. "I thought you were watching the movie."

"No one could watch that movie. It's one of the worst TV flicks ever made."

"But you said—"

"You were edgy when you walked in. I thought watching the tube for a few minutes would help you relax. I was wrong." His palm cupped her cheek, angling her for a kiss. He took her mouth as alluringly as a promise, as definitively as a claim, and then slowly lifted his head. "I love the look of your mouth just after I've kissed you, Kels. But don't even try begging or bribing me. You're not getting any more."

"No?" His small joke left her breathless. Or else his kiss had.

"Not until we talk." His thumb rubbed her bottom lip, softly, evocatively. "I want you. You know that. You walked in here knowing that, and there's a yes in your eyes, a yes every time I kiss you. But you've also been building up nerves. You're going to have to tell me whatever it is you're afraid of."

"I never said I was afraid—"

"You didn't have to." Rorke stole the couch pillow from behind her head and tossed it. He wanted her head on his pillow. He wanted her close. "You trust me?"

She met his eyes. "Yes." Of that, there wasn't and never had been any question in her mind.

"You've always been honest with me. Are you going to be less now?"

She took a long breath. His voice was as soothing as hot buttered rum, but there was a perceptive, determined glint in his eyes. Rorke could be stubborn. And she had to make this right. "There are," she admitted, "some things I'm afraid of."

"Starting with?"

"Starting with..." If she diverted him with humor, it had to go easier. "I'm skinnier than you may have realized. I have freckles in embarrassing places. And I haven't made love in eight years. For all I know I've completely forgotten how."

She expected him to smile. He didn't. His thumb, whispery as a butterfly's wings, simply stroked her cheek. Softly. Slowly. "Taking those one at a time," he murmured, "I love your bones. Your freckles turn me on like hell. And there isn't a damn thing you have to remember about making love, because making it good for you is my problem. Now what else?"

But she didn't, couldn't, answer him. Those things hadn't really been so funny to her. He could have made her feel foolish and instead had made her feel as if there were nothing she couldn't share with him.

Her gaze focused on the throat exposed by his open collar. The anatomical label of "Adam's apple" had never made sense to her before. It did now. This close to Rorke, she understood exactly what Eve's temptation had been. Eve had said to hell with tomorrow. She'd given away paradise for one moment, one time, with her man.

At that precise moment it sounded like a fair trade to Kelsey.

"You're afraid I would do something you didn't want?" he probed.

"No."

"You're afraid I would physically force you to do something you didn't want to do?"

"Never that, Rorke."

His fingertips caressed her throat. One rested on the soft pulse at the hollow. "I have protection. If you want to know the truth, I have no desire to use it. Bareback's a hell of a lot better than a condom, but I wouldn't risk you, honey. If that's what you were afraid of—"

"No." Her eyes squeezed closed. His blunt talk had sent heat spiraling up her pulse. He'd thought of birth control. So had she. And there was something almost humorous about that, because it wasn't the mental image of "bareback" that turned her on. It was the idea of making a baby with Rorke. His baby. Her baby. Their baby.

Dammit, she had to get tougher than this.

His knuckles brushed her jaw, angling her face so she was forced to look at him. Somewhere in the distance, a commercial was selling the new generation of Oldsmobile, and fireflies were flickering outside the screen door. She really saw only him. "I want to make love with you," she said softly. "I want to, I will, I need to make love with you—but only if we both stay...sensible about it."

"Sensible?" His brow rose.

"Sensible. As in . . . careful."

"Careful?"

"Careful. As in . . . only so involved."

His palm stilled on her throat. "I'm not as perceptive as you, honey. You're going to have to explain to me how two people can be 'only so involved' when they're naked in bed."

She didn't like the look in his eyes. He seemed to be remembering the way she'd come alive in his arms at the river, sharing feelings about her daughter that came from her soul, a kiss in a parking lot, a Sunday morning when she'd poured out her life. She wasn't exactly famous for being sensible, careful or uninvolved around Rorke. He knew that.

She tried to remind him of other things he knew. "I'm just trying to say that we're different," she said desperately. "You know what I mean. You're a law-

and-order man by profession, a neatnik by nature. A type A who organizes and plans things. Even being around me has to drive you basically bananas. I never put a spoon back in the same place. I start ten things and finish two."

"And that's what you're afraid of? These... differences?" His tone sounded utterly perplexed.

She shook her head wildly, shakily. "I'm just afraid... of being unrealistic about them. You and I would never work. Not long-term. We'd drive each other crazy and we'd argue all the time, and it matters to me that I know you can walk away before it comes to that. That you won't get so involved that you might start counting on something more. Counting on babies. A future. I can't guarantee a future, and if that's what you want, this is all wrong."

It took a moment for Rorke to wade through what she'd said. Kelsey did not always think along rational patterns. She seemed to take the transition from spoons to fears as logical, for example. She seemed to be telling him that the only damn thing she was really afraid of was that he'd fall in love with her.

He looked at her for a long time—her so vulnerable soft eyes, her wary stillness, her tremulous mouth—and then he bent his head.

One by one, his fingers loosened the buttons of her blouse. When he reached the last button, he moved down the last inch to flip the catch on her shorts. His palm stole inside the skimpy nylon panties at the same time he took her mouth.

Her eyes widened and she stiffened, not in rejection but in startled reaction to the sudden intimacy. He knew he'd shocked her. He'd wanted to shock her.

He also knew that Kelsey liked her first kisses dry, not slippery. She liked the flavor and rub of her mouth against his. She liked to tease, lips closed, as if she were considering denying his tongue entry, as if her mouth were virginal and his tongue her first lover. She'd excited him like hell the first time she'd played the game, more so because she did it unconsciously. Rorke played the game fully conscious, fully aware of everything she liked and using it.

He felt her fingers climb his arms when he used his tongue to paint her bottom lip with dampness. Her breath started coming faster. He cupped the soft triangle between her thighs even as he drove his tongue deeply, possessively, to the back of her throat.

You think all you want is a quickie, blue eyes?

He'd planned the first time in his head. He'd planned on being patient; he'd planned on being sensitive, on going real slow, real easy, no pushing her, no hurrying her. He'd planned on making it perfect—the best sex she'd ever had—and if she had any rotten memories left over from her husband, he'd had it in mind to obliterate those off the map.

Unfortunately he'd never once planned on being so damned mad at her that he couldn't think.

When he finished with her, there wouldn't be any more stupid talk about his walking away. When he finished with her, she'd know damn well she was loved whether she wanted to be or not. When he finished with her...

He heard a feverish sound escape her throat. He stroked her until he felt moisture, warm and silky, coat his finger. He severed the contact as he severed the last kiss, on a rasp of a breath. He had only two hands—he wanted ten—and his injured body was only amenable to so many contortions. He had to set priorities, and he did so. Ruthlessly.

He burned a blaze of kisses down her throat. Her scent surrounded him, not just the perfume but Kelsey, the woman scent on her skin. God, she was soft. Her blouse was already unbuttoned. He pushed the fabric aside and found the triangle of freckles cresting her breasts that had been driving him nuts from the moment he saw them.

When I finish with you, Whitfield...

He kissed all three freckles and then swept them with his tongue. He discovered a fourth freckle on the underside of her right breast and assaulted that one, too. She was built small, so small a breast barely fit his hand, the tips as tiny and hard as pearls. He'd known the shape of her through clothes before. Nothing was better—or more vulnerable—than bare. He rolled the nipples with his tongue, then nipped with his teeth until her spine arched and he heard her call his name.

You think you can handle it short and sweet, Whitfield. Well, you're not getting it short and sweet.

He found another freckle. He kissed it good, then trailed lower yet. She'd had Janey. Maybe she had stretch marks. If she did he was going to find them, because it would be just like her to be sensitive about those, like the freckles. His palm hit fabric, annoying him no end. He pushed the last of her shorts down over the curve of her hip, then the curve of her thigh. Her panties rolled, then tangled and caught.

He fixed that by dragging off her shorts and pants at the same time, and while he was at it he peeled off his own khakis. Kelsey seemed to think he needed help, because her fingers were scraping at his shirt buttons at the same time his were fumbling for the foil packet.

Somewhere the newscaster was politely mentioning a new terrorist problem in the Middle East. All Rorke saw was the reflection of light on her skin, slick now, slick like satin, and her eyes, fierce and blue with passion, and her fingers, beckoning him.

At some point he realized he was out of control—excusably, wildly, mindlessly out of control. And Kelsey, who should have had the sense to beat him with a two-by-four, was making it worse. Her breathless kisses were landing everywhere she could reach. Her hands were all over him, kneading, clutching. And she kept saying his name.

He wrapped her legs around him. His ribs screamed; he didn't care. He drove in, hard, deep, and Kelsey arched like a fragile bow. She was small and tight and her teeth closed on his shoulder. And then she framed his face in her hands and reached...for a kiss that lasted as he set a bucking rhythm that had them both rocketing toward flame.

A first flame burst for her, but she wasn't getting off that easy.

The blaze lapped at her a second time. She wasn't expecting it, didn't seem to know that could happen. Her lashes flew up and her eyes held his and then sheened.

When the flame exploded for her that time, it exploded for him, as well. He couldn't hold back.

When Johnny Carson started his monologue, Rorke was still holding her.

Then he couldn't imagine a time when he could ever let her go.

Chapter 9

The crack of a branch woke Kelsey at three in the morning. She opened sleepy eyes. A streak of lightning illuminated the trees thrashing in the yard. The curtains were billowing at the west window of her bedroom and rain was pouring in. She groped out of bed just as a tall dark shadow strode through the doorway.

"I'll close the window, Kels. Go back to sleep. It's the middle of the night."

"The rest of the house—"

"It's already closed up, and the puppies have just been fed. Everything's fine. Go back to sleep."

When he closed the window, she caught the gleam of his wet head and the bulky shadow of a towel loosely draped around his hips. Rorke had been a busy man. At three in the morning he'd been taking showers, feeding puppies, closing windows. Everything but sleeping.

She remembered him leading her to bed sometime after midnight. He'd dozed off first, giving her ample time to test her mind for regrets, for the flavor of a mistake. Kelsey knew exactly how those tasted because she'd made so many of them.

It hadn't been a young girl's dream of seduction. There'd been no slow lead-up, no buttered words, no tame and pretty foreplay—just a storm coming at her from nowhere, a man coming apart in passion. He'd scared her. Initially she'd sensed his anger without having any possible time to understand or deal with that. She responded to what mattered more—the instinctive knowledge that Rorke needed her.

His lovemaking had been explosive, wild, passionate and primitive. Mr. Stoner had forgotten to be careful. Mr. Stoner had forgotten to treat her like cut glass. Rorke had let go like a man who had no idea there was that much emotion in him, that much need, that much love. He'd scared her, thrilled her, satisfied her in ways she didn't know a woman could be satisfied. Regrets?

No matter what happened now—and Kelsey would be nuts to pretend the future didn't hold more hurt than hope—there was absolutely no way she regretted making love with him.

She switched on the bedside lamp. The pale circle of light illuminated his tall lean form in midstride for the door. It was more than obvious that Rorke didn't feel the same way. "Where are you going?"

"I still have a few things to clean up in the kitchen."

She nodded as if his comment made perfect sense, then got out of bed and walked toward him. Her pagan seducer was gone. Rorke was not only wide-awake, he had enough restless energy to climb mountains. His face was also harsh with exhaustion, his mouth a straight line, his shoulders as rigid as stone. He wasn't going to clean up any kitchen.

The muscle bucked in his jaw when she walked into him and slid her arms around his waist. He was so cold. He didn't move, didn't breathe when he felt her soft warm breast nuzzle against his bare chest. For a moment his arms hung there motionless, and then they wrapped around her, carefully, as if her shoulders might break if he touched her. Another stick of lightning cracked; rain pelted at the windows in a furious deluge.

"Are you afraid of storms?" he murmured.

"I love storms."

"You have to work in the morning. You need your sleep."

"Would you sit on the edge of the bed for a minute?"

She could see he didn't want to. He sank to the edge of the bed because she'd asked him to, but he looked ready to lurch for the door two seconds after he figured out what she wanted. He clearly didn't want to talk, and he was avoiding any glance below her neck as if exposure to her skinny hundred and ten pounds was just too dangerous a source of temptation.

She crawled across the bed herself and switched off the light, then in the darkness knee-walked back over the scramble of sheets and blanket to his broad back.

"Honey—"

"Shh. I'm checking for damages," she said gravely.

"Damages?"

"Yeah." She could have used his spine for a straight edge. The tendons at the back of his neck were as tight as fists. A gentle, sensitive touch just wasn't going to cut the mustard. "I know I was a little rough with you." Her fingers pushed, probed, kneaded. "I don't know what got into me. I meant to be so careful because of your ribs. Even more than that, I meant to be nice and polite. Mr. Stoner, would it be all right if I undid the third button on your shirt? Mr. Stoner, would you think it too brazen if I stroked your thigh? I mean...that's how it's supposed to be, right? Company manners. No one getting too real, no one being too honest, and for God's sake, no one losing control."

"Kelsey—"

"Shh." His upper arms were all tight cords, all unyielding muscles. She worked them, hard. "I have this horrible feeling I bit your shoulder. If I find any teeth marks, I'm going to die. I mean...I certainly don't want you to get the mortifying idea that I was turned on, that I wanted you so much I forgot my own name, that I completely lost track of what century we were living in."

"Kels—"

"I'll tell you something else. You really disappointed me." If she had any doubt what was eating him alive, she didn't then. Every vertebra in his spine was locked rigid. Diligently she attacked them, one at a time. "It had been a long time for me, Rorke. You knew that. I expected to be treated like precious china. I certainly *never* expected to be treated like an adult woman, fully capable of some responsive give-and-take, an equal participant who just might conceivably be even more aroused by a demanding lover. You are a demanding lover, sugar. You made very sure I knew you wanted me, needed me. I swear, it's enough to give a Southern woman the vapors. My heart's going pitty-pat just trying to talk about this. Here I thought you knew I was a doll and instead you treated me like I was a real live woman."

"Whitfield?"

"Hmm?"

"There can't be another woman alive who would come up with this much sass at three o'clock in the morning."

"I'm not through."

"Yeah, you are." His ribs still creaked when he turned; not that that stopped him. A streak of lightning silvered her kneeling form, her innocent blue eyes, the halo of tangled taffy hair framing her face.

His angel had the grip of a wrestler. The tension she hadn't whipped out of him in words she'd beaten out of his flesh. He didn't have a muscle left worth jelly. For that, the lady was going to pay.

She scooted back to the pillows. He kept coming until his shadow loomed over her, dark and intimidating. She knew she was in trouble, and he could tell she was scared from the way she crooked her finger at him. He slid in beside her and scooped her close. He kissed her once, because, dammit, she was asking for it, and then he kissed her again. Because he had to.

She responded by opening her arms and taking him in, her mouth yielding with abandon, her body welcoming him to her warmth.

"Where did I ever find you, Kelsey?" He meant to sound gruffly teasing but failed. His tone was as harsh and raw as a man who had no idea how to deal with his own vulnerability. She gave so much. And asked absolutely nothing from him in return. Not even to be loved.

In the dark, her soft white hands framed his face. "The point," she said softly, "is whether you were listening to me—"

"Yeah, I was. And I'd tell you I was ashamed as hell I lost my head, but you're not going to listen to that, are you?"

"No."

"I didn't think so." He turned his face and pressed his lips into the palm of her hand. "Like I said, I was listening. You thought it was pretty damn good when it was rough. Now I'm wondering if you'll think it's pretty damn good if we try it soft. And real, real slow. In fact . . . I'm kind of wondering how you'll take to torture, Ms. Whitfield."

Kelsey waved goodbye as the battered van with the local animal shelter logo backed out of her driveway. The puppies were headed for their next set of baby-sitters. That was one problem out of the way. She aimed for the house to tackle the next set.

On her agenda was a tutoring session with a ninth grader, finishing the curtains for her French doors, taking the wash out of the dryer before it rotted, sending out bill payments before her electricity was turned off and grading some sixty papers on the fate of the nation if the South had won the Civil War.

As her gaze swept the lawn, she woefully added mowing the grass to the list. It wasn't fair. If it had only rained one inch last night, how could the grass grow three?

There was no way she could get it all done before midnight, particularly since she hadn't had but three hours' sleep the night before. Temporarily she had the stamina of a worm—and an attack of sleepy yawns that had been building through a long afternoon. Some might consider her night's agenda daunting, even torturous, under those circumstances, but Kelsey knew what real torture was.

Stoner, rubbing a whiskered cheek on the inside of her thigh.

Stoner, dragging things out of her in the darkness that a woman should have enough sense to keep quiet about . . . like, for instance, confessing to the birth control device she'd bought. The one with the unconquerably complicated instructions, the one she'd never used before. The one he'd figured out how to use—and had a mortifyingly good time doing it—because he was determined to show her that bareback was better.

Stoner, proving that bareback was better.

Stoner, standing in the bathroom doorway with a mug of coffee in his hand while she took her morning shower. And waiting until she had her mouth full of toothpaste before casually mentioning, "You know, toots, we're not going to do it your way. We're going to try it for keeps. It'd just be a lot easier if you'd accept that."

Stoner, sorting through her spoons in the kitchen while she grabbed coffee and toast and scoured the whole house for her pair of red shoes. "I want you to watch this trick, Kels. It goes like this. You throw your spoons in any one of four drawers, and I organize them. That's what people do who are different. It's called compromise. That's not so tough, is it?"

If Rorke had just been about a hundred and eighty pounds smaller she could have taken him over her knee with a hairbrush.

Picturing that was so enormously satisfying that Kelsey chuckled as she let herself into the house. Her smile died as she kicked off her shoes, dropped five tons of papers on her walnut table and sank in the nearest straight chair.

Twenty-four hours ago she'd felt in reasonable control of her life.

That control was important to her. Acceptance and control had been her first steps out of the abyss. In the beginning she'd woken up with the shame every day, guilt that had defeated her will to climb out of bed. The guilt and shame were real, but they didn't help. She had to get past them or take cyanide. She couldn't change what she'd done. She could only make herself into a woman she could respect.

She was doing that now. Change was an ongoing process. She'd conquered some pretty steep mountains and she was proud of herself. No day passed that she wasn't aware of the bottle of Chardonnay in the cupboard. Her dragon wasn't sleeping, it never slept, but its power to claim her was linked to self-worth. A woman who thought nothing of herself had no weapons to fight with. A woman who valued herself earned the power, the strength, the right to say no.

She was failing, totally, at saying any kind of no to Rorke.

She pulled the white enamel combs from her hair and let the strands sift through her fingers. For eight years she'd been strong and in control and managing her life just fine alone. For eight years men had been asking her out. She'd occasionally gone, she'd definitely made friendships and not a single one of them had tempted her with a longing so strong that judgment, morality and sanity flew out the window.

It was just him...the man who excelled in exquisite torture when the lights were out, the man who was determined to cover ground at the speed of sound, the man who'd already so stubbornly enmeshed himself in her life that he was part of her heartbeat.

Wisdom warned her to slow down that heartbeat. Now. Yet the web of love had already become intricately complicated.

Before he'd left that morning, Rorke had asked her to go to some police picnic with him. He'd made light of it but she'd sensed a worry under the surface—Rorke hadn't totally resolved his feelings about his job since the robbery—and she'd leaped in with a yes. She'd meant that yes. If he needed her, what other answer could she possibly have given him? But she was desperately aware that she was becoming more and more involved in his life.

As he was becoming, inexorably, part of hers.

Tomorrow he was going to Biloxi to see Janey.

When traffic was good, the drive from Natchez to Biloxi took five hours. Rorke started predawn on Wednesday morning, stopped once for coffee and was parked in front of the Church of the Sacred Heart by ten o'clock.

The church was part of the private school grounds, and the grounds were fenced, landscaped lush and tropical. He could smell the salt breeze blowing off the gulf and was tempted to wander a few minutes and get his bearings, but there was no time.

He'd called the school office yesterday. The secretary had promised him that no one would mind if he visited the church. She'd also volunteered what time each class had a Mass for their grade. The lady had seemed to assume he was considering enrolling a child in the school. Rorke hadn't lied; he just hadn't corrected her.

He pocketed his sunglasses and pelted up the church steps. As he pulled open the massive oak door, the seventh grade was starting to file in through a door near the altar. Stained glass windows cast blue and crimson rays on the white marble altar. Even so, his eyes had to dilate after being in bright sunlight so long. By the time his vision was sharp again, his only view of the kids was on the back of their heads.

They took up the first four rows of pews. Rorke had his choice of any other seat in the house. Feeling like a trespasser—he wasn't even Catholic—he slid into the first seat in the tenth row.

Having no doubt Kelsey would grill him on every detail, he took a swift inventory of the church, but most of his attention was focused on the children. The girl's uniforms were plaid and the boys were in dress pants. They were at the age where the girls had all shot up and the boys were still shrimps. There wasn't a sound coming from the first four rows. The boys all had slicked-back hair; the girls fresh-scrubbed faces. The little angels all had their heads bowed in a suitably reverent posture.

Rorke saw a spitball fly from pew four to pew three. The target—a tall blond girl—retaliated by attempting to decapitate the pug-nosed boy with her prayer book. The priest walked in. Reverence resumed.

Wiping the grin from his face, Rorke mentally stored the tale for Kelsey, but throughout the half-hour Mass, he had little luck identifying Janey. Only half the kids went up for Communion—there were obviously children enrolled in the private school who weren't Catholic—but he caught a good look at every face coming back down. Janey's wasn't one of them.

When the Mass was over, a teacher led the troops out the side door. Zip. It was a well-ordered stampede but still a stampede, too many crushed bodies for him to see well. Cops, Rorke reminded himself, were known for patience.

Patience or no patience, he wasn't going back to Natchez until he found her. In the back of his mind, Rorke already knew that finding Janey wasn't going to solve a problem but open up one. As far as he was concerned, that real problem should have been opened up years ago. He didn't want to see Kelsey crying like that ever again. There had to be a way to get mother and daughter together. He'd find it. But right now he'd settle for bringing back a reassuring report that would at least ease her worries.

Unfortunately his report, so far, lacked the lead in the play. He bought some fast food for lunch, walked the perimeter of the school grounds and eventually took a seat in the bleachers. By the time he'd watched two gym classes, he'd have sold his soul for a cola. The sun was hotter than fire. The bleachers didn't have a stroke of shade, his throat was parched and there was only one class left in the school day.

School wasn't his only choice. He could trail her home. He had Whitfield's home address and Kelsey would undoubtedly want to know what the place looked like where Janey lived. Still, Rorke didn't want to do that if he wasn't forced to. For Kelsey, he'd find Janey, but his gut tightened like a knot at the idea of running, even inadvertently, into her ex-husband. He didn't want to know what Whitfield looked like, didn't want to know anything about him and he sure as hell didn't want to risk being within socking range of the dude.

Come on, Stoner. It was all a long time ago. She's put it behind her and the whole thing had nothing to do with you.

He knew that.

The knot in his gut just kept warning him that rational instincts and wisdom weren't fully operable where Kels was concerned.

A moment later it didn't matter. The seventh-grade girls poured from the locker room toward the soccer field, all of them dressed in shorts and white shirts with a little monogram. The gym teacher had thighs as thick as tires and a whistle hanging from her neck. The girls all looked alike, all legs, all giggles and gangling clumsiness.

Except for one.

Janey.

He fell in love with the daughter the way he had with her mother, on sight, hard, as if something painful squeezed his heart and wouldn't let go. He had a vague memory of seeing the finespun marmalade-colored hair in the church, but he'd never caught her face. The blue eyes were Kelsey's. The delicate bones and slight frame, the fragile mouth—they were all Kelsey's.

He watched. She went running down the field with the herd. The ball came her way; she kicked. Missed. A couple of her teammates jeered. Janey stiffened like a wounded fawn.

Rorke forgot the heat, forgot the beating sun. The girls played for a half hour. She was the smallest in the class, and she put her whole soul into the sport. She couldn't kick, couldn't block and had absolutely no sense of the game. Toward the end he saw the ball fly in the air, coming toward her. Her head was turned. He thought, *Sweetheart, look, dammit*. But she didn't, and the ball slammed square in the back of her head.

He winced. She didn't. The teacher jogged toward her, put a hand on Janey's shoulder and asked her something. He saw Janey mouth, "I'm okay." But she wasn't and couldn't be. Rorke knew she was going to have a goose egg. The ball had broadsided her at a good speed. The teacher blew the whistle—gym was over for the day—and the mite walked toward the locker room with her head held high.

Rorke frowned at the empty sports field, then glanced at his watch. School let out in fifteen minutes. He climbed down from the bleachers and strode toward the parking lot. An empty bus was just pulling in, and the street was starting to be lined up with expensive automobiles. No economy models for these kids.

Janey was one of the first kids out. She glanced at the lot of cars, juggled a load of books that looked heavier than she was, then sat on the school steps and opened one. The wind twirled some of those soft golden strands of marmalade.

Other kids started flooding out the doors, chattering, shouting, mostly in pairs or groups. Janey was the only one alone. A few shouted a greeting at her. She looked up but then hunched back over her book. She didn't reach out, didn't join them, didn't take part in their clowning around.

The bus filled and left. Parents were still arriving. A boy came from the far side of the parking lot, looked at Janey, shoved his hands in his pockets and swaggered over. Rorke unconsciously grinned. The boy said something. Janey glanced up, flushed and then ignored him.

The kid grabbed the book out of her hands and gamboled around the parking lot with it. Janey stood up, white-faced now. Rorke remembered the game—it had to be as old as time. The boy flipped the book, juggled it, balanced it. The kid was just trying out his moves, testing his male prowess in the way all seventh-grade boys tested their prowess. Yesterday all girls had cooties. Today he'd have died for a girl's attention. Specifically for Janey's attention. No harm or cruelty was intended.

Yet Janey, from nowhere, burst into tears.

The boy first looked stunned, then beet-red miserable. He sneaked the book back on top of her pile like a snake slinking in cold weather. He stayed two seconds, balancing on one foot, then the other. Janey never looked up. Her head was bowed and her face buried in her hands.

So small.

So small to be so damned miserable over nothing. For two cents Rorke would have crossed the lot and swooped her up.

He had to remind himself that he had no rights anywhere near her. He also reminded himself that every kid that age had emotional ups and downs. It didn't help. The kind of "alone" he saw in those sensitive blue eyes was more than moody hormones and being twelve.

When a silver gray Mercedes pulled into the lot, Janey immediately grabbed her books and walked toward it. By then her eyes were dry, her head high. A small woman with a carefully coiffed hairstyle stepped out of the car and asked Janey something. Rorke guessed she was being asked if she'd had a good day.

He guessed that because he saw her response. "Just great, Gram." She offered her grandmother a wreath of a smile that no one could tell was fake. Unless they looked hard. As far as Rorke could tell, no one had looked at Janey—really looked at Janey—all day except for him.

Chapter 10

Kelsey knew it was bad.

Rorke had given her an enormous kiss when he'd picked her up for dinner. The kiss had been her first clue. He'd wrapped her up tightly enough to recrack his ribs.

Her second clue had been the time. She hadn't expected him until late, yet he'd arrived just past nine. He had to have kept the gas pedal on the floor to get back to her this quickly.

And her third clue was the restaurant. He'd picked the crowded pizza parlor. Willie Nelson was whining from the jukebox about all the women he'd loved. The tang of pepperoni and garlic bread flavored the atmosphere. The place was bright and glaringly normal. Pizzas and traumas didn't go together. Ergo, everything was hunky-dory.

When the waitress brought the pizza, Kelsey calmly plucked a piece from the tray and lifted it to Rorke's plate. He'd already—fast and blithely—told her about Janey. He'd also ordered enough food for a herd, catered to her choices—double olives, when he hated them—and treated her to an endless parade of smiles.

The circles under his eyes were as big as half-moons, and beneath the table, his ankle nudged against hers. Since he'd come home, some part of him had been in constant contact with some part of her: ankle, wrist, shoulder, it didn't make any difference. His body language was protective. She had no doubt he'd mow down anyone who dared upset her.

She guessed a double shot of whiskey would have helped him, but the restaurant didn't serve liquor and Rorke, regrettably, wouldn't have drunk it in front of her anyway. Leaning over the table, she used her fork to dig the olives out of his pizza. He wasn't looking at his plate—he hadn't taken his eyes off her—and there wasn't a chance of his eating it as it was. "Tell me again what she looked like."

"She was beautiful. Like I said. Eyes just like yours, hair your same color."

"You didn't tell me how she wore her hair. Long? Short? Curly? Up? Down? Barrettes?"

"Barrettes?" he asked blankly.

"Come on, Stoner. I'm dying under this wealth of detail. Could you try to think a little less *male* for a minute? Think like a woman. Think *specifics*." Her teasing tone wooed a smile out of him—the first natural one that she'd seen so far—but she couldn't get him to eat.

"Specifically, her hair was long, to her shoulders, with a little fringe on the forehead. And she was wearing a uniform—a white shirt, a blue-and-white plaid skirt. Shoes."

She nudged his plate closer. "You said she was beautiful. What kind of beautiful? Pretty, cute, lovely, pert, beautiful-beautiful, impish?"

"Yes." When she groaned at that answer, Rorke's eyes took on a little life. "I don't know what kind of beautiful. I just know that if I'd been a seventh-grade boy, I'd have been hanging around her locker. Does that answer your question?"

She nodded approvingly. "Much better. Now go on."

"Next time I call in a suspect for questioning, I'm going to include you on the side of the good guys. You're much better at this grilling business than I ever was."

"Eat your pizza. And go on."

"Okay, okay...she was smart. Into books, you could tell. And a good kid. Obedient, manners, respect, stuff like that. She wasn't going to cause anybody any trouble."

"Okay, what else?" Kelsey prodded him.

"I already told you about the school. Good security, all the advantages, high on academics and discipline. Small classes. Landscaped grounds, lots of space, real nice."

"So you said," she murmured. "Rorke?"

"What?"

"I gave up believing in Santa Claus a long time ago," she said calmly. "What on earth do you think is going to happen if you tell me something I don't want to hear? You've described a model child, a model school, a model day. Nothing's that perfect, sugar. I never expected it to be."

At the next table, a two-year-old blithely flung a piece of garlic bread from her high chair. Whitney Houston was belting out one of her best from the jukebox. A harried waitress passed, popping gum. All Kelsey saw was the battle in Rorke's dark eyes. It wasn't easy for him to lie. It was even harder for him to hurt her. And she felt a terrible guilt for putting him through this.

"What I told you was true," he said gruffly.

She nodded. "Just not the whole truth."

"I just don't want you upset, Kels—"

"Do I in any way look upset?" She wound a strand of mozzarella cheese around her finger, demonstrating a calm, cool picture of unshakable normality. "I faced up to this a long time ago, Rorke. Honestly, I was expecting far worse than anything you could possibly tell me. It's okay."

But he wasn't going to budge quite that easily. "She was physically healthy. There was nothing wrong like that, and kids that age are up and down. The whole drive back here I told myself I was probably misreading the whole situation."

"I doubt that," she said gently. "You're excellent at reading situations involving people. Come on, tough guy. Spill it."

"I just felt . . ." He stopped fidgeting with a fork and dragged a hand through his hair. He hesitated and then let it go. "I feel she needed her mother, toots. It's as simple as that."

Five tons of steel squeezed around her heart. She didn't let it show. "There was no chance Janey wouldn't have some problems. All kids do, and she had a tougher start than most." Because Rorke's eyes were on her like beacons, she lifted the wedge of pizza as if she were going to eat it.

"You really are okay," he said gruffly.

She nodded. "Of course I am. It *couldn't* be perfect, nothing ever is. Just describe her how she really was, all right?"

He started slow, with the tale of the soccer game and the scene in the parking lot. But once he was assured that Kelsey was more thoughtful than upset, it started pouring out of him. "She just took my heart in that game. Couldn't play worth a damn, couldn't kick, couldn't defend, no concept of the strategy and too bite-size to be a contender. Like, so what? But it was such a big 'so what' to her, Kels. She kept forcing herself in that front line like she was determined to prove herself. Or not prove herself. She was just so damned determined to please."

Kelsey briefly clutched her napkin under the table.

"And her smiles. That's what she showed people. When she got hurt, she smiled like she'd die and go to hell before causing anyone any trouble. When her grandmother came to pick her up, she gave her this big smile and told her she'd had a great day. She'd had a lousy day. Lousy days happen to anyone, but she's just a kid. She should have been able to tell that to someone, get it off her chest." Again Rorke shoveled a hand through his hair. "I don't know how to say it. It was like she had no one she could trust, no one she could be honest with, and I'm telling you that she scared me. She was alone, Kels. Alone on the inside. Does that make sense?"

"Yes." Kelsey wrapped her ice-cold hands around the cola glass.

"It wasn't like anyone mistreated her, but all day I kept expecting someone to look at her, realize how unhappy she was. And this one boy tried, but—"

"She didn't give him a chance?" Kelsey asked quietly. "I can hear in your voice that you were worried about her."

"About her, yes." His gaze suddenly landed on her face. "But about you, ten times more. The whole ride home, I didn't know what I would say to you. You worry so much, Kels. It's in your voice, in your eyes, every time you try and talk about her. I didn't want to make that worse."

Kelsey shook her head. "You haven't. I wanted you to be honest with me."

He was still studying her when his voice lowered, as gentle now as it was determined. "Honey, there are answers for both of you," he started to say, but he was interrupted when the waitress brought the check.

Kelsey smiled at her and smiled at Rorke, then murmured, "I need to make a short trek to the ladies' room."

Rorke aimed for the cash register. She made it to the restroom before the blank smile on her face started to crack. A woman with a toddler was fussing at the first sink. Kelsey surged past, locked herself in the farther of the two stalls and slid the latch.

She sat on the toilet, unraveled two feet of toilet paper and jammed it in her eyes. *I think she needs her mother, toots.* The stab of a knife would have hurt less. *Determined to please. Alone on the inside.* Rorke couldn't possibly understand why those specific words had caused a thick, awful knot to block her throat. It wasn't his problem. She'd involved him enough, and she'd be fine. In a minute.

But in another minute, memories were surging through her mind faster than she could stop them.

She'd been in labor thirty hours and had forgotten every moment of the pain when she'd first held Janey. So scrawny, with a fuzz of blond hair and exquisite toes, the smell of her, the warmth and wonder of her. Kelsey couldn't stand to hear her cry. The whole world warned her she was spoiling the baby and she still flew if Janey let out a murmur. There had been one night, though. Janey had been teething and fussing all day, and Kelsey had been so exhausted. At three in the morning she'd heard that plaintive wail yet again, and Kelsey had let her cry for a full ten minutes.

The guilt for that ten minutes was as sharp as if it had happened yesterday. She should have picked her up. She could remember a thousand times she'd picked her up. The first time Janey had gone down a slide, giggling so hard she couldn't stand it. The first time Janey had taken three steps and fallen squat with a thoroughly disgusted bellow. And when she was two, she'd scraped her knee playing in the sandbox, and Kelsey had picked her up and loved her and put on a Band-Aid—her first—and Janey had loved it so much she'd demanded the whole box. She'd put Band-Aids on everything in the house before she was through.

A horrible, wounded sound came out of Kelsey's throat. She heard it, but it was as if it were coming from someone else. *You should never have let her cry those ten minutes, Kelsey. You knew she wanted you; you knew she needed you.*

The old memories hurt, but not half as fiercely as the pictures Rorke had created in her mind of the twelve-year-old girl Janey was now.

Kelsey knew her. Intimately well. At twelve years old *she'd* been determined to please, to cause no one trouble, to smile whenever she'd hurt. It was obviously her fault that her father loved his bourbon, and any child of an alcoholic knew the credo. Don't talk. Don't feel. Don't trust anyone.

Janey, like Kelsey, was the daughter of an alcoholic.

But the pattern was supposed to be broken. The same things were not supposed to happen to Janey. Kelsey had given up all custody, all contact, all rights to see her daughter. The price for losing half her soul was the guarantee of Janey's happiness. The pattern that started with the alcoholic parent simply couldn't repeat itself if Kelsey stayed far away from her. Like mother, like daughter—God, Kelsey would die first.

She was dying now. *I love you, Janey. Don't you understand that's the only possible reason I could give you up?*

Only, dammit, you were supposed to be happy. And never like me. Never, never, never like me.

The knife kept twisting, sharper than a razor, deeper than pain. Her worst nightmare had been about helplessness. This was living it. Rorke thought Janey needed her—an unbearable joke.

She was the reason her daughter was hurting.

She was the last possible person who could help her, because she was the cause.

Her ankles were crossed, her elbows on her knees and her face thoroughly smothered in a jam of toilet paper when she heard a feminine shriek—and a masculine response.

"Open the door, Kels."

Her head jerked up. She swallowed, tried to say something and couldn't. Rorke's voice had an echoing gentleness, but he didn't understand. She'd already involved him enough—too much—in her problems. This wasn't his problem, wasn't his pain.

"Come on, blue eyes."

Her vocal chords moved, but no sound emerged. She jammed her fists in her eyes, breathed hard and tried again. "Rorke, good grief, this is the ladies' room. Go away."

"With you. Not without you. Open the door."

"I'll be out in a minute. I'm sorry if you were worried. I didn't mean to take so long. I had this slightly embarrassing digestive problem."

"That isn't why you went in there, toots, and you can either come out now or I'll break the door down."

When she came out, he took one look at her face and sucked in his breath. He'd been afraid she was crying. He was shaken far more to see that she hadn't, couldn't, wouldn't. He held out his arms and folded her in. "We're getting you home."

They were out of the restaurant in seconds, Kelsey tucked under his shoulder, the dark night soothing the burn in her eyes from unshed tears. Rorke handed her into the car. She felt the cool leather against her neck, heard the click of the seat belt, saw his shadowed eyes looking at her as he turned the key to start the engine.

"Are you going to be okay?"

"I'm fine," she said, but she wasn't. She felt isolated and disorientingly alone—nothing Rorke could help her with, and nothing she'd have let him if he tried.

Realizing Janey was unhappy was like facing a mirror of everything she'd done wrong in her life. Her daughter was suffering for her sins. That guilt distracted any other thoughts in her head. The old ugliness crept up on her, the old feelings of worthlessness and shame. The dragon was close, closer than it had been in a long time.

Streetlights blurred past. Crisp night air blew in the open window, chilling her, but she didn't close it. It was a long time before she realized Rorke was talking to her.

"I don't know what you've built in your head, but this isn't that complicated. You need your daughter. Your daughter needs you. So you go to a lawyer and you get a custody hearing started. I know a few lawyers. I know my share of judges, too. There isn't a judge with a brain in his head who'd deny you visiting rights to Janey."

She turned her head, staring at his determined profile, the strong clean line of his jaw. He was outlining a plan with the enthusiasm of a steamroller. She knew he wanted to help her, but this man she'd lain naked with—physically naked, spiritually naked—was suddenly a stranger. Rorke couldn't be talking like this if he had the least comprehension of shame, of dragons, of what she very honestly had to deal with.

"I know you think what happened eight years ago was something terrible, but you were a kid, sweetheart, half a baby yourself when all that happened. You had pressures no kid should have to handle and you took a wrong turn, but anyone could understand that. And anyway, it's done. It was over a million years ago and has absolutely nothing to do with you or Janey now." He hesitated when he felt those too-soft, too-old blue eyes resting on his face. "What's wrong?"

"Is that how you justified being involved with me?" she asked softly. "By convincing yourself that I was just a kid who took a slightly wrong turn?"

A few minutes later he turned into her driveway. He shut off the engine and lights. Neither moved from the dark car. Fireflies were courting in the air and her whole yard smelled like magnolias. It would be hard to find a more innocuously sweet spring-summer night, yet Rorke had the odd sensation that he'd just stepped into a land mine. "I never had to justify being involved with you—and anyway, that's not what we were talking about. I'm telling you that no judge would let what happened years ago outweigh the life you've built for yourself now. I know you can get your daughter back."

Something snapped. Emotions stretched too taut, feelings so confused they'd reached a breaking point. It wasn't a good time to deal with this, but Kelsey felt she had no choice. "Rorke, listen to me. You told me my daughter was in trouble. If I thought for one instant that I was the one to help her, I'd already be on the road. Andrew couldn't stop me, neither could a lawyer or any fancy judge, and neither, love, would a lawman with a gun at my back. No one could keep me from my daughter if I really thought I could help her."

"Kels—"

"She doesn't need me." Kelsey's voice was almost as exhausted as she was. "I'm not her solution. I'm her problem. The best thing I ever did for my daughter was to get out of her life, and the best thing I can do for you is to get out of yours."

Kelsey had switched subjects on him almost faster than a knot could form in his stomach. "Wait a minute. What are you talking about?"

"I've let this go too far when I knew better." She reached for the door handle and pushed it open. "I tried to tell you it had to be short-term because of our differences, but this is the real reason. You, needing to make excuses. I wasn't a kid taking a wrong turn, sugar. You're lying to yourself because of me. I can't live with that, and neither could you for long."

He grabbed her wrist when she tried to climb out of the car. If she'd sounded angry, he could have argued with her. Instead she sounded calm and quiet and defeated, and it shook him more than anything else in the entire rotten day had shaken him. "Kelsey, I don't know what you want me to say. I never did. You want me to tell you that I see you as a lush? If so, you're going to wait from here to hell, because I don't."

"I know," she said gently, then she leaned over and kissed his cheek. Her tenderness was as real as the sheen of tears in her eyes. "And you were and are the best thing that ever happened to me, love. For a little while I forgot I was a drinker. You made me feel good again, clean-slate good and special and wonderful, as fresh as the woman I wanted to be. Keep your illusions, Rorke. Think of me as the good woman you wanted. I like that picture a whole lot better than the truth, anyway." She slid away from him and climbed out of the car. "Don't get out."

"Kelsey—"

"You found my daughter. There's nothing left to do. I'll find some way to pay you if I have to send you anonymous roses for the next thousand years. But don't call me, okay?" She repeated, "Don't . . . call me . . . please."

And then she was inside her door, shooting the bolts, drawing the drapes. Alone with her dragon, and braced for a sleepless night.

"Got time for a drink?"

Walt blinked, glanced at both brown paper bags in Rorke's hands and let him in the apartment. By no word or gesture did he indicate that Rorke had never visited him at this hour without calling before. "You've come to the right place, although it would seem you've brought your own. What's in the bag?''

"Bourbon for you. Sipping Scotch for me."

"Hard stuff," Walt noted. "Are we talking one drink or making a night of it?"

"You have to work tomorrow. I just wanted to visit for a quick hour. I could use some rational, intelligent conversation with another human being. Someone who talks language I can understand. Common sense. A male human being."

"Ah."

"The only thing I don't want to talk about is women. For an hour, for one short hour, I would like to pretend that the second half of our species doesn't exist. Do you have a problem with that?"

"No problem at all," Walt said mildly, and brought out two glasses from the cupboard. Scratching his chin, he watched Rorke pour a double shot of bourbon for him and generously fill the water glass to the brim with Scotch for himself. "You had any food recently?"

"Haven't had time to eat all day. Don't sweat it. I couldn't be less hungry."

"Ah," Walt murmured again. It took him a minute to fix a plate of crackers and cheese. By the time he carried the tray into his blue-and-chrome living room, he noted that Rorke had already turned the TV on and off, the stereo system radio on and off and was prowling the room like a caged bear.

Rorke reached for his glass of Scotch, took the first belt, grimaced as if his mother had washed his mouth out with soap, then took another. "There isn't a reason in hell I can't have a drink," he announced.

"I hope you aren't waiting for an argument out of me. Although I have to say—" Walt, dressed only in jeans, sprawled in an easy chair with one leg cocked over the side "—it has to be a blue moon since I saw you reach for anything harder than beer."

"Hard stuff is medicinal. And I have needed this particular medicinal belt for weeks."

"Since you met Kelsey?"

Rorke glowered at him. "We're not discussing women."

"Forgot," Walt said amiably.

"Have I ever discussed a woman in my life before? Ever?" Rorke took another slug. "I never took part in locker room talk, never played kiss and tell. What happens between a man and a woman is between the two of them. Any relationship worth anything is as private as a promise, and dammit, I don't break promises." He took another slug. "She is driving me *nuts*."

Walt waited for him to settle on the couch and then maternally put the tray within reach on the coffee table.

"You go in her house and the phone just keeps ringing. All these people know her. All these people expect her to drop whatever she's doing and run if they call. And she does. Somebody needs her, and she's off like a flash. What she does for those kids defies all description. She has a house that's practically falling apart around her, but you think she cares?"

"No?" Walt guessed helpfully.

"She can't cook. I mean, this woman can't fix a meal that a dog would eat. You give her frozen food and a microwave and she'd burn it. Like, so what? I can either cook or keep her in calories in restaurants, but cooking's her *hobby*. *Capisci?* She thinks she's good at it. What am I supposed to do, hurt her feelings?"

Rorke made it sound as if hurting her feelings were equivalent to beating her. Walt obediently shook his head.

"She's dying. You understand? She's dying, worrying about her kid. It's tearing her apart. On a day-by-day basis you can give this lady a flood, a tornado, a hurricane, and she's not going to lose her cool. She thrives on chaos. You mention her daughter, and it's all done. God, those eyes. So I tell her there's an obvious answer. We'll get her a lawyer and start pursuing custody potential. Does that sound unreasonable to you?"

"No," Walt answered obligingly.

"Does that sound mean, insensitive, cruel, unreasonable to you?"

"No," Walt repeated.

"She's got this idea that the best thing she could do for her daughter is to stay away from her. She makes it sound like she's a leper, like the kid could catch something bad from being around her. What's even stupider is that she believes it. You ever try talking to someone with a baseball bat between their ears?"

"Not recently."

Rorke clawed a hand through his hair. "She's scared. I don't have to understand it all to know she's scared, but you think she'd let me help her? Hell, no. She takes on my problems, mind you, drags the whole robbery thing out of me and any other rotten linen I never shared with anyone else.... She forgives, you understand. She accepts. When you're around her, she has this way of making you feel good, making you feel right, making you feel like you could face anything in hell if she was just there at the end of a day. She gives and gives and gives, but the one time I try to come through for her, she kicks me out."

Silence fell. As long as they'd worked together Walt had never seen Rorke lose it before. Walt figured he should feel worried as hell, and instead felt concern mixed with an instinctive relief.

He remembered meeting Kelsey and hearing some problem about the daughter. Rorke's flood of words hadn't cleared up any details. Walt didn't have a clear picture and didn't really need one. Rorke never lost it. Rorke depended on no one and nothing. He was a machine of control in a crisis. He took out a mountain if that's what he had to do. After the robbery he'd turned even more inward. So inward, so tight, that Walt had worried his friend was going to break.

Now, as Walt had already noted, there was some flesh on Rorke's bones, color in his face, life in his eyes. And he was talking. Really talking about things that mattered to him, for the first time since Walt knew him.

She had to be a miracle worker. More relevant than that, she had to be one hell of a lady.

"Matthews?" Rorke leaned forward and wiped his face with his hands. "There's more to it than her daughter."

Walt had already figured that out.

"It all happened so fast. One minute she's talking about Janey and the next minute she's kicking me out. It was like a low blow coming from behind, and you know the funny part about it?"

So far Walt hadn't seen anything on Rorke's face that remotely resembled humor. "What?"

"I was trying to tell her that I trusted and respected her. That's when it blew up in my face. Does that make sense? Wouldn't your average woman want to hear that you respect and trust her?"

"I would think so."

"Not Kels. You don't know how it is with her. She's fragile. And good. But so damned sensitive. You expect to reason logically with her like a man, you're going to grow old before your time, and I don't care." Bleak, dark eyes stared sightlessly at his friend. "She's the best thing that ever happened to me. Even having a fight with her is better than anything with anyone else. Even when she's being so blockheaded I could strangle her, it's better with her. Matthews?"

"Yeah?"

"She told me not to call. The one time she needed me to come through for her and I blew it. I hurt her. And unless I can find some way to make that right, I can't go back." Rorke's eyes dropped to the amber liquid in his glass, and as if it were a natural link in the conversation, he said, "This stuff is rancid."

Walt stood up when he did. "I noticed you went hot and heavy at it for all of five sips. Lost your taste for Scotch?"

"So it seems."

Fifteen minutes later Rorke was on the road. He aimed for home, but the Cutlass, of its own volition, passed the street to his house and steered out onto the open highway. When he was a kid, he took to the road to work out a problem. His mind emptied of all distractions when he drove, always had. Night driving was best. There was just the black sky, black asphalt and him.

He put the car in fourth gear, opened the windows and let the night wind whip around him. The road was so quiet he could hear the relentless pounding of his heart. Driving wasn't going to soothe him, not tonight. Trying to tell Walt hadn't helped, either. He was learning to let go with Kelsey, but it wasn't the same with anyone else.

Besides, there were only two people who really understood what he'd done. Himself. And the one woman on earth whom he'd sworn he'd never let down. But he had, and badly. Maybe irrevocably.

The black strip of road blurred in front of his eyes. It didn't *look* like he'd done anything to hurt her. He knew damn well he was right to press her about Janey. Kelsey might not be able to see beyond the black wall she'd built up in her mind, but he could. Her life was never going to be right until her daughter was in it. And you did not let the average sane, logical woman down by refusing to call her a lush.

He hadn't realized he'd done anything wrong until she'd already closed the door with him on the outside. Then her words had come back to haunt him. *Keep your illusions, Rorke. Think of me as the woman you wanted.*

He'd told himself a dozen times that he didn't know what she was talking about, but his heart recognized the lie. He'd loved the angel, not the lush. He'd fallen for a warm, vibrant, perceptive, sexy and full-of-life angel. No matter how often she'd told him about her drinking problem, it hadn't touched him. It had been so easy to block it out. She never reached for a drink. A cop saw plenty of boozers on the job. Kels was nothing like any of them. His mind recoiled every time he tried to picture her like one of them. So he hadn't.

And she knew it.

A fist of sharp nails kept churning in his stomach. He'd felt like such a hero, a regular armored knight riding in to save her out of that damned women's bathroom. Now he felt like slime. She'd been hiding out be-

cause she was alone, with a pain she couldn't share—
not with him. Her feelings about her daughter were
inexorably linked to her alcoholism. She'd needed
someone to understand. She'd needed someone she
could talk to.

And he's sloughed off what was really going on with
some platitudes and easy answers, as if her alcoholism
were nothing. That was how he'd been dealing with it.
Pretending it was nothing. Because it was easier for
him.

At three in the morning, he pulled into her driveway.
Her house was dark, her yard silent and ghostly still. He
turned off the car engine and sat there. He wasn't going
in. She'd kicked him out. He had no right even to be
here.

He was so tired he could hardly see, but the problem
wouldn't stop eating at him. If he dug deep enough, he
knew where he'd failed her. It wasn't his refusal to call
her a lush, it was his lack of honesty.

Alone in the dark he faced his deception. At a gut
level, at a soul level, he had no doubt about loving her.
And at a gut level, a soul level, he was scared like hell
of the bottle of Chardonnay she kept in her cupboard.
The fear was persuasive, invidious, real. If he wasn't the
right man for her—the right man, lover, mate—she
might reach for that bottle again. Rorke had always
been afraid of making mistakes. With her the consequences had an impossibly high price tag.

He leaned back against the seat and dug the heels of
his hands into his eyes. Either he found some answers
or he had to get out of her life. The truth was that her
drinking made a difference, and he'd been a shallow,
insensitive bastard for pretending it didn't.

The even greater truth was that he couldn't leave. There was nowhere else to go, not anymore, not for him. This was where Kelsey was.

At six-thirty in the morning, Kelsey opened the front door to find Rorke's car parked behind hers and his slumped figure in the front seat. Barefoot, hugging herself in the T-shirt she'd slept in, she came around to the side of the car and ducked in her head.

The shadows under his eyes were bigger than boats, his face was lined with exhaustion and there wasn't a muscle in his body that didn't look cramped.

Damn you, Stoner. Double damn you. Quadruple damn you. She'd paced the floor until two last night. She'd hurt enough people she loved. She wasn't going to hurt Rorke. Sending him packing had been one of the best things she'd ever done.

Only he was supposed to stay "packed." Instead, he was back, looking more emotionally battered than the rat the cat dragged home.

Although she made absolutely no sound, his stubby black eyelashes slowly lifted. His gray eyes blurred, then cleared, then rested on her face. He wasn't awake yet. The emotion in his eyes was naked. There she saw anxiety for answers he didn't have, and guilt for expecting himself to have those answers. Mostly she saw love, deep as a river and just as fathomless.

When he finally spoke, his voice was as hoarse and husky as gravel. "I screwed up with you, toots."

"Yes."

"You've been dry a long time. I thought that made it simple. It isn't simple."

"I know," she said softly.

"You want me to throw myself on a train track with a train coming by—I'd do that. You wouldn't even have to ask. But the wine—I'm telling you as honestly as I know how—you're going to have to help me understand."

"Stoner, there are hundreds, thousands, millions, *zillions* of women where it wouldn't be a problem. Couldn't you find one of them?"

"No."

"How about if I go find a club and hit you in the head? You think that might knock some sense into you? Nothing else I've done has seemed to get through."

"I'm sorry, Whitfield, but it has to be you. You're just going to have to give me more time."

"No."

"One more chance."

One more chance, so she could hurt a vulnerable man even more? So she could risk being cut to the quick when he made the final and irrevocable decision that he couldn't handle involvement with an alcoholic?

Kelsey told herself to get tough. Only she'd never been tough, not about people and never about love, and Rorke—her lover with the stark gray eyes—was hurting. For her, and because of her.

She said hesitantly, "There's coffee in the kitchen. One cup. That's all I'm offering, and then only because I can't send you back on the road in this shape."

The offer was a mistake. She knew it was a mistake. She understood a desperation for coffee, but he got out of the car and took her in his arms with a completely different kind of desperation. His kiss boxed, wrapped and tied her heart in knots.

She had no idea, then, how intricately tangled those knots would become over the next two weeks.

Chapter 11

"That's it. I can't take it anymore." Kelsey threw herself on the grass beside Rorke, her chest heaving and her forehead damp with sweat. "Those guys are vicious. I can't imagine how you work with them every day."

"Poor baby. Did they give you a hard time?"

"'Hard time' doesn't begin to cover it." She cast a dark glance at the volleyball game she'd just left and deliberately shuddered. "I should have realized what I was getting into when the wives sneaked off. And you, Rorke, could have warned me."

"About how rough they play?"

"About their jokes. I've never heard such terrible jokes, and they're all dirty. If they're an example of the sterling character of the fine men in blue who protect our streets..."

Rorke chuckled, a deep, throaty chuckle that tickled Kelsey from the inside out. He hadn't been so relaxed when he arrived at his boss's picnic, and neither had she.

The past two weeks had had their ups and downs for Kelsey, but this day was different. Balancing on an elbow, she flapped her T-shirt to cool off and looked past Rorke's shoulder to the scene in the yard.

Rorke's boss evidently put on the picnic as an annual get-together for his men. When Rorke had asked her to go, she'd sensed it was some kind of stress test for him. She hadn't understood why then. She did now, although at first glance the shindig was less a source of stress than a rowdy, uncontrolled free-for-all.

The Mississippi sun shimmered down, hot as Hades and twice as humid. A pickup stood under the shade of an oak, loaded with ice to keep the keg of beer cool. A picnic table still sagged under the weight of dishes, even though the entire gang had eaten like vultures not an hour before. Once dinner was over, the women—mostly wives and girlfriends—had the sense to cluster in shady spots. Not the men. The volleyball game, still in progress, was a blur of shirtless, sweating, hard-muscled action. That game was tame compared to the football action competing at the opposite end of the yard. "Good grief, don't they ever relax?" Kelsey murmured.

"Them? No. Get your eyes off that football game. That one's too rough, even for you, killer."

He thought he was being real funny. So did she, but she denied it. "You think I'd join them? After what they did to me?" She'd arrived looking law-and-order proper to meet Rorke's boss and co-workers, only to discover that sitting on the sidelines was no way to learn about the people he worked with. She'd learned plenty, which her appearance regrettably reflected. Her white shorts had grass stains and so did her knee; her French braid was now in shambles, and her cerise shirt couldn't look more wrinkled if she'd rolled with a dog. "Chivalry sure is dead," she groaned.

"It sure is. I was going to jump in and save the guys, but you threatened me with dire consequences if I left this shady tree."

"I didn't threaten you. I made the extremely mild suggestion that you keep your cracked ribs away from the action if you wanted to ever see the light of day again. Besides, you were perfectly happy talking shop with your cronies until a few minutes ago, and you can just wipe that grin off your face, Stoner. I don't know what it's from, and I don't like it."

His face loomed over her, darkly tanned and creased, with an unholy grin that had come from nowhere. His lips touched down, took hers, lifted. The kiss was short. Just short enough for her bones to melt in the cool springy grass.

She saw his smile fade and something hotter, more intense, flare in his eyes. They hadn't made love in two weeks. He knew it. She knew it.

For the past two weeks she'd shied from any physical intimacy. She was determined to be careful and cautious, but the devil was testing her patience.

She could not roust him from her back door. When she came home from work, he was there. He'd walked in on an AA meeting in her kitchen one afternoon. That hadn't scared him, nor had the time she'd flown off in the middle of dinner when Maggie called. And although he hadn't said anything, the bookshelf where she kept information on alcoholics had been raided. In a dozen quiet ways—none showy, none blatant—he'd shown his determination and desire to understand her problem.

In a dozen other ways, he'd mercilessly infiltrated her life. She'd shopped, graded papers and washed dishes with him underfoot. If he'd pushed her for even one kiss, she could have delivered her carefully prepared lecture on the wisdom of emotional distance. He hadn't pushed. He'd overhauled Bertha and then waxed her. He'd fixed her screen door, rented movies for her, dried dishes and, God love him, watered her pansies.

In Kelsey's opinion, it was a low-down, sneaky, demoralizing way to woo a woman. Keeping it cool. Making her laugh when she was frazzled, staying even when her moods had been mercurial, being there so constantly that she couldn't remember what it was like when he wasn't. Then, from nowhere, just a picnic and a sizzling-hot blue sky, taking a kiss that reeked— *reeked*—of tenderness.

Her fingers touched his cheek, clung. Rorke, damn him, had been a brick. She'd told herself a million times that loving him—needing him—was both selfish and unfair. It wasn't just her alcoholism but Janey. She wasn't sleeping for the nightmares, and her days were disrupted by an ache for her daughter that never eased. Rorke hadn't pushed her to talk about Janey. She would have denied him if he'd tried. She wanted to be strong enough not to pull him into her problems, but not to love him? Impossible.

Her thumb brushed the stubble forming on his cheek. Not a damn thing was right in her life. When she was with him, there was something about his eyes that made her want to believe. In hope. In love. In dangerous stuff.

Her forefinger tapped his nose. "You kiss me again, Stoner," she whispered, "and I'll knock your block off."

"Nah. You're still worried about hurting my ribs." His tone was teasing, but his eyes weren't. He looked cool in his open-necked shirt, his hair brushed back, his lips still moist from the last lick of ice from his lemonade glass. His eyes weren't at all cool. Rorke could light a fire in a woman when he had a certain look in his eyes.

"I thought we'd agreed to go at this slower."

"No. We didn't agree. We just did it your way for the last couple of weeks." His lips nuzzled the inside of her palm. "Both of us wanted some time. Both of us had some thinking to do, some testing to do. You decided that meant staying at arm's length. I didn't. I think we'd have done far better if I'd took you to bed. Several times. Every night."

She snatched her palm free. "Good grief, your boss could be wandering within listening range—"

"Amazing that he's stayed out of sight this long. You charmed him as thoroughly as you did the rest of the guys, on sight and no mercy." He didn't move an inch away from her. "You took on the whole crowd, Kels. One at a time. To protect me. Did you realize that? All soft eyes and invisible brass knuckles. I could have turned you over my knee—you think I'd use a woman to fight my battles?—but I have to admit I was equally touched. Particularly since I've been waiting all week for a lecture on caution and wisdom and emotional distance."

She wanted to smack him, but his palm had drifted to her ribs. There were people paired off wherever there was shade. They weren't the only two stretched out in the cool grass. They seemed to have found the only patch of grass, though, where lightning crackled on a perfectly cloudless spring evening. "Rorke?"

"Hmm?"

"You keep that thumb under control, buster."

"This one?"

The offending appendage walked up her T-shirt another inch. An inch higher and he'd touch breast, which Rorke knew. This was not the time and place, which Rorke also knew. Kelsey had wonderful memories of the time when Rorke had been repressed, closed up, a rigid abider of the rules. "*What* do I have to do to make you behave?"

"Maybe all you have to do is want me to behave."

"I do."

"That's not what your eyes say."

She averted her eyes and said righteously, "There are millions of people around—"

"And if they look this way, they'll see my back. No one can see where my hand is."

"You ever heard of honor?" Obviously he hadn't. Her voice rose to a near shriek when he lifted his thumb. "That's it!" Her palm leveled on his chest and pushed. Rorke toppled nicely to the shady grass, suddenly Mr. Obedience himself . . . and a convulsing Mr. Obedience when she scraped a fingertip down his right side. Stoner was ticklish. Not a little ticklish. Unbearably ticklish.

"Why, you hussy—"

"Promise to behave!"

His hand snaked out to claim hers. Fingers twined, held. The intimate laughter was there, but suddenly it was more. "You want promises from me, Kels?" She was close enough to catch the scent of his skin, feel the warmth of his body, see the pulse throb in his throat. He was breathing hard. So was she.

He released her fingers. She immediately rolled on her stomach safe inches away, rested her head on her arms and looked at him. Her heart...hurt. She loved flirting with him. She loved playing with him. She loved Rorke. Anywhere, anytime, any way.

His gaze met hers and wouldn't let go. *You want promises from me, Kels.*

I'm trying not to. I'm trying my best not to. Rorke, you haven't given me ten minutes to think since I met you. You don't play fair.

I want you. And you, at the moment, are equally hot for my body.

We happen to have some very real problems....

Not when we're naked, we don't.

Color streaked her cheeks, accenting every freckle. She broke the intimacy of eye communication by staring down at the grass, which she seemed to be sifting like mad through her fingers.

She'd spent a lot of hours mulling over the two of them. She knew just how seriously he was trying to handle her history with the bottle, and she knew he wanted a future with her. Sometimes, like now, the blind commodity of hope seeped into her heart. It didn't seem so much to ask...the right to love him openly, honestly, normally, freely.

But the word *normal* was where she seized up. No matter what she did or said, the balance of a ''normal'' relationship wasn't there. She was the one who had to ask him to deal with all her bad baggage.

It hurt. It hurt even more because there was nothing she could do about it except to love him, generously and silently, in ways where he might not guess. ''You're going back to work on Monday.''

"The doctor said I'd been lollygagging long enough," Rorke agreed, accepting her change of subject without a qualm.

Kelsey didn't trust his doctor. Probably she wouldn't have trusted any doctor's judgment about Rorke. She knew how hard he physically pushed himself. "This picnic's been an experience. I hadn't pictured you with stripes on your sleeve before, wearing a uniform and carrying a gun. Danger. What your job is really about."

His eyes were half-shuttered, watching her. "A lot of women have a problem with the job. Divorce rates are pretty high for a cop. If the lady's the kind who's going to sit up nights, it hardly ever works. Maybe you've thought about that?"

The last place she'd wanted to direct the conversation was near the murky waters of the future. "Maybe."

"I think you've thought about it a lot."

She took a swift peek at his face, then went back to pulling grass. "All right, yes, I have," she admitted. "It's pretty hard to like the idea of your facing risk. Being hurt. But I also thought about everything you told me about the robbery. I have no doubt how you'd be on the job. Careful, caring. Aware of all the dynamics going on around you. Cautious, controlled. You wouldn't hang out your neck unless there was something on the line, something that mattered."

He swung one arm up behind his head; his voice turned low and amused. "I remember telling you about the robbery. It seems to me you interpreted a lot of what I told you . . . imaginatively."

"Maybe I heard what you said quite clearly. And maybe you weren't really listening to yourself because you were so busy wearing a hair shirt and feeling guilty." She murmured, "You have a better perspective now, but not totally. That's why you were worried about coming to this picnic, wasn't it? You were worried about seeing them all again, knowing you were due back to work on Monday. You weren't sure how they felt about you, and you weren't positive how you felt about your job.''

''*Where* do you come up with all this stuff? Pull it out of a magician's hat?''

Actually, she'd been working like a dog ever since she arrived at the picnic, watching interactions, sensing atmosphere, learning about the people he worked with. She said quietly, ''You can't wait to get back to work. Didn't you know that? You were lapping up every detail on every case the guys were talking about, and they were cutting you in, bringing you back in the fold like you'd never been gone. I learned a lot in the kitchen before dinner—the wives *do* love to talk—and I learned even more taking on the boys in the volleyball game. I won't even *tell* you what your captain had to say to me as we were crossing paths to the bathroom, but there's a lot of respect for you floating around here, sugar. Absolutely astounded me—''

''You keep this up and you're going to get a thumb lashing you'll never forget.''

She opened her mouth, then closed it. It wasn't as if she had anything left to say, and Rorke had gotten the message or he wouldn't be such an unprincipled rogue as to retaliate. She had a brief fantasy involving his thumb and her bare breast that defied all laws of propriety in a public place.

''No comment, toots?''

''You're under the mistaken delusion,'' she murmured, ''that I can't take you out simply because you have a mere seventy pounds on me. When I decide

you're physically fit—and no doctor's release is proof
of that, because you probably lied to the turkey to prove
you were a tough guy—you can expect retribution of
earth-shattering proportions."

"Oh, Lord. Are you going to give me another history lesson?"

"Stoner?"

"Yeah?"

"There are two reasons I'm not going to swat that
masculine grin off your face. The first is that I'm a lady.
And the second is that you are inviting—no, *begging*—
for a physical confrontation."

"Whitfield?"

"Yeah?"

"You're not always a lady, not when it matters. And
you're damned right I want a physical confrontation,
only I'd put it a little less formally. I want your hands
on my body." He murmured, "Two weeks. You're not
sure yet, but you're a lot less scared than you were. And
scared or not, if we went home right now, Kels, you
wouldn't say no."

"Could we please talk about football?"

"No."

She was showering his face with slivers of green grass
when she saw a redheaded giant striding toward them.
Abruptly she dropped the grass, patted her T-shirt,
shoved both hands through her hair and rearranged the
expression on her face, all in the space of a second.

"Am I interrupting something?" Walt asked.

"Yes," Rorke said with no hesitation. His gaze was
still fixed on Kelsey.

"No." Kelsey glared at Rorke, then whipped up her
hand. "I met you before, Walt, but at the time I didn't

really understand you were old friends with this ill-mannered blockhead.''

"Hey,'' Rorke said.

Walt eased down to the grass with a cup of foaming beer in his hand. "Hurts to be pegged accurately, doesn't it? And, yeah, I remember meeting you, Kelsey. Ever since then I've felt this deep sense of remorse for inflicting Stoner on you.''

"Hey,'' Rorke repeated.

"Do I sense an ally?'' Kelsey murmured.

"You bet. Cops have a habit of living on top of each other—no choice, it just comes with the job—but that inevitably means that anyone connected to those cops ends up pretty close, too. Right off the bat, I'd like to mention that you and I can get just as close as you want. I'd also like to mention that I'm single, got all my teeth, and I'm a hell of a lot better looking than he is—''

"I've heard variations on this cheap talk all afternoon. No one's willing to get down to the bottom line. Will you or won't you fix my parking tickets?''

Walt let out a roar of a laugh. "She'll do,'' he said to Rorke.

"I thought you told me you couldn't make it this afternoon,'' Rorke said, but it was hard to get his friend's attention. Walt had clearly come to size up Kelsey, and Rorke watched her charm him with the same merciless zeal she'd shown to every other male at the picnic.

He hadn't seen her around other men before, and the guys could be rough on an innocent. A bad sport was shown no tolerance, and if they thought she'd blush at a dirty joke, there'd be no end to them. She'd blinked at the first bad punch line, subtly roughened her language and flirted as ruthlessly as they did . . . but not really.

Her fanny backed up to his side as she took on Walt, in body language announcing where she belonged. She knew how to play the game, but her shrewd eyes had seriously assessed every person—husband, wife, girl-friend and child—before they'd been there five minutes.

It took Rorke even less time to realize that Kelsey had come here to protect him, to shield him from any trauma he might encounter much like a primitive cave-woman would wield a club when her mate was sleeping. Rorke wasn't sleeping. Kelsey balked at any mention of the future, but he saw in a million ways how she really felt about him. The obstacles in their path were problems, not a lack of love.

Walt glanced at his empty cup. "Well, I'm up to get another beer. I'd offer to get you one, Stoner, but I can see you've got a full glass of—what is that?"

"Lemonade."

"Lemonade. May wonders never cease. How about you, Kelsey? You aren't a saints-preserve-us teetotaler, are you?"

"'Fraid so," she said blithely. "Discovered a long time ago that alcohol and I don't get along. You could filch me a soda while you're up."

"Will do." Walt lurched up and wandered toward the picnic tables.

The exchange had been so short, so easy, that Rorke hadn't had time to react. Kelsey had. She'd moved an almost imperceptible distance away from him. A distance where they were no longer touching. "He's a good man," she murmured.

"Yeah."

"But younger than you, Rorke. In more than years." She stole a sip of his lemonade. Her throat was suddenly too parched to wait for the soda. "You're the strong one when you work together."

Rorke shook his head. "Detectives don't work the same way as cops on the beat. Even so, there's no compatibility if two like men are paired together. I've always been the planner, the 'head' man, the decision maker, where Walt's faster on his feet, quicker reflexes, action instincts. When it counts, he knows when to watch his back. And mine."

"There's no woman in his life?"

"Not for lack of trying," Rorke said dryly. He watched her pluck a handful of grass, let if sift through her fingers, then pluck another handful. He hadn't missed the change in her magnolia drawl. "So I screwed up again?" he said quietly.

"No."

So far, anytime Kelsey had uttered that single syllable, he'd been in deep trouble. "You thought I should have told him about your drinking."

She lifted her head, her eyes as vulnerably blue as the sky. It was new, his need and desire to talk honestly about her alcoholism. It was new, her having to deal with the raw edge between shame and pride. "I can handle myself in a group, Rorke. I don't need you—or anyone—to cover for me, to protect me from questions about having a drink. But, yes, I'd hoped you felt free to tell him because he's your friend." She hesitated. "I understand that it's hard for you. I'm not living in your shoes, I'm living in mine. For all I know, it's your best choice—to say nothing to anyone."

His hand hooked her wrist faster than a lariat. "Why am I getting the impression that you think I'm ashamed of you?"

She couldn't move. The clasp on her wrist was tight enough to bruise, but it was his dark, luminous eyes that held her. Rorke was furious.

And she suddenly felt older than time. Eyes closed, she said gently, "Look. It isn't just friends, it's family. I'm not exactly the girl-next-door you bring home to a man's mother, Rorke. Nothing's sure. Try and believe that I understand, would you? You don't inflict that kind of thing on a family unless you have to."

"I told my father about you a week after I met you." That made her eyes blink open. "But you're right. I should have told Walt. The reasons I didn't had nothing to do with being *ashamed* of you, lady, but because I can't—don't know how and never did—ask for help from people close to me." He loosened his grip yet didn't release her. The pulse in her wrist was beating, beating, beating. His thumb rubbed the throbbing vein, soothed it. "And I'm not the only one with that problem."

"I don't understand."

"I think you do. I'm talking about Janey. I'm driving to Biloxi tomorrow to try and see your ex-husband."

A warm spring evening suddenly chilled. The color washed from her face. She tried to snatch her hand free and found her fingers locked with his. Rorke's features were taut with determination. "No, Rorke."

"Look at you," he said quietly. "It happens every time we try and talk about your daughter. You get all shook, all still. Do you think I don't know you aren't sleeping nights? Your whole house can be in shambles, but those photographs get dusted every day. She's never off your mind, Kelsey, and you're nuts if you think you can live with it like it is."

"I have to."

"Yeah, I know you believe that. The leprosy thing. You think she'll catch it from you. I've been reading those books on alcoholism you have around the house." His eyes met hers square. "The statistics on alcoholic parents having alcoholic kids are pretty rough. Your dad was a drinker, so were you. So that's two generations, making it rougher yet. That's what you were trying to tell me a few weeks ago, wasn't it? Maybe the cycle can get broken if the kid gets a lot of counseling, but the pattern can't happen at all if Janey isn't around you. Have I got it?"

She took a long breath. "I didn't think you understood before." She swallowed hard. "I'll do anything, Rorke, anything I have to do, to make sure Janey doesn't end up like me."

"Sweetheart..." If he thought it would help, he would shake her. Unfortunately, he could never shake Kelsey any more than he could make her see she had dimensions to offer her daughter that went far beyond her alcoholism. Kelsey was understanding, uniquely perceptive, loving, as a woman and a lover, and, Rorke had no doubt, as a mother. She also had a mental block that was, he'd finally understood, a fear she simply couldn't get past. "You've put yourself in a corner. You think you can't go to her, but you also can't live with the situation as it is."

"Rorke..." Her eyes unconsciously pleaded with him.

"I'm not going to talk to your daughter, not going to contact her direct, not going to do anything that's in any sense a problem with the custody agreement you have. But there's no way I could hurt the situation by talking with your ex-husband. If he won't talk to you, he'll talk to me—believe it—and at the very least, I could find out

more about how Janey is really doing. Honey, I'm
going. You can argue with me, but you're not going to
change my mind.''

Twenty yards away, Kelsey saw Walt wending his way
toward them. She stared at Rorke, too sick to talk. She
knew he intended well; she knew he believed he had the
right to interfere, but he didn't know what he would be
getting into in Biloxi.

She did.

He suddenly reached over and softly brushed a strand
of hair from her cheek. "Come on, sugar. Smile for me.
If it doesn't help, it isn't going to hurt, either you or
Janey. It'll be all right."

But Kelsey doubted anything would be all right again.
She smiled because he'd asked her to, but there was a
stone sinking like a lead weight in her heart. Rorke had
needled a sliver of truth she could not deny. She
couldn't live with the situation as it was. If there was
anything she could learn about her daughter, any way
to help Janey, she had to try.

Even so, she wanted to beg him not to go. She stayed
mute only from a sense of terrible weariness. He hadn't
said the words, but she knew he loved her—or believed
he did. He also believed she was good at heart.

There was no way he could come back from meeting
her ex-husband feeling the same about her.

And maybe it was time she faced that reality, too.

At four o'clock the next afternoon, Rorke parked his
car on the road in front of a white, two-story stucco
house in Biloxi. The pool in the side yard glinted aqua-
marine diamonds in the distance. Yucca and palms
landscaped the golf-course-perfect lawn.

He climbed out of the car and stretched to shake out the kinks from the long drive. He was looking forward to meeting Kelsey's ex-husband as much as he'd enjoyed cuddling up with a viper.

He wasn't worried about his ability to handle the situation. Handling tough people in tough situations was his business, and Kelsey had built any confrontation with the bastard all out of proportion in her mind. At one time Whitfield had had enough brains to fall in love with Kelsey, which said something positive about the man's basic intelligence. And if he had some brainpower, Rorke could reason with him on a man-to-man basis.

It was just going to be tricky, trying to reason with a man he'd like to kick in the teeth. Whitfield had hurt Kelsey. Rorke wasn't likely to forget that in this lifetime.

He headed up the circular walk of the driveway, forcing himself into a different frame of mind. He was here to open doors of communication, not close them. They didn't have to be chums for him to be civil, calm and reasonable.

Even if it kills you, Stoner. And don't forget it.

He rang the bell at the Whitfield front door, aware that there was no sign that a child lived there—no bike, no mess, no swing set, no nothing to mar the elegant landscape.

The angel answered the door, Kelsey's soft blue eyes looking wary and worried when she saw a stranger.

"Is your dad home?" Rorke asked her gently. She was wearing shoes and a Sunday-spotless white jumpsuit thing—*not* attire that a kid would dare get dirty. From the corner of his eye, he saw the book tucked under her thin arm.

"Yes, but he can't come to the door right now." She pushed nervously at her ragamuffin bangs. "Could I help you?"

So polite, so sweet. Her voice was as proper as a thirty-year-old matron's—another thing Rorke was inclined to damn Whitfield for, but momentarily he had a more obvious problem. He could see from the look in her eyes that her father wasn't home. She'd obviously been instructed never to inform anyone she was alone.

"I need to see him," Rorke said carefully, "but I realize you don't know me. I wouldn't ask to come in the house, but if it's all right, I'll wait outside here until he's back."

"He's here. I told you. He just can't come to the door."

"Okay." Rorke took a breath rather than smile. She fibbed no better than Kelsey. "Do you think he might be able to come to the door sometime within the next hour or two?"

"I think he might be able to come to the door by five o'clock." She readjusted the book in front of her chest protectively. "But I'm not sure if it's all right if you stay."

Rorke wished he could have saved her this worry. A phone call ahead would have done it. Unfortunately, a phone call would also have given Whitfield the chance to say no to a meeting, and an unexpected visit gave Rorke the advantage of being prepared. It had to be this way. "I think," he said carefully, "that if you lock your doors and I sit out by the pool, you'll be able to see me from a window. You won't be worried then, will you?"

The twelve-year-old, serious as a judge, studied his face long and hard. So long and so hard that Rorke was tempted to say, *Sweetheart, please be that tough judg-*

ing men when you reach dating age. Somehow the humor wouldn't hold, though. Her reserve was more than caution, more burdened than the basic stranger-at-the-door problem should call for. Where was the child with the dancing eyes and vital effervescence that Kelsey had been holding in her arms in that photograph?

"Okeydoke," she said finally, her phrasing the first glimmer of "pure kid" he'd seen. "I'll send Dad out as soon as he's . . . as soon as he comes down from upstairs. It shouldn't be longer than five. He's never late."

A classy gray Karmann-Ghia drove in at a quarter to five. Rorke was on the pool patio, on his feet and braced at the first sound of the car, but Kelsey's ex-husband didn't notice him from the driveway. Andrew lifted a bag of golf clubs from the car and strode toward the house.

It would take a few minutes for Janey to tell him he had a visitor. Very few. Rorke stared at the glitter of sun-tipped blue waters in the clover-shaped pool, feeling sweat collect at the back of his neck and tension knot in his stomach.

The short conversation with Janey had only intensified his resolve. Both daughter and mother needed each other. Twelve years old—she should be running like the wind, making noise with piles of friends, getting yelled at for her messes, laughing. Rorke knew where the blame lay, and that wasn't helping him feel rational and objective about this meeting with Whitfield. The bastard clearly needed strangling on two fronts.

You're gonna be nice. So nice, butter wouldn't melt in your mouth, Stoner.

Janey was a fast informer. Andrew stepped through the glass doors onto the patio almost before Rorke turned around.

From his first look at the other man, Rorke felt an oddly off-kilter sensation. The instant animosity he'd expected to feel was there, razor sharp and real, yet it was like sensing a second bullet slamming toward him from the unexpected sniper.

He'd been so sure who and what Whitfield was.

He'd known he would see privilege and did. The hair was professionally styled; the watch was jeweler-fancy; and the golf clothes all had the best label. Andrew was blond, blue-eyed and as tall and good-looking as a tennis pro, but Rorke had expected to see insensitivity and arrogance. There was none of that. He'd expected to see a soft, spoiled man and maybe a look of cruelty. There was none of that. He'd expected to see a total bastard.

The man ambling toward him had world-weary lines around his eyes, tired brackets around his mouth and an openly blunt, assessing manner as he met Rorke's eyes. He didn't judge a man by his clothes but by eye contact. Andrew was used to being sociable, but not with anyone who was going to waste his time.

Rorke had the sudden appalled feeling that in another time and place he might have met Andrew Whitfield and liked him.

"Janey doesn't always remember to catch a name, I'm afraid."

"Rorke Stoner."

"And you were obviously persistent enough to wait. I can't very well apologize when I wasn't expecting you. If we know each other—"

"We don't, but I'm hoping that we will." Rorke extended a hand at the same time Andrew did. "I'm here for Kelsey. To talk about your daughter."

The curiosity in Andrew's eyes died. A sheen of ice replaced it. The hand extended dropped back to his side. "You can either get the hell out of here immediately or I'll call the police. Your choice."

The attack was stunningly fast. Rorke had expected awkward rhetoric, not a door locked before it was even opened. "If you think I'm here to cause you trouble, you're mistaken," he said quietly. "If you'll sit down for a minute, I believe I can convince you that a conversation is worth your time. There are things you need to know, things that need to be talked about—for your daughter's sake. And before you say anything else, I think you should be aware that Janey's in an open second-story window looking down here right now."

"Janey can hear anything I have to say to you. She already knows her mother's a drunk and a lush. I don't know how Kelsey found us, but this interview is all done. I don't care who you are, what you are, or how you're representing my ex-wife. She goes anywhere near my daughter and I'll have the court on her so fast it'll make her head spin. Get out."

"Whitfield—"

Andrew was halfway through the glass doors and never turned. He jerked the open one shut and latched it.

Rorke could have clawed air. *Do you have the feeling this chat's over, Stoner?*

He looked up and saw the small white face pressed to the pane of the partially opened window. He couldn't tell if she was too far away to have heard the conversation, but she was looking at him, her expression sober. And old. Far too old for a twelve-year-old girl. Kelsey's eyes could look old like that.

The little one suddenly pushed at the window and leaned over as though she were going to say something to him, but then she jumped, as if her name had been called by an impatient parent. She looked at him one last time, then closed the window and disappeared.

For a moment he couldn't seem to move, couldn't seem to catch the cadence of even a heartbeat. He was as close to shaken as he could ever remember being. Pictures of Kelsey shot pell-mell through his mind. Some of them stung. All of them hurt. He didn't want them there, but they persisted.

Andrew's words knifed through him. *Janey already knows her mother's a drunk and a lush.* And Kelsey's words. *How many times do I have to tell you, Rorke? I put Andrew through hell. He'd never let me anywhere near Janey.*

Rorke had never believed her.

He'd thought he had. He'd thought he'd dealt with all those illusions she'd accused him of. But he'd never once truly pictured her with a bottle in her hand, never once tried to picture how her drinking had affected other people's lives.

In time he found the energy to move. Striding toward his car, he put a lid on the chaotic thoughts churning in his mind. He wasn't here to think; he was here to act. One thing was still true—the bastard, as he'd expected, showed as much understanding and sensitivity to his daughter as a dead toad. The little one had grandparents in the same town. Rorke wasn't driving back to Natchez yet.

The grandparents couldn't possibly be as impossible to deal with as Andrew.

Chapter 12

Kelsey's lights had been off for an hour. She'd already tried the rituals of a soothing bath and a cup of mint tea to relax her. She had school tomorrow and was going to be worthless if she didn't get some sleep.

Apparently she was going to be worthless, because she sure wasn't sleeping.

Her teeth gnawed at a broken thumbnail. There was no chance of seeing Rorke until tomorrow after work. They'd both agreed that was logical timing. He couldn't get back from Biloxi until late, and he had to work tomorrow, just as she did.

At the level she was building anxiety, she'd have a heart attack before tomorrow night. Knowing where he was, guessing what he'd been through, had caused her stomach to churn acid all day. When she was a little girl, she used to be afraid of alligators under the bed. This was like turning on the lights and discovering the alligators were real.

She could have stopped him from going. If she was a stronger woman, she would have stopped herself from loving him, from caring, from allowing hope to take root. You protected those you loved. She'd failed to protect Rorke, but it seemed an unbearable irony that Andrew would do that for her. Rorke had gone to Biloxi because he believed in their future. No man, meeting her ex-husband, could fail to understand that she was not "future" material.

You've been doing this to yourself for hours, Kelsey. You have to try to relax, and I know just the thing. How about pouring yourself one small, soothing glass of Chardonnay? Just one, sugar. What's the harm?

Eyes closed, she nipped the thumbnail right to the quick. She hadn't let the dragon this close in a long time. Its power was real, potent, familiar, and for the past few weeks had been gaining strength like a noose tightening around her neck.

She thumped the pillow, shifted to her side and huddled under the covers as if she could hide from the shadows. For eight years she'd thought the abyss was behind her. Instead, between Rorke and Janey, she was again facing her oldest enemies. Guilt. Shame. Helplessness.

She thought she'd moved past them. She hadn't. Knowing Rorke was meeting her past made her mistakes burn as fresh as raw wounds. They weren't healed. They weren't even scabbed over. Becoming a decent woman now didn't erase the sins of the past. She didn't deserve Janey. She didn't deserve Rorke.

I agree, Whitfield. You're absolutely worthless. So what on earth is stopping you from having that glass of Chardonnay?

Nothing, she told herself, but she didn't get up, didn't head for the kitchen, didn't reach in the drawer for the corkscrew—although she imagined herself doing all those things. She even imagined the first taste of the wine.

She imagined herself doing a dozen terrible things, but for the life of her, she couldn't imagine facing Rorke tomorrow.

Over the hours she tossed and turned, positive she caught no sleep at all, yet she must have. When she next opened her eyes, she felt groggy and disoriented. Outside, the crickets and night bugs had stopped making noise. It wasn't midnight now but predawn, the time of total silence, total darkness.

And she wasn't alone.

At first she thought Rorke was part of a dream. There'd been no moon the night before, and she could barely make out the shadowed hulk lying beside her. Where she was cozied under a comforter, he was lying flat on top of the covers. One arm was behind his head and he was fully clothed—even black on black outlines revealed that much—and his eyes were wide open and staring at the ceiling. Eyes had a luminous sheen that transcended darkness, too.

Confusion affected her heartbeat more than surprise. Maybe she'd half guessed he wouldn't wait until tomorrow night to see her. He had no patience. When Rorke had something tough to handle, he tackled it head-on. She assumed he'd come to tell her, tactfully, that meeting Andrew had forced him to do some thinking. Yet if he'd come to talk, he should have wakened her. And she was braced for a lover who wanted to call it quits, not a thief in the night who'd stolen in her house to lie near her.

"Rorke?"

He jolted when she touched his arm. "I didn't mean to wake you, honey. Go back to sleep if you can."

That was as likely as cows flying. Even from that slight contact, she could feel the tense, coiled muscles in his arm. There was anger in him, although it didn't seem to be directed at her. The timbre of his voice was husky, deliberately soothing.

"How long have you been here?"

"I don't know. An hour, maybe two." He turned his head then. "I'm not leaving. We don't have to talk, not until tomorrow when you're more awake. But I'm staying here tonight."

His possessive tone was dominantly male, and lying next to him made her even more conscious of Rorke's sexuality. The charge crackling between them this night, though, was not desire. He hadn't moved to touch her, yet he was here. And even more troubled than she was, judging from the hard sheen of black in his eyes. "I couldn't be more awake and, yes, we do have to talk," she said quietly. "I'm sorry I let you go."

He faced away from her, the darkness between them as big as a chasm. "That was my choice, not yours. In one sense I didn't get anywhere, but losing a battle isn't losing a war. Without making that trip, I would have had no idea what you were dealing with, or what your daughter was dealing with. You can't plan a strategy without knowing the weapons the enemy has in his arsenal. We were flying blind before. That's no good. If I learned one thing it's what you already knew, you're going to have to fight like hell for her."

Silence. "Rorke, I've told you a dozen times how I feel about Janey—"

"You've told me what you think you're supposed to feel. What you think you're supposed to do. And 'supposed' is one of those words I rate right up there with cow manure, toots, so I think we're going to leave any discussion of Janey and strategies for another night."

Kelsey had the brief sensation that she was walking through patches of quicksand blind. There was no way she could handle a discussion—or argument—about her daughter. One blow at a time. "I didn't know," she said awkwardly, "that there was necessarily going to be another night."

"If you thought I'd leave you high and dry on Janey, you'd better rethink it. I'm in for the whole count, Kels. Don't doubt it."

The tone in his voice begged her to argue with him, and it couldn't have bewildered her more. "You had more to deal with than Janey if you met my ex-husband," she said carefully.

"You have that right."

The stubbornness had dissolved from his tone, and in its place was the bleakness of pain. She was the one who'd expected to feel pain when he told her his feelings for her had changed. Totally confused, she reached up to turn on the light, but his hand snagged her wrist.

"I have something I need to say to you, but it's best said in the dark. It's nothing I'm proud of."

She heard weariness, she heard anger. "Rorke—"

"I couldn't go home. I had to come here. I'm still not sure if that was a right or wrong choice, but I wanted, I needed, to be near you. There's no guarantee once I tell you this that you'll want me around. It's going to hurt you, Kels," he said gruffly. "And the most I can ask is that you hear me out—all of it—before you decide what you want to do."

Her eyes closed. "It's all right, whether you believe it or not. There's nothing you could say that I wasn't expecting."

"It's *not* all right, and no, I don't think you're expecting this." He pushed up against the headboard, his head thrown back against the wall. "There's no easy way to get into it, so I'm just going to say it. Early on, I had a partner who drank. Russ. At the time I told myself I did my bit to help him, but it wasn't true. I felt contempt, not compassion. I'd worked too hard to turn my own life around. Watching him throw his away turned my stomach. A man wasn't a man who couldn't handle his liquor. I thought it was as simple as that."

"Stoner—" It took her a moment to comprehend that the mountain of anger he was dealing with came from the inside. Rorke's eyes, in the dark, were lost in their own private trial.

"Listen. Just listen." He never took a breath, and his voice was as hard as nails. "I *am* a simple man, Kelsey. I'm not perceptive like you. I don't analyze things. I make a straight, honest judgment on right and wrong and do my best to live it. A thief's a thief. Everybody has a bleeding-heart motive, but in the long run you can't let people kill other people because they had some sad background. Sometime, somewhere, a line has to be drawn. Wrong is just plain wrong, and dammit, drinking is one of those lines I drew with a thick black pen."

"Sweetheart—"

"Shh. Listen. Please." He sighed, like a whoosh of air exploding from his lungs. "After Russ, Walt and I hooked up as partners. We worked a black and white to start, a night shift, and with those hours we inevitably got calls to handle drunks in bars. Walt was a soft touch, but I never had a tolerance, especially if it was a woman. A woman who drank added up in my mind to cheap and easy, a tramp who usually got what she was looking for. That's how I saw those women, and that's how I judged them on sight. Dammit, please don't jerk away from me. Whether or not you believe it, this is harder for me to say than it is for you to hear.''

But Kelsey hadn't moved, much less jerked away from him. Something was breaking loose inside her that she could never have prepared for, never have protected herself against. It wasn't the emotion of hurt but the emotion of hope—and not the hope of fairy-tale dreams, of whimsy and wanting to believe. This hope was real, and so fragile it whispered through her pulse.

"So I met your ex-in-laws this afternoon," he ground on. "It didn't take me long to peg them as bitches and bastards, but you know what that was really about? Coming face-to-face with me. The whole drive home, that's all I could think about. They'd judged you, written you right off the slate, and there was no difference between them and the way I'd related to every drinker I'd ever met. You think that didn't make me sick?''

Coiling the sheet around her, she leaned forward. "And you're feeling guilty?" she asked softly.

Again anger, virulent and explosive. "I *am* guilty. Of being a sanctimonious bastard. Thinking I was different than they were, better than they were. I separated myself from the problem no differently than they did, Kels. I told myself I understood, when at gut level I never heard you.''

"I never thought," she said slowly, "that you'd come this far.''

He dragged a hand through his hair, stopped. "Come this far?"

"Are you ever going to stop judging yourself so harshly, Rorke? You were never a sanctimonious bastard, not with me. You just hated it. My drinking. How on earth could you possibly expect yourself to feel any other way?"

"Kelsey." Exasperation climbed in his tone. "I'm trying to tell you that I wasn't there for you any more than they were. I'm trying to tell you that I feel like a sludge of humanity." His voice grew hoarse. "And I'm trying to ask you—not for the first time—to give me another chance. I'm not the same man I was. I can show you the difference if you'll let me. I *want* to understand. Not the books. You. What you feel, what you have to deal with."

It wouldn't wait any longer. She thrust her fingers in his hair to hold him still, and then kissed him. Softly. Thoroughly. Exquisitely. It was the only way she knew to tell him that she loved the sinner, not the saint—the sinner with the scruffy whiskers and dark lost eyes who was so, so angry he wasn't a perfect man.

At the first contact of her lips against his, he grabbed her bare shoulders as if he were going to push her away...but the callused fingers denting her soft skin suddenly lingered. "I'm not through talking to you." She was quite sure he was. The anger was gone from his voice. His tone had thickened, deepened. "Honey, is there anything you can't forgive a man?"

"Forgive you for being real with me? Honest with me?" But she couldn't talk, so she just kept kissing. Hard kisses. Silk-and-satin kisses. Wet soft rubs and dry caresses, kisses involving tongues and kisses involving teeth.

She thought she'd lost him. She'd been so positive they never had a chance. Rorke had opened that terrifyingly powerful door on hope. He was so sure he'd hurt her, so sure she'd judge him for being a terrible man. It was never that way. He had no different gut feelings about drinkers than anyone else. Those feelings weren't criminal but human. And if he could be honest with her at that human level, promises worth nothing before now had a chance of meaning something. Maybe everything.

Maybe she was asking for heartache. She didn't care. Maybe the risks were still unbearably high. She didn't care. She'd always held something back before. Not tonight. Tonight she had no defenses and a terrible need to express how much she loved him, honestly and from the soul, and as if he caught her mood, he was suddenly pushing at the sheet separating them, first with a hand and then his leg. Callused hands, rough and frantic, raced up and down her side, her spine, anywhere they could reach. She hadn't been the only one afraid of loss this night. His mouth latched on hers like he wouldn't, couldn't, let go.

His buttons and belt surrendered to her hands. In little time she had him bare. Total darkness aided the rush of abandoned emotion sweeping through her, and without the sense of sight, all her other senses intensified. She could hear every change in his breathing, taste the coffee he'd had hours ago, smell the male musk heating his skin. And she could feel.

Her lips explored corded muscle, supple skin, scars. Her hands glided over his hair-roughened chest, the taut skin below his navel, and then moved lower. His manhood was long, hard and hot. It had a pulse all its own. When she trailed a fingertip along the blood line to that most sensitive spot, she heard Rorke make a low desperate sound. The sound a man might make if his control was stretched taut enough to snap.

Her heart was beating so hard she could hear the roar in her ears. Somewhere there was a spiraling fear that she could lose herself in him, that she could cross the line and never go back. She sensed the danger, yet courted it. There was no shame, no guilt, not with him. There was nothing she wouldn't do for him, nothing she wouldn't give him, and she slipped from his arms, coiled up on her knees and bent down.

Her palm stroked the inside of his thigh as her lips grazed the satin length of him. He tasted salty, almost as salty as the slick perspiration starting to coat his skin. His response fed the sweet, wild recklessness already dominating her heartbeat . . . but not for long.

Abruptly Rorke reached for her, blind in the darkness, and crushed a kiss on her mouth as he lowered her flat beneath him. He tested himself on her lips and came close to losing his mind. "You didn't have to do that," he said hoarsely.

"I wanted to. I want—"

"Tell me." She plainly couldn't, not right then, but what he saw in her eyes jammed all the oxygen in his lungs. He murmured roughly, "We're going to slow this down, sugar."

"No."

"Oh, yeah, we are." His hands skimmed the length of her arms until he had both her hands captured over her head like pirate's booty. Her legs instinctively coiled around him. He embedded himself inside her in one smooth thrust, but he didn't start the rhythm.

Kelsey was helpless, the way he wanted her, and coming vibrantly alive for him as a woman . . . what he wanted for her even more. For every hurt she'd ever suffered, he kissed her. For all the people who'd never been there for her, he took her mouth again. For being Kelsey... maybe that was why he kissed her the third time, the seventh time, the tenth time.

When he finally lifted his head, her eyes were glazed and shimmering and she didn't want her hands captured, not anymore. She understood she was vulnerable now and wasn't quite so sure. He arced above her, where his possessive gaze had free reign over all her shadowed honey and cream. His free palm cupped her aching breast, the flesh swelling for him, heating. She had a problem with that, too, because a song of longing—of fierce, restless, feminine need—whispered from the back of her throat.

His thumb brushed, then lashed, then soothed the taut nipple. Her whole body tightened beneath him, and she called out. His name. Still he started no rhythm. Pleasure wasn't enough, even bottomless pleasure, not for Kelsey and not for him. He was patient now, lover now, an artist painting landscapes where he touched. He stroked throat, breasts, abdomen, then let his fingers tangle into crisp dark curls and stroke where the two of them were joined.

"Let go," she whispered wildly. "Let go of my hands."

"Not yet."

"If you don't, I'm going to die. Like this. Wanting you." She saw his lips curve in the darkness, saw his eyes, fierce with tenderness and intent. He wanted more from her than wanting. He wasn't going to let her agony end until he had it, and there was no way, not this night, she could deny him anything. *I love you, Rorke.*

For a moment time was suspended. There was just
the scent of magnolias and dew, the stillness of a night
that belonged to them and the look . . . the look of fire
and lush emotion in Rorke's eyes. "And I love you." He
whispered it first, too aware she had rejected hearing
words of love from him before. "I *love* you." This time
his voice was stronger, half a call to her heart, half a
demand from his soul. "You didn't want to know that
before. You were afraid before. You didn't want promises from me before. Say it, Kels. I need to hear you say
it."

And it spilled from her in broken whispers. "I want
you to love me. I want to be loved by you, with you, be
part of you. I want to believe . . . Oh, Rorke, you don't
know how much I want to believe—"

In the two of them. He saw the love in her eyes. He
released her hands and kissed her—a kiss far more
powerful than a spoken vow. And then he took her with
a driving power and force that had her clutching him,
clinging, aching.

Fire lapped at her from the inside, a fire that kept
burning hotter, wilder, more unbearable than pain,
more exquisite than pleasure. She'd felt need with Rorke
before, but not like this. She'd felt the climb of desire
with him before, but not like this. This was feeling heat
explode through her body in shattering rays. This was
feeling claimed, taken, owned; a burning up, a giving
in, a total yielding. This was discovering her right to
love . . . with the one man she could give that kind of
trust to.

When a pearl-gray sunrise started to peek in the east
window, Kelsey's cheek was in the tuck of his shoulder

and his entire right arm was numb. Rorke hadn't moved and didn't want to at least until seven.

Her alarm was set for seven-thirty, but he had to get going earlier than that. Before going to Biloxi, he'd stashed a uniform and razor in his car—the habit of being prepared for any eventuality was hard to break. He *wasn't* in the habit of facing a day of work with no rest, but sleep, even a dozing nap, wouldn't come.

At the moment he was both worried and aroused, conditions he had become accustomed to since meeting Kelsey.

Her future was enormously secure, although she didn't know it yet. He had never understood "belonging" until last night. Kelsey could take a man's broken soul and make it whole, turn his emotions inside out, heal anyone of anything with her passion and giving. Once he'd said he didn't give a damn about her drinking. It wasn't true. He gave a huge damn. He'd also sell his heart before giving her up, and if he had to fight for her, he would.

It would be a lot easier if fighting for her involved heroic measures like leaping tall buildings in a single bound.

Kelsey stirred in her sleep, unconsciously nuzzling closer to him. Rorke let his hand drift through her hair, his touch light so she wouldn't waken. The way she'd given herself to him last night left him no doubt that she felt the same power of love that he did.

Few relationships could have had a rockier start. His coming into her life had raised complex emotional issues for Kelsey about her daughter. His feelings about her drinking had caused his own emotional maelstrom. Nothing had been easy. Yet it was through the toughest problems that he'd found her...a woman he could come to, share with, cleave to. Love had taken root from the stoniest of all possible soils. And it had grown, tenacious and strong.

Rorke, though, was worried she wouldn't wake up in precisely that frame of mind. A permanent agenda had never been on Kelsey's agenda. She wasn't afraid of commitment, but of the effect her alcoholic history had on a relationship, and Rorke felt a disquieting unease every time he thought of Janey. At one level he understood Kelsey's fears about her daughter, but for some time he'd known he was missing something. A clue. A reason. The piece of the puzzle that would explain Kelsey's nightmares where her daughter was concerned. He needed that puzzle piece—not just for Janey but for himself. Nothing was going on Kelsey's permanent agenda until she'd climbed over that emotional brick wall.

Mulling over that problem was getting him nowhere, and when he glanced at the clock, he realized how late it was. Gently he tried to withdraw his right arm. Her hold instinctively tightened and she only snuggled closer. Asleep, she didn't want him to leave her. He mentally willed her to keep that attitude when she woke up.

He sneaked away as quietly as he could, covered her with the comforter and headed first for his car, then the shower. Fifteen minutes later he silently opened the door to the bathroom to let some of the steam out, and immediately heard her sleepy voice. "Stoner, get your naked body in here."

Razor in hand, her pink towel hooked around his hips, he took his grin as far as the bedroom door. She hadn't budged from where he'd left her, nestled in covers with pillows piled around her, but her lashes were opened. Marginally.

"I like the towel," she murmured.

"Pink's always been my color," he said dryly.

"What time do you have to leave?"

"A half hour from now."

Immediately she pushed at the covers. "I'll make you some pancakes."

"Please, God. No."

Her brows quizzically lifted. "Rorke, I make wonderful pancakes."

"I'm sure you do. I'm just not a breakfast man." He crossed the room and bent down. He kissed her softly, lingeringly, aware she was coming to full wakefulness now. Bare and sleepy warm, her arms came around him like a memory of the night before. "I love you," he murmured, light and easy, but just enough to test her memory, too.

Her eyes searched his as he pulled away. "If you love me, you're going to be careful today."

"Yes, ma'am."

"No chances. No risks. No pushing those ribs."

"Yes, ma'am."

"You managed to catch a few hours' sleep?"

"Yes, ma'am," he lied. His soul was already in hock for the little one about the pancakes. One more fib couldn't make it any worse.

"Stoner? Right or wrong, I love you, too. Really. Love you." She said it in her softest magnolia drawl and then swallowed hard. If she'd ever looked more fragile, he didn't know when. "Well." Abruptly she blew a strand of hair from her eyes and bounced back against the pillows. "For heaven's sakes, take off that silly-looking towel and let me see you put on your blues. I've never been much impressed by uniforms, but you can give it a try. And notice I'm not asking why there's a uniform hanging over my bathroom door. Type A's are always prepared for every contingency. It's a disgusting trait, sugar."

"Yeah?" He heard the unspoken plea in her voice. It was no time for heavy subjects; she wanted to keep the mood light, keep it easy. Her "I love you" sang in his veins like bluesy jazz. He'd have happily given her gold and diamonds, but if all she wanted was to keep things light just for this morning, he aimed to please. Deliberately his gaze took a meandering trail around her bedroom.

"Don't you dare say it," she warned him.

"Say what?"

"Don't you dare say, 'We've got to get you organized.' The state of this room is not my fault."

"No?"

"Absolutely not. Those piles of clean clothes on the chair—the maid keeps forgetting to put them away. Some slob left the camisole on the floor—it certainly wasn't me. There's this drawer fairy that comes in every night and leaves all the drawers hanging open. And some stranger, some slovenly stranger, has obviously been in my closet. You don't think I'd throw all the shoes on top of each other like that?"

"The thought never crossed my mind," Rorke assured her.

"The more I look, the more it's obvious the place has been vandalized. Thank heavens I know a cop."

There was no help for it. All he had on were his pants and one sock when he stalked over to her again. Her eyes were full of sass, her arms lifted to his—Kelsey at her most impossible to resist. He kissed her good. "You want me to arrest this ... um ... drawer fairy?"

"I think it would be a heroic thing to do," she said primly. "Not that I ever expected to find a hero in my life." All her jokes and teasing suddenly faltered. Her eyes met his. "Nor did I ever want one. All the wildest, most impossible dreams I ever had were about a flesh-and-blood man. Someone real, someone human. Not too perfect, because by no stretch of anyone's imagination could I ever qualify for a halo myself...." Her voice suddenly broke. "*Dammit*, I'm scared, Rorke."

He sank next to her on the bed, but she laid a finger on his lips when he tried to talk. "I thought I'd lost you last night," she said fiercely. "I know how much you mean to me. I'm not going to forget it. I'm not going to pretend last night meant nothing because it did. But it's not easy, believing I'm right for you. When I start thinking—"

"Don't think. Feel." He wrapped her close and took her mouth, offering no nuzzling kiss this time. Lips molded, tongues yielded and passion sparked faster than lightning. So, though, did a sense of rightness, the seal of what they brought each other, what they were together. Kelsey felt it. He didn't release her until he was sure of that. "That's how you make me feel—more, always more as a man than I've ever been before. You're right for me, Kels. You and only you. There's nothing we can't handle together."

He said it because he believed it, but every instinct warned him to get a gold band on her finger as soon as possible. Kelsey had always had the problem of believing she needed to protect him. He wanted to protect her, but the right to do that only came with a committed relationship. Trust and time were the keys. And love.

God knew, he had the love. But as for sneaking a ring on Kelsey's finger...

Leaping tall buildings in a single bound was a cupcake job in comparison. Rorke felt a lump form in his throat. He couldn't shake the feeling of apprehension that he was quickly running out of time.

Chapter 13

Rorke turned the key and opened the door. "You're not going to like it."

Kelsey brushed past him with an impish grin. "At least give me a chance to get a look, Mr. Paranoid." She rounded a corner and stopped dead. "Good grief." A few seconds later he heard another appalled "Good grief!"

Rorke chuckled, pocketed the house key and scooped up the mail en route to the kitchen. He planned to eventually throw some steaks on the grill and take her to a movie. First, though, it was past time she saw where he lived . . . and once she gave him hell about the place, he could subtly bring up the subject of where *they* might live. Together. Permanently.

Guessing that Kelsey would take a few minutes to explore, he detoured outside to get the charcoal started. He'd whisked home from work to change clothes before he'd picked her up. His gray jeans and charcoal sweatshirt were as old as the hills. Lucky clothes. He'd cashed in on a friendly poker game in the jeans, saved a kid in a bike accident when he was wearing the sweatshirt. He'd paired them together, praying for double luck.

He knew he was going to need it. A mixture of anxiety and anticipation was pumping in his veins when Trouble rounded the corner. He could hardly miss the swirl of color or the schoolmarm pursed lips. "You're sure someone lives here and we didn't get into the wrong house by mistake?"

"I'm sure," he said dryly. She was wearing a new scent, something exotic and sassy, seal-brown slacks that molded to her nonexistent fanny and an apricot shirt designed by a man hater. It buttoned up the back, bitty buttons, about five million of them the last he checked. He figured she'd done it deliberately, gone braless in the one blouse it would take him five hours to get her out of.

He briefly considered seducing her into saying yes to a marriage proposal. The option lacked any claim to honor. He didn't care. Kelsey beautifully lost her mind when they were naked together and so did he. It was going to take all his wits to sneak a ring on her finger, especially since Kelsey was clearly in no mood for serious talk of any kind.

"I had no idea real people lived like this. No finger smudges on the glass coffee table. No dust balls under the bed. No drying dab of toothpaste on the sink. Oh, my God." Her hands flew to her cheeks. "Look out there at the grass. In the middle, a little to the left. There's a spear of grass that's about three inches taller than the rest. Your mower missed it. Will lightning strike?"

Lightning wasn't the problem. *He* was going to strike if she angled by him one more time with that provocative little swivel in her hips. "You're slipping, Whitfield. I thought you'd come up with a lot more lethal insults than those."

She found the bag of potato chips on the counter and popped one open. "Who's talking insults? I'm talking grave concern. Neatness, thrift, order. We're obviously dealing with the bad habits of a lifetime. You can't just reform those kinds of problems overnight. That kind of job would take years—whatcha want me to help with dinner?"

"Trust me—nothing. It's all under control." He tried to divert her away from the refrigerator. Too late. She came away from the shelves with a crackling fresh head of lettuce and a fat tomato.

"The least I can do is make a salad," she said firmly.

He briefly considered what destruction she could wreak on a head of lettuce. The risks seemed minimal. Either way, it didn't much matter. Kelsey was wired with energy. The kids put her on the ceiling every Friday—it always took her a little time to level down—but this was more than that.

She'd been full of the devil all week. He loved this side of Kelsey, but in his own way he sensed she was trying to outrun a freight train. She made love in the night fueled by desperation as much as passion. She found ways to make him laugh when the day's mood hadn't been laughter, and she flew—typical Kelsey—but these last days she'd been flying at breakneck speeds.

He figured she was afraid.

Once he had a ring on her finger, he figured he had fifty, sixty years to show her she didn't have to be. Right now, though, his immediate goal was to set the appropriate scene. Some men might vote for candlelight and music. Rorke knew better. A calm, reassuring, relaxing, innocuous scene of domesticity was his intent. If he could erase every worry from her mind, he'd do it. Kelsey had been through too much lately, and it took too little to raise her defenses.

He put a marinade on the steaks, lined a couple of plates on the table and then absently reached for the penknife in his pocket to open the mail. There had been a mountain of it. He slit envelopes while Kelsey chopped lettuce, cucumbers, tomatoes and a fresh green pepper. Since she sampled more than she put in the bowl, the salad took a long time to create.

To his satisfaction, she was relaxing. Their chitchat was lazy, desultory, starting with his work—Kelsey liked to hear every detail—and the meandering into hers.

"Kids give you trouble today?"

"Are you kidding? Kids aged twelve to fourteen live to give a teacher trouble." She went back to the refrigerator and peered in, looking for something more lively to put in the salad. "Actually, that's why I chose those ages to teach."

"Didn't you tell me that you used to teach elementary?" He went back to opening bills.

"Just for a few years." On a back shelf she found a jar of maraschino cherries. Her vice. "Kids that age were born to give a teacher trouble, too. Maybe I'll try high school next."

Rorke figured she'd do just that, because Janey would be high-school age a few years down the pike. He'd picked up on her history of teaching a long time ago. When her daughter was in third grade, Kelsey had been teaching third grade. Now that her daughter was twelve, Kelsey was teaching middle school. And no matter what age kid she was teaching, her door and telephone line were always open for any question, any problem, at any time of the day or night.

She never saw the connection. It was evidently subconscious, unconscious, at the heart level. Rorke wanted to call her on it—but not yet, not until he had the ring on her finger. Part of the freight train chasing her was Janey. Kelsey was happily willing to discuss sex, religion or politics. Anything. Just not her daughter.

Bed and wed was different than wed and bed. There was a trust implicit in a marriage vow that cavemen, Rorke felt, understood completely. Right now Kelsey wouldn't let him help her. She was too damn busy "protecting" him ... but that was all going to change. *Easy and slow, Stoner,* he reminded himself.

"Hey. No onions, lady."

"Aha." Winsome blue eyes leisurely dawdled over him head to toe. The provocative sass in her grin made his blood simmer, but it was the love in her eyes that turned up his body heat. "Is that a subtle hint that you intend to seduce me later?"

"I'd scare the pants right off you if I told you what I had in mind for later." There was a little more truth in that than he wanted her to see in his expression. He lowered his head to trash the junk catalogs in the wastebasket, when one lost envelope slipped to the floor.

When he flipped it, he saw the Biloxi return address.

"It takes an awful lot to scare the pants off me. Could you be more specific?" She put the onion back and snatched a salad dressing, waiting for his comeback. When he didn't respond, she glanced at him.

His gaze was riveted on the single page in his hand. Where he stood in the open window, the sun cast a triangle of light on his forehead and shoulder. For that moment he looked so...Rorke. Intense and private, all contained energy and vital sexuality, stubborn and determined. She took the picture in her mind the way she would take a snapshot, something to savor and remember for no particular reason except that she loved him. And then he looked up. When their eyes met, she felt her smile die and her heart seize up.

"What's wrong?"

"Sit down, honey."

But she stood frozen, bewildered by the sudden change in him. One minute he'd been happily prowling around the kitchen and the next his skin had turned ashen, his features were carved in harsh lines, and his eyes were fastened on her face with fierce anxiety. He swallowed, threw back his head and then moved.

From one cupboard he brought out two glasses and clapped them on the counter, then opened another cupboard. Kelsey found herself suddenly not breathing.

From where she was standing, she couldn't see all the contents on the shelves, but he was reaching for the shelf with his liquor supply. Bottles of Cutty Sark, Seagram's and Jack Daniel's were all still packaged in gold boxes, the kind people gave you for Christmas. He foraged behind those, then said flatly, "It seems I don't have any Chardonnay. Or any other wine, either." Then he ripped the seal on the Seagram's. He splashed the whiskey in the glasses and set them on the table, one near him, one near her.

"I'm not sure," she said, real softly, "what you're doing."

"Neither am I." He wiped his face with his hand. "Just once—just once in this life—I'd like the right to make something easy for you. Instead I'm the one stuck making it tougher. We're going to test it all tonight, toots. That sure as hell isn't what I wanted or planned, but I'm afraid it's all going to come together right now.''

''Rorke, you're not making a lick of sense.''

''I only wish that were true. Sit down. And then read the letter.''

''Read what?''

She hadn't associated his volatile change of mood with the letter until he motioned to the single sheet of stationery he'd thrown on the table. She picked it up, half expecting some terrible news like someone had died.

No one had died. No one was hurt. Nothing terrible had happened at all, yet Kelsey hadn't read more than a few lines before she had the sensation of the earth falling beneath her, a cliff giving way, a bottomless tumble down a dark dark tunnel.

Dear Mr. Stoner,

My name is Janey Whitfield. I met you at my house last Sunday. I guess you must be wondering why I am writing you. I heard you talking to my dad.

I want to see my mom. If you know my mom, would you tell her that? Tell her that I love her and I miss her and I need to see her real bad. As soon as she can. Please.

And please don't tell my dad that I wrote you.

Thank you,
Janey Whitfield

She sank in the kitchen chair and read it again, then again. Her gaze finally fixed, then blurred, on the round-lettered scrawl. All the *t*'s were crossed with a slant, the *i*'s dotted with little circles. The paper was purple, with a little spray of pansies at the border. Janey had loved pansies, even when she was a toddler. "I want to see my mom" had been written over twice so the sentence stood out in relief. The words "real bad" had been underlined three times.

The temperature in Rorke's kitchen seemed to have dropped thirty degrees. She was suddenly cold, numb cold, while deep on the inside her heart made a raw keening cry of grief. She had to work to make her voice normal. "How could she possibly get your address?"

"Who knows? She obviously caught my name. Maybe I told your ex-husband or in-laws I was from Natchez—I don't remember now. One way or another, she went to some trouble to put it together. I don't know or care how she did it any more than you do."

His tone was knuckle-under tough, startling her enough to raise her eyes. The compassion Rorke had always offered her was missing. His brow had creased in hard lines. He wasn't moving toward her. He hadn't moved at all. A spear lanced in her chest, sharp, hot and unbearably painful. "If it's all right with you," she said swiftly, "I think I'll skip dinner. I'd just like to go home—"

"You're not going anywhere, toots."

Again, that ruthless tone. "Rorke—"

"She needs you."

"It's not that simple."

"Maybe it wasn't before, but it is now. She needs you." Rorke hadn't sat yet. He stood there, watching her, aching for her. "Something's always been missing that you didn't tell me. I know what you're afraid of—

that she'll become an alcoholic and go through what
you did. You sold half your soul to make sure that pattern was broken. And that's real stuff, Kels, but there's
a missing piece. I don't know what it is, but you're
going to tell me."

"I don't know what you mean." Her trembling fingertip retraced the letters. Tell her I love her. Tell her I
need to see her real bad.

When something hurt this much, you were supposed
to be dead...and Rorke was being so cold. "There's no
'missing piece'—"

"Sure there is. It's killing you not to reach out to her.
It's killing you because you know exactly what she's
going through. I read the credo in one of your books.
Don't talk, don't feel, don't trust anyone. That's where
she is. I think that's where you were once upon a time.
If anybody's going to break the pattern for her, it's
you—not in spite of what you are, but because of what
you are. You understand what she's up against—your
ex and in-laws don't. It has to be you, so let's take the
wild cards out of the poker hand. Come on, Whitfield.
What's the missing piece? What really kept you from
going to her all this time?"

Kelsey latched her arms around her chest. She
couldn't believe Rorke would be this cruel—ever, not to
her—yet his tone was relentless, gnawing at scars she'd
thought were healed, digging at feelings she simply
couldn't handle. Her gaze focused blindly on the glass
sitting in front of her. Sun rayed on the amber whiskey, making its color look like liquid gold. If she stared
long enough, she could see the mesmerizing, alluring,
golden eyes of the dragon.

"If you're not going to tell me, I'm going to guess.
You always had two choices—to sneak off and see her,

which is hardly your way. Or to risk taking it to court.
If you took it to court, you knew you were going to face
hell. They'd label you a boozer and a lush. And it's
possible that's where you hold up, but somehow I don't
think so.''

My God, he wouldn't let up. "Forget it, would you
please, Rorke!''

But he wouldn't. "I think the problem—the real
problem—is that you'd have to fight them. You'd have
to stand up there and tell the whole damn world that
you're good, and you're strong, and that you're wor-
thy of being a mother. You'd have to say it like you believe it. And that's where it breaks down for you, isn't
it, Kels? Answer me. Answer me!''

And it suddenly blew. Guilt, so long bottled up, rip-
pled and tore to the surface. "You don't know,'' she
said hoarsely, "how I was. You don't know.''

"Tell me.''

She shook her head, tears scattering from her eyes
like rain. God, she was ashamed. "In the last months
before I left...I wasn't a mother. I was a machine,
waking up every morning with new broken parts.
Blackouts, headaches, a stomach that wouldn't keep
down food, hands that wouldn't stop shaking. No, I
didn't drink around her, but I was no mother, either.
Janey was my baby, and if I'd been any kind of human
being I would have stopped it. Only I couldn't. She was
so little, and I was so ugly, and I'll never in this life forgive myself, Rorke. Never!''

Rorke expelled a long breath. If ever a woman needed
holding, it was Kelsey, now. He had to brace himself to
stay tough a little longer. Quietly, deliberately, he said,
"You had me so fooled, toots. I thought I was the
judge, the one who couldn't forgive himself mistakes.

You're the one who taught me all about acceptance and forgiveness, so how come it never took for you? You decided, judge and jury, that you weren't a good enough human being to be a mother. Eight years of penance, sugar. Don't you think it's time you forgave yourself?''

"It's not that easy. I can't.''

"Guilt hurts; it doesn't help. You taught me that. Throw it, Kelsey.''

The command came from nowhere. Her eyes flew to his, then dropped to the hypnotic golden liquid in the glass.

"You love her so much, honey, and you're so good. Good from the inside out. Look inside if you don't believe me. There's no evil there, not then, not now, not ever. It's time you believed it. *Throw* it, Kels.''

Her gaze latched on the liquid like a moth to flame. She felt a splintering inside, a boiling up of an emotion she couldn't identify. But she'd felt it before. Once she'd lived on the edge of an abyss, a lonely abyss that no one else seemed to understand. The dragon had promised to soothe the loneliness, fill up the hollowness, offer her comfort. It never seemed so terrible, to need comfort. Only the dragon hadn't kept its promises. Any of them. She'd let herself be destroyed for absolutely nothing…and Rorke's voice kept coaxing her, goading her, needling.

"Don't you dare cry, Kels. You've cried enough—now, dammit, get mad. Throw it, babe. Now. Do it. Throw that thing as hard as you can.''

She didn't do it. She could have sworn she never moved, yet suddenly the glass was hurled against Rorke's pristine white wall beyond the table, hard enough to make a dent in the plaster before it shattered. Whiskey flew, the yellow liquid dribbling down the virgin-white wall, making a hell of a mess.

Rorke hauled her in his arms while she was still shaking. He peppered kisses all over her face before covering his mouth with hers. The warmth of his arms seeped into her chilled flesh, offering all the comfort she had once been so desperate for. The strength of his kiss demanded a yielding... a yielding of shame, a yielding of pain.

And when he lifted his head, she was aware, as she hadn't been, that there was a blur of moisture in his eyes. Her arms swept around him and she held him, hard and tight. He'd called her good. He'd called her strong. And at that moment she believed him, because he held her like she was his anchor, his ballast, his heart.

He kissed her again. And again. And before he kissed her a third time, he scooped her up in his strong arms and started walking. There was simply no stopping him.

"Rorke, I have to clean up that mess—"

"Later."

"You started the charcoal. It's going to burn out—"

"Later."

The curtains were closed against a pitch-black night. The single bedside lamp illuminated clothes dropped like Hansel and Gretel's trail of pebbles. Neither Rorke nor Kelsey had eaten, and neither had done much moving in the past twenty minutes. Both were buried under the cocoon of sheets in one lump, not two, and Kelsey still felt the liquid glow from Rorke's lovemaking.

She saw the same liquid glow in his eyes. There was an element of desire in that glow. The way he'd made love to her had been demandingly, dangerously, deliciously carnal. He'd wanted her naked, in body and soul. He'd taken what he wanted and given her what she'd only dreamed of. A feeling of being valued, more precious than treasure. A feeling of being needed, for who and all she was. A feeling of being understood, too mortifyingly well, by a man who loved her. She had an itsy-bitsy problem feeling good about herself. He'd obliterated, sabotaged and submarined that problem off the map.

At least for now. Some problems didn't disappear overnight. They became tangibly surmountable, though, when the love around you was a contrastingly insurmountable defense.

She stroked his cheek, savoring the look of him. Both of them claimed they were sleepy. Neither was sleepy at all. Her limbs were still tangled with his and her whisper as soft as secrets. "I thought you were being cruel."

"I know you did."

"You were afraid I was going to take that drink."

He never considered lying to her. "Yes."

"But you poured the whiskey, Rorke. You put it in front of me."

"I figured if you were ever going to be tempted, it was then, with all of it coming down: you, me, your daughter, the past. It was all linked to that glass and whatever power it still had over you." His palm slid down the fragile slope of her shoulder, lingered. "All I knew was that if you took that first sip, I was going to be there. With you. That's how it's going to be from now on, toots. If I'm going to marry you, we both share the problem."

"How did marriage get in this conversation?"

"You don't have to say yes right off the bat. You can think about it. You just can't leave this bed until you give me the answer I want. It'll work out okay. I'll bring you food if you're worried about starving."

"I'm more worried about your sanity."

"I'm going to worry about my sanity, too, if your right hand wanders any lower." He captured her slim fingers, twined them with his. "I got a measure of your dragon tonight, love."

Her grip tightened. "You think so?"

"I know so. He sits on your shadow. That's a hell of a load to carry. You warned me once that you couldn't give out guarantees. I just want you to know I'm not asking for any, but if the time comes when you can't beat the sucker, we won't be talking judgment. I'll be there. It won't be just one fighting the bastard but two."

"Rorke?"

"Yeah?"

"I love you."

"I've been doing my best to give you no other choice."

She took a long breath. "It's *your* choices I'm trying to think about. There's a big deck of cards out there. You could draw a better hand."

"From where I'm sitting, this hand doesn't get any better. I found a woman who's giving and special and wonderful from the heart. She's hot as hell in bed, she can handle a chronic neatnik and you can tell her anything. *Anything.* And she understands. So she has a small problem—correction, she has a major life problem. Did I plan on that? No. But I'll take the cards I have, Kels. I want this deck. No other. I've had thirty-seven years to figure out what matters to me, and believe me, I know."

Her heart turned inside out, but Rorke, possibly, was too afraid she was going to say no to give her a chance to respond.

"We don't have to rush this. We can live together in some good, wholesome, wanton sin for the next two days...and then we'll get the license on Monday. The same day we see an attorney for Janey. Lord, a cop seeking out an attorney. Even thinking about it is enough to make a man break out in hives."

"Stoner, you're moving faster than the speed of a gallop. Slow down. You most subtly slipped my daughter into the conversation—"

"You were going to if I didn't."

She whispered, "Yes." And then, softly, "I *am* going to fight for her, Rorke. Somehow, some way I'm going to win the right to see her, but after that... I don't know. What's right for Janey has to be the basis of any decision we make."

"Toots?"

She lifted her head.

"You just said 'we.' For that, you pay a penalty." He leaned over, sieved her hair through his hands and kissed her, long and lingeringly. "I know you're worried she has problems. I know you're worried about seeing her that first time...but she had a starting investment of love, Whitfield, and coming from you that's pretty potent. She'd perceptive like you are. You tell her where your head was; she'll figure out where your heart was."

"You think it's that easy?"

"I think nothing in this life is easy. Getting a yes out of you, for instance, is proving to be difficult."

"You're attempting dishonorable methods of persuasion."

"You bet I am."

"I can't think when you do that."

"Good."

"Stoner, if you'll let me up for air, I'd like to tell you that I adore you and I'll marry you and I need and want you. I even love you."

"Honey, you just lost your chance to be let up for air for the rest of this night."

"Rorke—"

"Shh. I have a good woman—the best woman I know or have ever known—in bed with me. She just caught the mood. I don't have time to talk."

The courtroom was almost empty. Anyone who'd had their two cents to say had done it over the past two days. There had been a few unwilling to label Kelsey a good woman, namely the Whitfield contingent, but she'd had an enormous rooting section on her side, from teachers to cops to the pair of psychologists who'd evaluated her daughter.

Robertson, their dark-haired attorney, was mulling over the brief of another case. There was nothing else he could do on this one. As soon as the judge came out of his chambers, the decision would be set. Robertson had advised them to go for visiting rights now and shared custody a few months down the pike. Rorke had chafed at the interim step, but Kelsey had sided with the attorney. She was unwilling to force anything on her daughter that Janey didn't want.

Rorke could hardly take his eyes off Kelsey. Her white dress was simple and demure, dressed up only with a gold chain, gold earrings and her wedding band. She'd raised holy hell with him about the dress and the chain. Kelsey wasn't used to presents, wasn't used to having anything, but he'd take care of that in time.

She looked proud and beautiful and confident, and she'd projected that quiet image throughout the two days of the custody hearing. She'd taken blows for her past. She'd been unfalteringly honest, and she'd had to do what he warned her—announce that she was strong, a good woman, a loving woman, a woman who had earned the right to be part of her daughter's life.

No one could have guessed Kelsey's battle with self-worth. She'd come so far in their two months of marriage that Rorke felt as if he were watching her come alive, secure, vibrant, vital, confident. There were moments when she occasionally slipped back. One of those moments was now. For all the serene assurance she projected, the small hand, locked with his, was wet with nerves.

Her hand tightened when the judge walked back in. Her eyes met his. . . .

It'll be okay, love. Trust me.

Ten minutes later it was done. The outcome was never a question to anyone but Kelsey. Janey was in an antechamber, waiting to see her mother.

Kelsey shot Rorke a look, full of wonder and relief and love and anxiety. And then, still squeezing his hand tight enough to break bones, she sprang for the hall leading to the back room as if she had rockets in her heels.

Rorke gently broke her hold when he reached for the doorknob of the small, darkly paneled room. When she walked in, he stayed back, deliberately near the door.

Kelsey wanted him there; she'd insisted he stay, but he figured that was more love talking than honesty. The reunion between mother and daughter was a private thing. He planned to stay long enough to see everything was okay and then slip out.

Janey lurched out of a leather chair the moment Kelsey entered the room. There was no question that she only had eyes for her mother. It was an accident, of course, that they'd both dressed in white—but no accident at all that they both had unforgettable blue eyes, a dance of freckles across the nose and the same set of fragile lips now sharing the same tremor.

"Mom?"

Happiness shouldn't hurt this much. Kelsey never meant to cry, but when she saw Janey's arms reach out to her she flew. She gathered up her daughter and hugged, so hard, so tight, that suddenly both of them were laughing and crying at the same time. Kelsey didn't know what she said, what Janey said, but they were both interrupting sentences, talking bubbling fast. Neither could seem to stop. Neither tried.

At a deeper level inside Kelsey, she was absorbing the sound, smell and look of her daughter, who was so vulnerable, so scared. The damp hands matched her own; the fragile laughter tugged her heart. She had work to do with Janey. A mother's work, to listen, to teach, to build up, to instill self-worth made strong and secure with love.

It was work she couldn't have done eight years ago. It hurt to accept that—it was always going to hurt to accept that—but that acceptance was at the core of her strength now. And the man who'd finally made her see that was trying to sneak out the door. Kelsey's hand reached back.

Rorke saw her hand, but it wasn't like that. He didn't want to intrude. The moment belonged to the two of them.

Kelsey didn't see it that way. She backed up a step, her hand still extended, and snagged his wrist. "You met Rorke before, Janey—he's the man you wrote, the man who found you for me. And he's my husband."

Kelsey knew she'd done the right thing the moment she saw the look in his eyes…and then his head bent to Janey.

For all the nerves she'd suffered through the course of the custody hearing, she had felt no hesitation, and no hesitation on the day they'd married. The sense of rightness was that powerful, and it was Rorke who'd made her sure. Nothing she'd built of her life in the past eight years would make sense if she'd refused herself the right to love him. If she was worthwhile, if she'd built the self-respect she claimed she had, if she'd forgiven herself for being human as she'd urged him to do—then she had the right to this moment . . . and the future.

"This is a heck of a place to try and talk. When we pick you up for the weekend, we'll have to start with a dinner on the town," Rorke suggested. "We don't have to go fancy, but I think at the very least we need a celebratory pizza. Sound okay by you?"

"That sounds great," Janey said softly.

"Wouldn't you rather have our first dinner at home?" Kelsey said. "It would be nothing for me to make a casserole and throw it in the oven. You used to love my chicken when you were little, sugar—"

Janey shared a shy and most meaningful glance with Rorke.

By damned, he had himself an honorary daughter. "I'm sure she did, toots," Rorke said tactfully, "but your first night together you don't want to waste time cooking. I insist—the treat's on me."

*   *   *   *   *

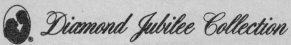

Double your reading pleasure this fall with two Award of Excellence titles written by two of your favorite authors.

Available in September

DUNCAN'S BRIDE
by Linda Howard
Silhouette Intimate Moments #349

Mail-order bride Madelyn Patterson was nothing like what Reese Duncan expected—and everything he needed.

Available in October

THE COWBOY'S LADY
by Debbie Macomber
Silhouette Special Edition #626

The Montana cowboy wanted a little lady at his beck and call—the "lady" in question saw things differently....

These titles have been selected to receive a special laurel—the Award of Excellence. Look for the distinctive emblem on the cover. It lets you know there's something truly wonderful inside!

DUN-1

Take 4 bestselling love stories FREE
Plus get a FREE surprise gift!

COMING SOON...

For years Harlequin and Silhouette novels
have been taking readers places—but only in
their imaginations.

This fall look for PASSPORT TO ROMANCE,
a promotion that could take you around the
corner or around the world!

Watch for it in September!

★